MURDER SPIKE

Mysterious deaths stump Welsh detectives

NICOLA CLIFFORD

THE BOOK FOLKS

Published by The Book Folks

London, 2022

This book is a work of fiction. Names, characters, businesses, organizations, places and events are either the product of the author's imagination or are used fictitiously. Any resemblance to actual persons, living or dead, events or locales is entirely coincidental. The spelling is British English.

ISBN 978-1-80462-028-1

www.thebookfolks.com

To William Hill,
For the support and encouragement

Chapter one

Stacey Logan, reporter for *The Mid Wales Times*, drove carefully on dark, country roads, heading for home on the Epynt Mountain. In her mind, she wondered how to begin the review she would write for the paper. Maybe, "The last night was a success?" Of course, last nights were always claimed as successes, but Stacey wasn't sure the local am-dram production of *Bouncers* came anywhere close. Nearing Llanwrtyd Wells, she glanced at the dashboard clock and was surprised to see it was past one o'clock. That was the trouble with wannabe actors, they always had a lot to say, especially at a wrap party.

She slowed as she approached The White Bridge in the centre of Britain's smallest town, and caught a glimpse of a group of lads standing on The Square. In reality, The Square was a living room-sized patch of grass, with a couple of benches and a striking, nearly three-metre-high sculpture of a red kite with its graceful wings unfurled and several wooden planters placed around the base. The young men's faces were raised and Stacey, wondering what had captured their rapt attention, pulled in. She grabbed her Nikon from the passenger seat and walked back over the bridge spanning the river Irfon. Anxious not to startle the group, she was still ten feet away when she announced her presence with a quiet cough.

Three heads shot round and three pairs of eyes peered into the darkness.

'Bloody hell,' a tall lad said. 'Who's there? Cops?'

Stacey chuckled. 'Not cops. Why? What are you up to?' She walked closer until she stood on the grass beneath the statue. 'I'm Stacey by the way. I live in Llanagethin. What's going on?'

The teenager raised a hand and pointed at the kite.

'There's a bloke up there,' he said. 'Got no kit on.'

His companions, late teenagers like himself, laughed uneasily and Stacey detected the sweet smell of cannabis in the still night air.

'Did you lot put him up there?' Stacey asked, surreptitiously taking a couple of shots with her camera.

'No, babes, not us. Found him like.'

'Do you know who he is?'

'Think he lives in Abergwesyn. One of the cottages on the right before the village. Don't know his name though.'

One of the others piped up. 'I seen him in the Stonecroft earlier, drinking with a group of buds.' The kid snorted. 'He was wasted, man. Boisterous.'

Stacey smiled. 'Good word.'

The tall lad said, 'We was wondering whether his mates put him there like. Stripped him and stuck him on the bird for a laugh, but he hasn't moved and looks cold.'

'Would be,' an overweight lad said, 'got no bloody kit on.'

The group tittered.

'Have you checked for a pulse?' Stacey asked and received three shaking heads – like toy dogs on a dashboard – for an answer.

She stepped closer. The man, probably in his late twenties, was sprawled face down on the back of the bird, pale as a ghost with his arms outstretched, limp hands dangling between the wings and neck. Stacey lifted a tentative hand and gently felt for a pulse already knowing, due to the clammy coolness of the skin, she wouldn't find one.

'Is he dead then, babes?'

'It's a possibility,' Stacey said, trying to get a better look at the man's face while simultaneously slipping her mobile from her pocket and tapping in a number.

'Who you calling?' the tall lad asked.

'My fella. He's staying at my place up the road. He's a copper.'

'We'll get off then. Don't wanna get involved with the five-oh.'

'Hang on, you should stay. You're witnesses. The police will want to talk to you.' Her call was answered and she held the phone to her ear. 'Hey, Sherlock. Ditch your slippers and meet me at The Square in Llanwrtyd, beneath the kite ... What? ... No don't be daft. Bunch of local lads have found a body ... On top of the sculpture.'

'Let's go, boys,' the tall lad said. 'They'll haul us in for this before we can fart. Time to leave.' He glanced at Stacey as she returned the phone to her pocket. 'Will you be OK?'

'At least you bothered to ask,' Stacey said as the others slunk away into the darkness. 'The police are bound to work out who you are and it's not like you did this. You really ought to stay.'

'Not keen, to be honest.'

'My partner will be here within minutes,' she continued. 'His name's Ben and he's a really good cop, fair. Please wait until he arrives, tell him what you told me. If someone did kill this poor man, someone else needs to catch them so it doesn't happen again.' She placed a hand on his arm making him face her. 'I promise, he won't arrest you.' She grinned. 'Be a good idea not to have anything in your pockets you shouldn't have, though. What's your name?'

'Idris,' the lad said, removing a plastic baggie from his pocket and slipping it into his sock. 'Named after the bloody dragon on *Ivor the Engine*. Da was a fan.'

'What do you do, Idris?'

'Work at the builder's yard. Only been there a few months but it's OK.'

'Thanks for waiting with me. If someone did do this they might still be around.'

'Shit, never thought of that.' Idris twisted his head from side to side and squinted into the darkness.

A sweep of headlights and the sound of an engine announced Ben's arrival. Idris looked ready to bolt so Stacey held his arm a little tighter. Ben pulled up next to The Square, turned off the engine and stepped out of the car. Stacey smiled when she saw he hadn't bothered changing out of his slippers.

'Ben, meet Idris and vice versa,' she said. 'Idris is one of the young men who discovered...' Stacey raised one hand, index finger pointing upwards.

Ben gazed at the bird, eyes widening as he spotted the limp, pale body.

'You checked for a pulse?' he asked.

'I did and couldn't find one,' Stacey said. 'He's cool to the touch.'

'A team is on the way,' Ben said. 'SOCO too.' He pulled a phone from his pocket and woke the local pathologist, Carrie Salmon, then he put the phone away and turned to look at the lad.

'What's your last name, Idris?' he asked.

'Jones.'

'Do you live in town?'

'Yeah, got a flat above the old Barclays. Share it with a mate.'

Ben nodded. 'How long ago did you find the body?'

'Just before she turned up,' Idris said indicating Stacey. 'We thought he was pissed and someone stuck him up there for a laugh like, but your girlfriend checked and said he's dead.' Idris lowered his eyes, spotted Ben's tatty leather slippers and smirked. 'Are you really Old Bill? Shouldn't I see a warrant card or something?'

Ben sighed. He removed a wallet from his back pocket and held it in front of the lad's nose. 'Happy?'

'DCI Ben James,' Idris read aloud and nodded. 'It's just I never seen you before. You could have been the killer.'

'You have a fertile imagination, young man. We don't know the chap has been killed yet.'

Two cars drove over the bridge and parked outside the local cafe. DS Jack Trent and DC Oliver Langdon stepped out of one, Carrie Salmon emerged from the other, and they walked across the road to The Square.

'Morning, guv,' Jack said and smiled at Stacey. He glanced up at the metal bird and whistled softly. 'Looks like something out of a Harry Potter movie or installation art. Any idea what he died of?'

'Only just got here myself,' Ben said. 'Surely this isn't all of you?'

'No, guv,' Jack said. 'SOCO and the guys with the white tent are on their way.'

'Good, we need to protect the scene.' Ben pointed at Idris. 'Boy over there with Stacey found the body. His name is Idris Jones and he lives in town. Can you have a chat with him while I stay with Carrie?'

'Will do,' Jack said, turning away. 'Idris, a word please.'

Ben turned his attention to Carrie who was balancing on a small set of step ladders, sweeping the beam of a torch back and forth across the body.

'Anything?' he asked.

'Give me a chance,' she said. 'All I've been able to confirm so far is there isn't a dagger sticking out of his back. That and the fact he's dead and hasn't been that way very long.'

An ambulance appeared around the bend and pulled up at the kerb. The paramedics got out and walked closer. 'Need a hand?' one asked.

'Please,' Carrie said. 'We need to lift this poor man down and lie him on a stretcher, face up. Be very careful. We don't want to disturb any evidence.'

Ben stood back as the crew followed Carrie's instructions; they placed the body on a wheeled stretcher and rolled it inside the vehicle, away from prying eyes. Carrie followed and examined the corpse under a decent light.

'What d'you reckon?' Ben asked, hovering by the open back doors.

'Patience really isn't your middle name, Chief Inspector, and that is unfortunate because there is no obvious cause of death. No injuries I can see and no sign of a struggle. I can't tell you anything more until I've had him on my table.'

Carrie backed out of the vehicle and dispatched the crew to the local morgue, then she climbed the ladder again. She shone her torch on the dark surface of the statue.

'Can't see anything here either,' she said. 'SOCO might have more luck.' She stepped down and stripped off her gloves. 'I'll get going and will ring as soon as I know something.'

'Thanks,' Ben said. 'Sorry to have dragged you out of bed.'

Carrie smiled. 'No worries, it's my job. Speak later.'

As her car pulled away, SOCO arrived and a white tent was soon erected. Jack walked over to his boss.

'I've sent Idris home,' he said. 'He reluctantly supplied the names and addresses of his mates and also told us the dead man had been seen in the pub earlier.' He closed his notebook and slipped it into his pocket. 'Ollie and I will make some house calls. Not much else we can do at this time of night.' He looked down at Ben's footwear and frowned. 'Why not get off, guv? We can meet up at the nick at a more sensible hour. Might even have something to tell you by then.'

'I should stay.'

'Up to you, of course, but for all we know this is a case of misadventure.' Jack chuckled. 'Would have been different if Carrie had found a dagger.'

'Yeah, OK, thanks. I'll be in early. See you then.'

Jack watched Ben and Stacey drive out of town. He checked the SOCOs were happy, then set off through the dark towards the Stonecroft Pub, DC Ollie Langdon in tow. Ollie hammered on the door and it was eventually opened by a short, bald man. He was muscly like a weightlifter, with heavily tattooed forearms, and was dressed in baggy jogging bottoms and a grey vest.

'Oi, oi, oi,' the man said. 'Who the hell are you banging on my door in the middle of the night? You're making enough noise to wake the bloody dead.'

Jack held up his warrant card and watched as the aggression slipped from the man's face.

'Police, sir,' Jack said. 'I apologise for the intrusion, but we need a chat.'

'Can't it wait until the morning?'

'No, sir, it can't. Best if we come in.'

The man stood to one side and the officers walked inside the dark, low-ceilinged bar, the scent of stale beer hanging thickly in the air.

'Go through to the back. Might as well have a cuppa – now I'm awake.'

'What's your name, sir?' Ollie asked, his notebook open, pen ready.

'Derek Brumby, landlord here for the last ten years or so.' He led the way to the kitchen, filled the kettle and switched it on. 'So, tell me what this is about.'

Jack perched on a high stool next to the worktop. 'We've found a body on The Square and have been informed the dead man had been drinking in here before he died. He was seen with three other men. Wondered if you could put a name to him.'

'Lots of people drink in here,' Derek said. 'You'll have to give me more than that.'

'Our witness told us he thought the dead man lived in a cottage on the outskirts of Abergwesyn.'

'Ah, you're talking about Robin Townsend. Apart from the blokes he was with, all the other customers lived in town.'

Derek poured boiling water into a teapot and took three mugs from the drainer. He seemed unmoved by the death and Jack thought that if the man had a personality, he'd left it upstairs in the living accommodation.

'No idea then who these buddies of Robin's were?' Ollie asked.

Derek shrugged. 'How would I know? Not like I ask my customers to prove their identity, not if they're adults. We get all kinds in here, seeing we're on the tourist map. The place is really busy when there's an event on, Man versus Horse, Bog Snorkelling, stuff like that.'

'Did the group leave together?' Jack asked.

'No the three guys left first and Robin stayed on. He was pretty bladdered.'

'What time did Robin leave?'

'Not sure. He had at least one more drink and the next time I looked over, he'd gone.'

'Approximate time would be useful.'

'Around closing?' Derek yawned. 'Can't this wait? I'm dead on my feet here and got a delivery due first thing.'

'Nearly there, sir. Anyone else work the bar with you last night?'

'Just the wife.'

Jack tried to construct a sympathetic face. 'Sorry but we need a quick chat with her too, then we'll be out of your hair.'

Derek got to his feet. 'Wait here and I'll fetch her. I warn you, she won't be best pleased at being dragged out of bed.'

The landlord left the room and reappeared a little while later accompanied by a short, curvy woman in her early forties wearing a puce-pink dressing gown; her bottle-blonde hair was in curlers and her eyes were puffy from sleep. She held the gown closed across her ample bosom and began speaking as soon as she entered the room.

'Who the bleeding hell do you think you are, dragging me out of bed? Speak now while I'm still listening.'

Jack introduced himself and asked the woman her name.

'Denise, married to this useless article.' She nodded at her husband. 'So, what do you want to know?'

'Your husband has told us Robin Townsend was drinking in here yesterday evening with three friends.'

Denise smirked. 'Well, it is a bloody boozer.'

'Did you see Mr Townsend with anyone else yesterday evening?'

The woman shook her head. 'Don't think so. His mates left first. He wobbled out around closing time, although...'

'What?' Jack asked.

'I think he had a word or two with Big Bron.'

'Who?'

'Sheep farmer, runs a flock the other side of the Devil's Staircase. We don't see her often.'

Jack nodded. 'One last question,' he said, 'then you can get back to bed. Did any of the group pay using a card?'

'One of them did.' Denise went to the bar, opened the till and removed a small bundle of receipts. She held them out to Jack. 'I can't tell you which of these was his, you'll have to work that out yourself. You can take the lot but I need them back sharpish. I got books to keep so don't bloody lose them.'

'You from London?' Jack asked. 'East End?'

Denise cackled. 'Course I bleeding am. D'you think I'm putting the voice on? Now, if you don't mind, this ain't no social club, so sling your hook. I need my beauty sleep. You know where I am if you need me.'

Chapter two

Jack made it back to the station just after four. Knowing Ben would clock on early, he propped his feet on a desk, got comfy in a swivel chair and dropped off to sleep. He was woken just before six when the fax machine sprang into life, whirring and buzzing. Jack rubbed his eyes, lowered his feet and hauled his large frame off the chair. He wandered down to the end of the room, set up the coffee maker and by the time it dripped a mugful, the fax machine had finished printing.

Jack picked up the sheets, carried them and the coffee to his desk and began reading through an early autopsy report from Carrie Salmon. He peered at the medical information and saw that Robin Townsend had suffered a period of oxygen deficiency, coma, followed by heart attack and death. A little further in, the report explained a mix of alcohol and GHB – gamma-hydroxybutyrate, well known as a so-called date rape drug – were likely to blame. Carrie had also sent copies of fingerprints collected from the body on the slab. Jack turned to his computer, checked the database and unusually got an almost instant hit.

He leaned back in his seat, hands behind his head, and stared at a mug shot belonging to the man in the morgue.

Jack was still staring at the screen when Ben entered the squad room.

'Morning, guv,' Jack said.

Ben nodded. 'You been burning the midnight oil?'

'Pretty much, but I grabbed a couple of hours of shut-eye.' He waved the bundle of faxes. 'Seems Carrie's also been up all night. She sent her early findings by fax about ten minutes ago and woke me up.'

'Useful stuff?'

'Confirms Robin Townsend is definitely our man. He's on our records and there's a fingerprint match.'

'Why is he on the database? Have we arrested him in the past?'

'Not us. The Met nicked him a few years ago. Only suspect in a pretty nasty attack on an ex-girlfriend who ended up dead.'

'Did the case get as far as court?'

Jack nodded. 'Twice. First trial, the jury couldn't reach a verdict. End of the second, a new jury found him not guilty on a majority. Having no other suspects, the Met dropped the case.'

'What the hell is he doing in Mid Wales?'

'Probably keeping his head down, living in fear of being recognised while trying to start a new life.' Jack pointed at the mug shot on the screen. 'I reckon he did it – look at his eyes.' He sighed heavily. 'Another guilty man who managed to walk away.'

'Were we informed he was moving here?' Ben asked.

'Why would we? The court said he was innocent.'

Ben poured coffee and asked, 'What did Carrie say about the cause of death? Nothing too gruesome, bit early in the morning for that.'

'Overdose. Large quantities of alcohol and GHB in his system which caused coma and death.'

'No ligature marks, defence wounds, anything?'

Jack turned back to the report and read more. 'Can't see anything, not even a bruise.' He held the paper to the light. 'Fax isn't working brilliantly, can't read the last few lines.'

'Don't worry, I'll nip over to Brecon and have a chat with her. You should clock off now. You look done in.'

Jack yawned. 'You're right, I am. If you need anything though, just phone. A couple more hours' sleep and I'll be ready to go again.'

* * *

Ben sat in Carrie's tidy, ordered office, and listened as the pathologist led him through her findings.

'No visible cause of death, no injuries, nothing. His feet were interesting though.'

'Oh, why?' Ben asked.

'They were clean, no pavement dirt but I found a few fibres, looks like they've come from a carpet. What I'm saying is he might have arrived at the kite dressed and under his own steam, or was carried from a vehicle. Any sign of his clothes?'

'Not yet, we need to take a look inside his house. What did the autopsy show as cause of death?'

'As I wrote in my report, he'd smoked some pot and there were large amounts of alcohol and GHB in his blood. GHB has a short half-life so it metabolises rapidly. Lucky the victim was discovered so soon after his death. Made my job easier.'

Ben sighed. 'So he might have done all this to himself? Case of misadventure?'

'I can see why you'd think that,' Carrie said, 'but I reckon you're way off the mark.'

Ben raised his eyebrows. 'You found something didn't you?'

Carrie smiled and held up an evidence bag, a small piece of white card in the bottom. 'This was folded in half and pushed inside the victim's mouth, hence its soggy condition.'

Ben took the bag and held it beneath the desk lamp. Written in what looked like black marker, was the capital letter U and a number 2. Ben turned it over but the back was blank.

'U2, the band?' he asked.

Carrie laughed. 'I'm pretty certain Bono had nothing to do with this. Do you remember the #MeToo movement? The demos? The rubbish spouted by the authorities following the death of yet another young woman?'

'What rubbish?'

'Not to go out after dark, keep your keys in your hand, let BT track your movements and to flag down a bus if you need help. Hah! How on earth would that work out here?' she said.

'You sound angry?'

'I'm furious! Very little changes. Did you hear a government minister say recently that misogyny is wrong whether it's directed at women or men?'

Ben held up his hands. 'Whoa, Carrie. Step away from the soap box.'

She took a breath. 'Sorry, things have been a bit... tough lately.'

'Why? Something happening with you?'

'My niece,' she said.

'What about her?'

'She's enrolled in a performing arts college in Cardiff and was walking home one evening when she was grabbed by a couple of lads.'

'Was she raped?' Ben asked quietly, dreading her answer.

'Thank the stars, no, but they roughed her up, tore her clothes, put hands where they shouldn't, gave her a black eye and stole her bag.'

'Why don't I know about any of this?' Ben asked.

Carrie shrugged. 'Not your patch. I went with her to Cardiff nick.' She sighed. 'They asked why she was out so late. Why didn't she take a cab? Why was she on her own?

We left when they wanted to know what she was wearing, how short her skirt was.'

Ben topped up their mugs from a hotplate in the corner of the office.

'How is your niece now?' he asked.

'Very angry about the police's response, feels betrayed. A less positive reaction is she rarely goes out alone and never after dark. She's curtailing her life for something that isn't her fault.' Carrie dabbed brimming eyes. 'Thought I might invite her to Brecon for a break.'

'Sounds like a plan,' Ben said. 'Do me a favour though, give me the names of the officers you spoke to in Cardiff? I'll try to find out what they're doing about this – and why they showed such a lack of understanding.'

Chapter three

The CID team met in the squad room at the end of the day for a debrief. Jack Trent had made it in as promised and Ben had to admit his sergeant was back to his usual self, dressed in a sharp suit and handmade shoes. Ben removed his jacket, sat at the table and waited for the others to join him.

'Won't keep you long,' Ben said. 'It's been a hard day for some of you and we all need a decent night's sleep so we can be at our best in the morning. Be warned. Seven o'clock start.' He lifted his mug and saw the team's nodding heads above the rim. 'OK, this is what we have.' He got to his feet, walked closer to the incident board and tapped an enlarged mug shot of the victim. 'Robin Townsend, twenty-eight, lived in a rented cottage just short of Abergwesyn village. He has a file. Only suspect in a nasty attack in London which left his ex-girlfriend dead. CPS failed to prove his guilt so Townsend walked... all the way to Mid Wales.'

'He was looking for a hideaway,' Ollie said. 'Knows he's got enemies in the city and wanted to get the jump on them.'

'Seems to me,' DC Tegan Hedges said, 'that he didn't pull it off and one of them found him.'

'That does seem the most likely explanation,' Ben said. 'The killer left a calling card.' He pointed at an enlarged copy of the white card with the handwritten text. 'Carrie wondered whether U2 was a response to the #MeToo movement, as in You Too.' Ben sat. 'Priorities tomorrow are house-to-house. Knock on every door in town. I'll round up half a dozen uniforms to help with the legwork. Ollie and Tegan will be in charge. I want to know anything you're told, including any gossip, and we need to track down the victim's drinking buddies.' He rubbed his face. 'Is Elsa Duffin still posted in the station?'

'Yes, guv,' Jack said.

'She's good at tracking people online. I'll have a word with CS Warren, get Constable Duffin on the team.'

'What will we be doing tomorrow, guv?' Jack asked.

'We'll go out to the body dump, have SOCO look over Townsend's cottage, track down Big Bron the sheep farmer, then back here to trawl the records to find out if anything like this has happened before.'

'You think there might be more of these?'

'This killing was extremely well planned, more like a work of art than just a murder. Wouldn't something like that require practice?' He gazed around the room. 'Any questions? No? Good.' Ben got to his feet and picked up his jacket.

Jack moved closer to his boss. 'I had a bit of a chat with my opposite number in Cardiff nick like you asked.'

'And?'

'The DS I spoke with said she was also less than impressed with the treatment received by Eve Salmon and intends to do something about it.'

'That's a good start, but I want the boys who attacked Eve caught and brought to book.'

Jack grinned. 'So does my contact. We've worked together in the past, she's a very determined woman.'

'Do I know who we are talking about?'

'Erica Bevan. Heidi's ex-girlfriend. You can put money on the fact that if these scallys are catchable, Erica will move mountains to make sure they do.'

* * *

Ben left Noddfa, Stacey's cottage, for work before the sun had risen and Stacey also got up early. She drank coffee in the garden to wake up and plan her day. Stacey's editor, Sam Jenkins, disturbed her train of thought soon after nine to complain about the lack of substance in her last article. She explained that as she didn't know much, she couldn't write much. She hung up and, slightly irritated, made the decision to work in the back garden while the weather was kind.

Autumn was without a doubt her favourite season of the year, especially when the Epynt was bathed with soft, yellow sunshine. She sat on the bench and watched bees and butterflies stocking up on nectar before the long winter. The morning was warm enough for a short-sleeved T-shirt and Stacey enjoyed the touch of sunshine on her skin, topping up the charge in her internal batteries in readiness for short, dark, winter days.

She got to her feet and disassembled the bean stick teepees, pulled out past-their-sell-by-date courgette plants, dug up the last of the carrots and spread compost on empty beds. The ravens which roosted in tall forestry larches, also loved sunny weather and soared out of the plantations, twisting and somersaulting in the warm air, flying for flying's sake. The pairs sang to each other, strengthening the bonds which would last a lifetime, and Stacey stopped work to listen to the extraordinary range of grunts, snorts and low whistles.

At lunchtime she made a plate of sandwiches. She sat on the bench next to the back door to eat and admire the progress she had made. Lunch over, she began dragging old strips of carpet out of the shed to cover the weeded and composted beds. She was struggling with a length which refused to unroll when she heard the click of the side gate. Stacey straightened up and smiled as her friend, Heidi Holtz, strolled around the end of the cottage. Until she resigned, Heidi had been a detective constable working for Dyfed-Powys Police. The women had met when Heidi helped Ben home, and they had become firm friends.

'Hi, you,' Stacey said, wiping her hands on her gardening trousers. 'This is a nice surprise. Coffee?'

'You need to ask?'

Heidi followed Stacey into the kitchen and plonked herself at the table.

'To what do I owe the pleasure?' Stacey asked as she put a fresh pot of coffee on to brew. 'Everything OK?'

'Not really. I'm bored and I detest being bored.'

Heidi tore a blank sheet of paper from Stacey's jotter pad and began folding and tearing with quick, nimble fingers.

'Why don't you go to your father's place?' Stacey asked. 'He loves spending time with you at Milebrook.'

Milebrook Manor was the Holtz family home in the Cotswolds. A graceful residence, built of honey-yellow stone and set in many acres of parkland.

Heidi shrugged and half-inched another sheet of paper. 'I've been there for the last couple of weeks and yes, Pa loved having me at home. Spent many long evenings in the library nursing balloons of his best brandy – proper lady of the manor stuff.' She suddenly snorted with laughter. 'Except of course for the evening when Freddie showed off his reggae collection, at full volume. Cook was not impressed.'

'One day that long-suffering woman will up and leave. Who would feed your dad's waifs and strays if that happened?'

Heidi grinned. 'Freddie's got her sussed. He apologised profusely in the morning and arranged a huge bouquet.' She chuckled. 'Cook was Pa's nanny so he really can do no wrong – as long as he prostates himself properly and gives her a hug.'

Stacey handed her a mug of black and sweet and asked, 'How is everyone at Milebrook?'

'Fine, good actually. Felix and Pixie have finally moved to a cottage in the grounds and the estate employs Felix as a groundsman and handyman. Pixie covers for cook three days a week and rustles up some amazing meals. She really is a funny little thing. Squeezes the life out of me every time I see her.'

'How about your sister, Greta, and beautiful baby Grace?'

'Not a baby anymore, nearly three. I'm teaching her music and have given her a dinky cello.'

Stacey smiled. 'Sweet, a future duet partner.'

'That's the idea. Can I borrow your laptop?'

'Knock yourself out but nothing illegal.'

Heidi opened the laptop, cracked her knuckles and logged on while Stacey began peeling carrots.

'Looking at anything interesting?' she asked.

'Your body on the bird article.' Heidi rattled the keyboard then said, 'There could be more of these.'

'What?' Stacey asked.

'More killings. Might not be here, but I predict that somewhere in the country more men will die, if they haven't already.'

'That's some prediction. No details relating to the actual death have been released.'

Heidi made a rude sound. 'Consider the facts. The body was posed – displayed – in the centre of a small town, an enormous risk for the killer. Whoever this is will be an adrenaline junkie, loves the rush.' She gulped a mouthful of coffee. 'The manner of death – booze and a large quantity of a date rape drug. Discovered naked – shaming the victim.'

'How do you know he didn't do this to himself? Took too much and overdosed. It does happen.'

'Yes, it does, but he was murdered. The killer left a calling card.'

'I didn't see a card.'

'You wouldn't, it was in his mouth.'

'Did it say anything?'

'U2.'

'The band?'

Heidi shook her head. 'This killer will take some catching. Look at the planning involved. It's almost ritualistic.'

'Any idea who might do something like this?'

Heidi shrugged, cracked her knuckles for a second time and began lining up tiny origami mice. 'You know Townsend had form don't you?' she asked.

'I didn't know his name until you told me,' Stacey said, 'never mind anything else. The police haven't released any details. How do you know the victim's name and all that other stuff?'

'If it's on the net, I can find it.'

'So tell me, what form does Townsend have?'

'He was the only suspect in a violent sexual attack on an ex-girlfriend and charged with her murder. Jury found him innocent and seems he ran to Mid Wales. My bet is someone tracked him down.'

'Where did the murder take place?'

'London. If I had to guess – not my favourite thing – I'd look at the friends and relatives of the ex-girlfriend.'

Heidi fiddled with her last paper sculpture and placed it in the middle of the mice. It was a large white cat with one raised paw.

'I think you should stay for supper,' Stacey said. 'Ben and Jack are coming over and are bound to be interested in your theories.'

Chapter four

Stacey carried a tureen of Welsh Black beef stew, loaded with fresh autumn vegetables, and placed it in the centre of the table, together with a dish of golden roast potatoes.

'This is nice,' she said with a smile, 'all of us together.'

Jack grinned. 'I'm always grateful to be invited. I'd never say no to supper at yours, especially when I have the opportunity to catch up with the marvellous Ms Holtz at the same time.' He raised a glass in Heidi's direction.

She frowned but didn't pass comment.

'You really will have to bring Julie over one evening,' Stacey said, 'with or without the twins.'

Jack snorted. 'Have to be without. They're on the go every second they're awake. I'm beginning to think they have ADHD or something, but Julie and her mam tell me they are perfectly normal four-year-olds.' He sipped from his glass and groaned with pleasure. 'Parsnip tonight, folks, and bloody delicious. My best effort at winemaking to date.'

Once the meal had begun, Stacey asked if there had been any developments in the case. Ben and Jack described what they had discovered so far.

'So, who is the dead man?' Stacey asked innocently.

'Robin Townsend,' Jack said. 'A London migrant who has lived here for a couple of years. Got into a bit of bother in the Smoke and cut and run. We're working on the theory that Mid Wales wasn't far enough and the "bother" tracked him down.'

'Heidi has a couple of theories. Listen to what she thinks,' Stacey said.

Heidi spooned in a mouthful of food to give her some thinking time, then said, 'The bother you refer to must be the attack and subsequent murder of Townsend's ex-girlfriend. He narrowly escaped conviction, so my money is on a relative or friend of the dead woman, seeking revenge.'

'How can you possibly know all this?' Ben asked.

'Honestly,' Heidi said, 'I'm gonna start wearing a T-shirt that says, "If it's on the net I can find it".' She broke off a chunk of homemade bread and dabbled it in her bowl. 'There's more,' she said. 'At a push, this could also look like an almost textbook killing by a sociopath or similar. The posing, shaming, manner of death and the note in the mouth suggests that.' Heidi glanced at Ben whose eyebrows had disappeared beneath his short hair. She sighed. 'Last time I'm ever gonna answer your questions, spoken or otherwise. A fax isn't as secure as you lot seem to think. The pathology report hit the net as soon as Ms Salmon sent you a copy.'

'So which is it?' Jack asked. 'And how do we catch him?'

'Him or her,' Heidi said forcefully. 'The victim had a gentle death, no gore, no injuries. Probably just slept himself away. A bloke – especially one acting out of revenge – might have been less gentle.'

'You think killing someone is gentle?' Ben asked.

'Can be.'

'How could a woman get a dead body on the red kite?' Jack asked.

'Strength and technique? Who knows, maybe Townsend was still able to move and was encouraged to climb up before the coma hit. Finding his clothes would be a bloody good idea.'

'We wondered about a vigilante,' Ben said, 'dishing out justice the courts failed to.'

Heidi nodded and wiped her bowl with another piece of bread. 'The card might have something to do with the #MeToo movement, as in You Too.'

'Carrie mentioned that,' Ben said.

Heidi continued, 'Someone doing to a man what some men do to women. Drink spiked to make him malleable, then stripped, displayed and allowed to die.'

'That doesn't sound dissimilar to some past attacks on women.'

'No, it doesn't,' Heidi said. 'Keep the idea in mind in case the friends and family of the poor woman in London all have alibis.'

'How would someone strip a man and plonk him on the kite without being spotted?' Jack asked.

Heidi just shrugged.

The stew finished, Stacey – knowing Heidi's love of ice cream – removed a glorious baked Alaska from the Aga and gave the honour of dissecting the perfectly cooked dessert to her friend.

'Stacey, did you know Carrie Salmon's niece had some trouble in Cardiff recently?' Ben asked. 'Couple of lads hassling, tearing clothes and robbing her?'

Stacey nodded. 'I heard something about it. *Cardiff Journal* ran a short piece I think.'

'I spoke with Carrie earlier and it seems the police handled the matter disgracefully, trying to put the blame on Eve. Carrie went with her niece to the station, but they walked out before the end of the interview due to inappropriate questioning.'

'Nothing new there then,' Heidi muttered as she filled glass bowls.

'Jack spoke to his opposite number,' Ben continued, 'a female DS who is as determined to nick these touchy-feely individuals as I am. We might get involved with the case if she needs assistance.'

Jack glanced up at Heidi. 'She sends her love by the way.'

'Who does?' Heidi asked.

'Erica Bevan. She heard on the grapevine you'd reappeared.'

'She say anything else?'

Jack shook his head. 'You should give her a ring.'

Heidi said nothing and Ben changed the subject.

'We met a very unusual woman today,' he said. 'Locals know her as Big Bron, lives above the Devil's Staircase. A shepherd who runs a flock on the tops.'

Stacey laughed. 'Big Bron eh? What was she, 5'2" and seven stone?'

'Oh no,' Jack said. 'She more than fits her nickname. Large woman, very tall and broad, with massive hands. Looked like she could have tucked your man here under one arm.'

'Shudder the thought,' Ben said quietly.

'So what does BB have to do with the dead man?' Stacey asked.

'Denise Brumby, landlady of the Stonecroft, thought she saw BB speak to him,' Ben said. 'We wanted to know what was said so we made a house call.'

'Some place that mountain pass,' Jack said. 'Such wild land, especially above the Devil's Staircase. BB has a place at the bottom of a deep valley, the journey was interesting to say the least. Nothing but mountains, streams, lumps of rock, sheep and the odd pile of stones that someone calls home.'

'That's a bit harsh, Jack,' Stacey said. 'Families have lived in those farmhouses for generations. Most are off-grid so life is different. "Have we got enough wood for the

Raeburn to cook supper?" rather than, "Shall we use Farrow and Ball in the study?"'

'Yeah, I suppose. I've just never seen places like it before.'

'Tell me what BB was like,' Heidi said. 'The suspense is killing me.'

'The whole thing was a bit too *Torchwood* for my liking,' Jack said. 'BB is built like a bloke. Her father lives with her. A small man in a wheelchair, strapped in because he can't support his upper body. Not sure what's wrong with him, but he has an old burn on one side of his face. English is their second language and despite Ben being born and bred here, his Welsh is pretty rubbish.'

'Is it just the two of them up there?' Heidi asked.

'Yeah, just them.'

Heidi nodded, then she turned her attention to a pink serviette on the table and began to turn it into a lotus flower.

'So, did BB speak to Townsend?' Stacey asked.

'Yes,' Ben said. 'She offered him a lift home apparently.'

'Which he refused,' Jack added.

* * *

After Jack and Heidi had left, Ben tackled the washing-up. Stacey picked up a tea towel.

'Do you think BB killed Townsend?' she asked.

'Wow, no beating about the bush there,' Ben said. 'I can always tell when you're in reporter mode. You're usually more subtle.' He scrubbed the stew pot. 'My answer is it's too soon to tell.'

'But you must have a gut feeling. All coppers have those.'

'Gut feelings aren't evidence.' He wiped his hands. 'SOCO will take a look at Townsend's house tomorrow and we have some short snippets of CCTV gleaned from local businesses in Llanwrtyd. What we need is a witness.

Like Jack said, how was it possible that someone could hoist a dead body up like that without anyone seeing them?'

'That's the trouble with places around here. Nearly everyone goes to bed early and when the council turns off the street lights, it's bloody dark. That's why I pulled in when I saw the lads on The Square, because it was unusual to see anyone out that time of the night.'

'Why were they out?' Ben asked.

'No idea, I didn't ask. That's your job.'

Ben sighed. 'I wonder if anyone actually did ask the question.' He yawned. 'Bedtime I reckon,' he said. 'I'm bushed.' He kissed Stacey's cheek. 'Thanks for a lovely evening. As you said, nice for us to be together. I hadn't realised quite how much I missed Heidi, good to have her back with us.'

Chapter five

Ben and Jack were standing in front of the incident board, when the squad room door opened and DS Erica Bevan walked in.

'Morning,' she said and smiled at those she knew. 'How is everyone?'

'Good thanks,' Ben said. 'What are you doing here?'

Erica chuckled. 'That's not much of a welcome. I spoke to Jack yesterday about a case I'm working on, and he said if I needed to run anything past you...'

'Yeah, of course.' Ben looked across the room. 'Constable Hedges, fetch the sergeant a cuppa please.'

Erica took a seat, leaned on the table and gazed at the photos pinned to the board.

'That's some case,' she said. 'How's it coming?'

'Early days,' Ben said. 'How about yours? Any closer to nicking the boys who roughed up Eve Salmon?'

Tegan placed a mug on the table and smiled at Erica. 'Good to see you,' she said. 'Things OK?'

'Not bad thanks,' Erica said.

'So, any clues?' Ben prompted.

'I'm on it and I'll get there,' Erica said. 'I actually wanted to chat about something else.' She sipped her drink.

'OK, tell me.'

Jack joined them at the table.

'We have a bit of a problem with spiking in the clubs in town,' Erica said.

'That's always gone on,' Jack said. 'Got spiked myself when I was with the Met. Someone dropped a tab of acid in my pint one night. Never left a pint on its own since – truly awful experience.'

'We seem to have an epidemic,' Erica said. 'I'm sure there are more victims out there than those who make it to the nick. The ones we do see feel stupid, embarrassed and dreadfully confused.'

'Is any of that after-effects of what was slipped into their drinks?' Ben asked.

Erica shook her head. 'Not really, there's more to this but I can't work out what. Hence my visit to pick your brains.'

'Pick away then, Sergeant,' Ben said and leaned back in his chair.

'We've had four very similar complaints over the last month or so. All young women whose statements are pretty much identical. They all report having a good time at the club, being bought a drink by a lad around their own age, then...'

'What?' Jack asked.

'They wake up in a motel room on their own, with a hangover from hell, not a clue how they got there, or what happened between the club and the motel.'

'Were they...?' Ben asked.

Erica shook her head. 'They agreed to be examined, in case what we found would help them fill in the gaps, but not one had been touched by anyone.'

'That is pretty strange,' Jack said. 'Why go through the hassle of drugging someone if not for the obvious reason?'

'You can see my problem,' Erica said. 'We've put warning posters up at the clubs, bus stops and taxi ranks. I've also spoken with club owners and their staff, told them not to slacken off on their entry searches, but it's still happening.'

'The lads who gave the women spiked drinks – does it sound like one lad or many?'

Erica shrugged. 'The women's memories aren't great, they have been affected by the drugs, but they all say white, medium height, no obvious distinguishing marks, wearing a baseball cap.'

'That could describe half the clientele,' Jack said.

'But if it is one guy,' Erica said, 'this could turn into something else entirely – if we allow him to get comfortable.' She got to her feet. 'Anyway, better make tracks, got some calls to make, not least to Carrie. I promised her an update.'

'Have you spoken to Heidi?' Ben asked.

Erica frowned at him. 'She knows my number, sir.' Erica turned on her heel and stomped from the room.

Ben sighed. 'None of my business,' he said, 'but I wish those two wouldn't be so touchy and just talk to each other.' He rubbed his face. 'How are we getting on with our case, Jack?'

'Using the credit card slips from the pub, we've identified one of the drinkers with Townsend just before he was killed. Ian Townsend, elder brother of the victim.'

'That's progress.'

'I rang him and he confirmed his younger brother, Kevin, was also in the Stonecroft on the night in question.'

'Who was the other guy?'

'As yet, unidentified. Ian said the man was Robin's friend, introduced as Pete. Doesn't know more than that.'

Ben nodded. 'We should speak to them both.' He sighed. 'Don't fancy traipsing to London.'

'No worries, guv, they're also migrants from the East. They invested in a holiday park just outside Tenby. Both live on site.'

'Well then, no time like the present. Where's Ollie Langdon?'

'Llanwrtyd, trying to track down more CCTV footage from local businesses, having another chat with the lads who found the body, and checking in with SOCO.'

'OK.' Ben looked up. 'Tegan? Elsa Duffin is due in half an hour. When she gets here, bring her up to date then work together to compile a list of friends and family of the ex-girlfriend of Robin Townsend. Find out as much as you can about them and the original case, but no direct contact – not yet.'

'Yes, sir.'

'Come on then, Sergeant, we're off to the seaside.'

* * *

Stacey was in her office writing an updated article regarding the body on the bird, as Heidi called the murder case, when the doorbell rang. She got up from her desk and opened the front door.

'Erica! Wow. Great to see you.'

Erica smiled. 'Sorry, it's been a while. Pressure of work.'

'Come in and head for the kitchen.'

Stacey shut the door and followed her friend to the back of the cottage.

'This is a lovely surprise,' she said, switching on the kettle. 'How are you? What have you been up to?'

'Coppering mainly,' Erica said and sat on the carver. 'After that business with Heidi, I moved out of her place in Brecon and found a flat in Cardiff. Been working out of the main nick ever since. The job kept my mind off things. How about you?'

'No major changes. Working hard like you.'

Stacey poured water into a tea pot and carried it to the table together with a couple of thickly buttered slices of bara brith.

'You know Heidi's back?' she asked.

Erica nodded. 'Did she say where she'd been?'

'Not really, something about needing time to slow herself down, and to learn to play the cello.'

Erica blinked. 'She could always play beautifully. I miss hearing her play.' She sighed. 'If I'm honest, I just miss her.'

'So why not contact her?' Stacey asked.

'Not sure it's a good idea. Things didn't end well last time. It took me ages to get over losing her, especially in such... difficult circumstances.'

'She was hurt too because she was the one who walked. Give her a call. If she doesn't want to talk, she'll probably just hang up. Telephone etiquette was never her strong point.'

'Yeah, maybe.' Erica took a bite of tea bread.

'How come you're in my neck of the woods?' Stacey asked.

'Day off. Promised I'd visit Carrie Salmon, let her know what progress we've made with her niece's case. Thought I'd nip in on the way past to say hi. Also, I wanted to ask what you know about spiking.'

'Vampires or lawns?' Stacey asked.

'What?'

'Sorry, being silly. You mean spiking drinks?'

'Yeah that, and its more sinister twin, spiking with actual needles.'

'I've been aware of a few media mentions.'

'Well, we've got it bad in Cardiff. I've spoken to several young women this has happened to over the last month or so. They've been spiked, removed from the club, taken to a motel room and left there without anything sexual happening.'

'Why would anyone do something like that? What's in it for them?'

'Unless there's someone out there who just likes watching sleeping women – there are bound to be some – that's precisely my point. Any chance you can ask around in case it's happening anywhere else and the victims aren't coming forward?'

Stacey smiled. 'Mid Wales isn't overly endowed with night clubs, but I'll keep my ears open.' She topped up the mugs. 'You said you were going to see Carrie. Have you caught the lads then?'

'I wish,' Erica said. 'My visit is more of an apology than anything else. I'm still on it but we'll be very lucky if we can make any arrests. Way too much of this sort of stuff goes on.'

'Do you think more coppers on the street would make a difference?'

'Gotta be worth a try. CCTV doesn't put anyone off, it just gives us a better chance of catching the bad guys. Oh, hang on...'

'What?'

'You can't quote me in that rag you work for. This isn't an official interview.'

Stacey laughed. 'Come on, you know me. When have I ever?'

'Fair point, sorry.' Erica drained her mug and nodded at the origami cat and the flock of mice on the mantle. 'So tell me,' she said. 'How was Heidi when you last saw her?'

Chapter six

Jack pulled onto the main A40 and headed west towards Carmarthen. Ben made himself comfortable in the passenger seat and gazed out of the window at the passing countryside.

'Autumn is amazing in Wales,' Jack said. 'I really enjoy seeing the trees change colour, it's like they catch fire.'

Ben smiled. 'Never had you down as a poet, Sergeant.'

'I have my moments, guv.'

'You thought anything more about what Erica told us?'

'Yeah, a bit. Trouble is, not being able to work out why the women were taken makes it difficult to get a handle on who we might be looking for.'

'Not enough CCTV in the clubs,' Ben said.

'Probably not, guv, but even if there were more cameras, we'd be lucky to spot anything. The victims didn't.'

'All these noxious substances are much too easily available,' Ben grumbled. 'Order online, dark web or whatever, and anything you want is delivered to your door by the posties.'

'I agree with you wholeheartedly. D'you reckon that's cos we're getting old?'

'No,' Ben said, 'I don't. It's because we have the wisdom to recognise there's a serious problem.'

'Never had you down as a philosopher, guv.'

Ben chuckled then asked, 'What do we know about the Townsend brothers?'

'At the time of Robin's bit of bother, his older brother Ian was also arrested, held briefly, then released without charge.' Jack slowed to tackle the humpbacked bridge on the edge of Nantgaredig. 'I rang one of my London buddies. He confirmed the brothers were picked up together, but at the station it quickly became obvious Ian wasn't involved, hence his release.'

'Anything else?'

'Not even a parking ticket. Ex-teacher, now joint owner of the caravan park. His wife and two kids decamped with him to Wales a year or so ago.'

'What about Kevin?'

'Baby of the family. Clean as the proverbial whistle. Got an arts degree at uni, invested in the caravan park with his brother, where he has a home and a studio.'

'What did Robin do before he was arrested?'

'Call centre work mainly; he moved around a bit in London. As far as I can discover he hasn't worked since he left the city.'

'So where did these guys get the money to buy caravan parks and enjoy lives of leisure?'

'Inherited from wealthy parents, killed together in a pile-up on the M25. His father was an investment banker and left behind a sizable packet.'

'I wonder if the brothers met up regularly for a drink,' Ben said.

'We'll find out soon. What's Tenby like? Never quite got there somehow.'

'Busier than it used to be. Lots of rowdy stag and hen dos these days.'

Jack chuckled. 'Thinking like that is because you're getting old.'

As Jack turned off the St Clears roundabout, Ben glanced at his watch.

'Almost lunchtime,' he said. 'Drive on into town. We'll find some fish and chips, you can take a look at the sea, and we'll conduct the interviews on the way back.'

'Fine by me, guv. I'd never say no to fish and chips at the seaside.'

* * *

Stacey flopped onto the visitor's chair in the editor's office at *The Mid Wales Times*. Her grumpy boss peered at her over the top of his glasses.

'Thought you'd emigrated,' he growled.

'Aw, give it up, Sam. You're fooling no one and we spoke on the phone yesterday.'

Sam flapped a pudgy hand. 'So, what have you got for me? Body on the bird killer arrested?'

'No, and I wish you'd stop calling it that. I never wrote that.'

'Catchy though, you have to agree. Now, why are you here?'

'I need a bit of time to do what I'm good at.'

'That being?'

'Investigative journalism. I had a chat with a source earlier and there's a worrying increase in spiking offenses in South Wales. I was told some strange facts about these cases and would like some time to dig around, unburdened by flower shows and disastrous first nights of not-very-good am-dram societies.'

'What's in it for me?' Sam asked.

'Hopefully, a thought-provoking exposé, enough to fill a couple of pages... at least,' she added when she saw her boss frown.

'That's not new, spiking drinks. Happened when I was young.'

Stacey tried to imagine Sam young, slimmer and with hair, and managed to smother a smile.

'I can't go into details,' she said, 'but from what I've heard, this is something different.'

'Different how?'

Stacey sighed. 'That's why I want time to investigate. I think there's a bigger story here.'

Sam rubbed his eyes and stared out of the window before turning back to glare at his reporter.

'Go on then, take a couple of weeks, but make sure you bring me a story.' He frowned. 'Any chance of a titbit?'

'Of course not, but hopefully it'll be worth the wait.'

Sam nodded. 'What about the murder case? Any progress?'

'None I'm aware of. Thought I'd ask around town, chat to any potential witnesses. Very peculiar business.'

'Not sure "peculiar" is the word. How was the fella killed? Do you know?'

'The police aren't releasing much, but I've got my ears to the ground.' Stacey removed a flash drive from the pocket of her leather jacket. 'Here's an article concerning the spiking incidents in Cardiff. Outlines the crimes, contains the facts I have been able to corroborate, and includes a warning to young clubbers to be aware of the dangers. A taster for the feature.' She got to her feet. 'I'll stay in touch and keep working the murder. You'll know as soon as I have something for you.'

* * *

Ben and Jack sat in the large living room of a recently built, four-bedroom property, close to the entrance of an extensive caravan park, three miles outside Tenby. The Townsend brothers sat on chairs in the bay window, while Ian's wife poured tea into pretty patterned mugs.

'So how often did you all meet up?' Ben asked.

'Every now and again,' Ian said. 'Wasn't like we'd get together once a month or anything.'

'Any special reason for your most recent visit?'

'Not really. Kevin had been offered a mini exhibition of his work at the Wyeside Arts Centre in Builth Wells. We arranged to meet up with Robin while we were in the area.'

Jack turned to look at Kevin and asked, 'What do you paint?'

The young man tucked his long hair behind one ear, then he clasped his hands together and rested them on the knees of torn and paint-splattered jeans.

'I take my inspiration from street art,' he said. 'Try to bring the work inside people's homes.'

'So you copy graffiti?' Jack asked.

'No. I said I'm inspired by street art, not that I reproduce existing pieces. I create new works in a similar style.'

Jack wasn't sure he'd learned anything, but scribbled in his notebook just the same. 'Where on site do you live, Kevin?'

'Down at the bottom on the edge of the wood. Back in the day the site was a farm. When the caravans arrived, the previous owner converted a small barn and some outbuildings into living accommodation. I live there, my studio is next door. Perfect for what I need.'

Kevin played with his hair again, his pale fingers twisting and separating the strands. He was a small man, short in stature and thin. If he was a woman he might have been described as willowy. He seemed edgy and nervous one moment, relaxed and dreamy the next and Jack wondered if he was high, or drunk.

'Did you travel home together?' Ben asked.

'No, actually,' Ian said. 'I'd hired a van to transport the artwork to the centre and needed to get it back. Kevin drove his own car and travelled home the next day.'

'I stayed with a friend of mine in Llanwrda,' Kevin explained.

'Name of your friend?' Jack asked.

'Steve Gibson. Lives just off the main road near the petrol station.'

'What time did you leave your friend's place?'

'Before ten. I got back here around lunchtime.'

Jack nodded and made more notes.

'Can either of you tell us about the man who accompanied your brother to the pub?'

'Not much to tell,' Ian said. 'He was called Pete. We hadn't met before.'

'Do you know where the man lives?'

'No, sorry. As I said, it was the first time we'd met.'

'Any idea why anyone would kill Robin?' Jack asked.

Ian hesitated so Jack prompted.

'Do you think his death had anything to do with the court case he was involved with in London?'

'Can't think of another reason,' Ian said. 'He was getting trouble where he lived, even though he was found innocent. That was why he moved.' Ian snorted. 'You probably know I was arrested at the same time and released without charge. The bad publicity the case generated was having an undesirable effect on my family, so we upped sticks a few months after Robin and bought the holiday park.'

'How did you hear about the place?'

'Kevin found it for sale on the net. We bought it jointly using the money our parents left us and have never been happier. The children just adore the countryside and the freedom, the space and clean sea air.'

'When you heard about your brother's death, how did you feel?' Ben asked.

'Devastated, obviously, and very angry. Robin was proved innocent, yet that wasn't good enough for someone.'

'You think the killer was connected with the dead woman in London?'

'Who else would kill my brother?' Ian said. 'I ask because I can't think of anyone.'

Chapter seven

Stacey turned off the narrow and twisted road of the Abergwesyn Pass and began to follow two-wheel tracks gouged into the grass. Heidi stared through the windscreen at the mountains looming either side.

'Thanks for coming with me today,' Stacey said. 'Jack said BB's first language is Welsh and I don't speak much.'

'You should rectify that,' Heidi said. 'It's not too difficult once you've learned the rules – and the alphabet.'

'I did take classes when I first moved into Noddfa but didn't make much progress. At school I was crap at French – and German.'

'Never had a problem with languages myself.'

Stacey chuckled. 'You've never had a problem with anything.'

Heidi shrugged and cracked her knuckles. Stacey winced and concentrated on navigating the track. A little further on, the car suddenly lurched, the nose dropped and there was a bang from underneath.

'Whoa, Stace,' Heidi said. 'That's not right. Pull up.'

Stacey applied the brakes. Heidi opened the passenger door and stepped out. Stacey cut the engine and watched as her friend peered at the front of the vehicle.

'Crap!' Heidi said. 'The nearside tyre burst. If I'd known we'd be off-roading, I'd have insisted on using my Land Rover.'

Stacey got out and inspected the damage. 'To be honest,' she said, 'I had no idea the track would be this bad.'

'DS Trent did say it was "interesting". Got a spare and a jack?'

Stacey nodded. 'In the boot. I'll dig them out.'

Heidi checked her phone. 'Absolutely no bloody signal whatsoever.'

Stacey carried the tools to the front of the car and returned to the boot for the spare.

'This isn't going to be easy,' Heidi grouched.

'Why not?'

'The high point in the track and the jacking point don't match up so I can't raise the car. We need to push it forward a little, find a place that's flatter.'

'OK, let's give it a go.'

'Slowly,' Heidi warned. 'We don't want the car to jump out of the ruts and damage anything vital underneath.'

The women leaned hard on the boot and managed to get the old car moving, but the uneven track made the going difficult. After a few minutes and maybe twenty feet, a front wheel dropped into a deep pothole and there was a crunch. Heidi stopped pushing. She rested her back against the boot and gazed up at the blue sky.

'Any vultures in Mid Wales?' she asked.

'Don't need them,' Stacey said. 'Half a dozen kites can strip a dead sheep in a day.'

'Comforting thought, thanks.' Heidi pushed herself off the car. 'Time for plan B then. How far have we travelled since we left the road?'

'Two or three miles perhaps.'

'And how far away is BB's farmhouse?'

'I'll be honest, I have no idea. Wish I'd asked Jack more about his interesting journey.'

'Well, we have an interesting choice,' Heidi said, 'not dissimilar to the one faced by Alexander the Great on his search for the Oracle at the Temple of Amun. Smaller scale of course.'

'What are you talking about?'

'Not important. Shall we go on and hope BB will help us? And give us coffee. Or do we trek back to the road and pray we get there before dark. I can't imagine there's much traffic in the pass after the sun goes down.'

'Not much anytime of the day,' Stacey muttered.

Heidi removed their bags from the car. 'Let's go on,' she said. 'If we're going to have an adventure, may as well go for the whole hog.'

They set off on the track running along the bottom of the valley, startling the occasional rabbit and mountain hare. A shallow stream ran alongside the path and Stacey spotted a dipper, bobbing up and down on a moss-covered boulder. A buzzard, riding high thermals, called to his mate. The sound echoed in the emptiness before the valley soaked up the wild cry like a sponge. Heidi was beginning to wonder if she had made the wrong decision when she spotted the top of a smoking chimney. She turned and grinned at her friend.

'Tell you one thing, Stace, I'm certainly not bored now.'

Heidi walked to the door and knocked loudly. It was opened by a very large woman, who peered at her visitors suspiciously.

'*Prynhawn da*,' Heidi said. '*Mae rhywbeth yn bod ar fy nghar.*' Good afternoon. There is something wrong with my car.

'*Pwy dych chi?*' the woman asked. Who are you?

'*Heidi ydw i.*' I'm Heidi. She nodded at Stacey. '*Fy ffrind, Stacey.*' My friend Stacey.

'Bronwen ydw i. Alla I'ch helpu chi?' I'm Bronwen. Can I help you?

Heidi smiled. '*Os gwelwch yn dda. Mae twll yn y teiar.*' Please. The tyre has a puncture.

Bronwen nodded, stepped out of the house and walked towards a battered Land Rover.

'Is she going to help us?' Stacey asked.

'Looks like it.'

The large woman stomped across the dusty yard, climbed into the vehicle and beckoned for the women to join her.

'*Diolch yn fawr.*' Thanks very much, Stacey said, using her limited grasp of Welsh.

Bron nodded, fired up the engine and headed slowly towards Stacey's car.

Encouraged, Stacey asked, '*Siarad Saesneg?*' Speak English?

Bron smiled. '*Tipyn bach.*' A little.

'Have you lived here long?' Stacey asked.

'Born here,' Bron said.

'And your da lives with you?'

Bron nodded.

'No mam?'

Bron shook her head. 'Died, years ago.'

The truck neared the broken-down car. Bron grasped the steering wheel hard and yanked it to the left so the wheels bumped out of the track and onto the short grass. She stepped out.

'Which tyre?' she asked.

Heidi pointed. 'We tried to push the car so we could use the jacking points, but we hit a pothole.'

Bron dropped the truck down behind the car and fastened a rope. She revved her engine and gently towed the car backwards until all four wheels were more or less level, and turned off the engine. Bron dragged out a heavy pillar-jack, rolled it beneath the front of the car and lifted it easily. She looked up and smiled. Heidi changed the wheel and Bron lowered the jack.

'There,' she said. 'Are you lost?'

'No,' Stacey said. 'We were coming to see you.'

'*Pam?*' Why?

'I work for the local paper and I'm writing an article about Robin Townsend? The man found dead in town.'

'I know, the police told me.'

'You saw him in the pub the night he died?'

Bron nodded.

'Did he say anything to you?'

'I offered him a lift. He wanted to walk.' Bron dumped the heavy jack in the Land Rover. 'Follow me to the house. You can turn round there and go.' Bron got into her truck, bumped it back into the ruts and set off.

Stacey started the car and followed gingerly.

'Do you think she'll talk to me when we get to her place?' Stacey asked.

'Wouldn't bank on it,' Heidi said. 'I saw her face change when you started asking questions.'

'Better not bank on coffee either then?'

'Better not.'

Stacey reached the end of the track without further incident and spotted Bron standing in front of the door, arms akimbo. Stacey pulled closer and wound down her window.

'Thank you so much for helping us,' she said. 'We'd have been in trouble without you.'

Bron nodded. 'Car no good. Dangerous road. Don't come back.' She went inside and shut the door.

'Definitely no coffee,' Heidi said. 'Let's get off this bloody track and back to the road. Be careful, I'm not sure Bron will help us a second time.'

'I agree, and it's my fault. Too many questions. Trouble is I have lots of those and not necessarily about Robin's death.'

'Oh? Like what?'

'How BB and her da manage to live like they do for one. I didn't know of their existence and I've been here for years. Feels as though I've discovered a lost tribe of two – something like that.'

‘It is certainly curious,’ Heidi said. ‘I’ll have a dig around when I’m home. See if I can find out anything about them and let you know.’ She chuckled. ‘I can already tell you this. BB is more than capable of posing Townsend on the kite. Did you see her forearms? Massive like a bloke’s.’

Chapter eight

Jack turned off the A40 at Llandovery and headed towards Llanagethin, hoping he'd be able to get across the ranges to home before dark.

'What do you make of Kevin?' he asked, slowing for a sharp left-hander.

'Not sure,' Ben said. 'His mood seems to change continually. I wondered if he was stoned.'

'Same here. I think we should dig a bit deeper into young Mr Townsend.'

'Why's that?'

'He was in the vicinity when his brother died. That seems a touch coincidental to me.'

'Is that it?'

'No, and this might sound a bit left field, but he's an artist. Street art inspired no less. If you ask me, it looks as though Robin was turned into street art.'

'Well, Sergeant, if you're right, we need to find an accomplice. Kevin would be lucky to lift a bag of sugar on top of the kite, let alone a dead body.'

'So Ian helped him. Didn't go back to Tenby like he said and they used the van to move Robin, from wherever he was when he lost consciousness, to The Square. Pulled up close to the statue, made sure the coast was clear, then put him in place and legged it.'

'OK, I'll buy it. Worth looking at. We need to find out who rented the van, what time it was returned and who returned it. Get the reg number and have Ollie check the ANPR again for any sightings.'

Jack nodded. 'We ought to nip into the Wyeside Arts Centre in Builth. Have a chat with the manager. Get her take on Kevin Townsend and have a look at his exhibition.'

'Top of tomorrow's list. Any word from SOCO and their visit to the victim's residence?'

'I had a phone call earlier. Not much I'm afraid. As expected, prints from the victim, a few still unidentified. Samples from the carpet match fibres found on Robin's feet.'

'Any sign of his clothes?' Ben asked.

'No dirty laundry anywhere. I reckon he could have been spiked in the boozer. Fits in nicely with my theory.'

'What motive would Ian and Kevin have for getting rid of their brother?'

'The obvious one is money,' Jack said, 'always is. Robin dies, leaves his worldly to the other two, and their third becomes more like half.'

'Valid notion,' Ben said.

'Alternatively, they knew Robin killed his girlfriend. Suffered the fall out he brought to their own doors, were disgusted by what he did and got away with, and made sure he never got away with anything like it again.'

'Why not kill him when they all still lived in London? Why wait all this time?'

'Dunno, guv. Maybe they thought something like this would be easier to get away with out in the boonies.' He grinned. 'Everyone thinks the Met is sharp, but...' He shook his head.

'Has to be worth putting the pair of them under the microscope to see what we can discover.'

Jack nodded and pulled in tight to the verge outside Noddfa.

'Sure you don't want a cuppa?' Ben asked.

Jack shook his head. 'I'm fine, guv. Told Julie I'd be home at a reasonable hour. Her parents are coming for supper. My job is to entertain the twins while Julie rustles up some food.'

'OK, we'll meet at the nick tomorrow. If you're in before me, have Tegan find out about the rental van. Ollie and Elsa can work through the tapes again while we pay a visit to the Wyeside in Builth Wells.

* * *

The next morning after Ben had set off for the station, Stacey was in her office researching recent incidents of spiking when the phone rang.

'Hello, Stacey Logan.'

'Hi, are you busy?'

'Hi, Erica. Not overly so, why?'

'I've just spoken with a young woman who has woken up in a motel at Sarn Park services, junction 36 on the M4.'

'I'm guessing she has no memory of how she got there?'

'You guess right. We spoke at length. She was fairly distressed at the start of the conversation but calmed down when I explained there were other cases and sexual assault was unlikely.'

'That's good, but I don't understand why you called me.'

'I told her a reporter was working on the spiking story. Told her that you want to warn others not to fall prey to this and she said she'd be happy to speak to you.'

'Wow! Thanks for setting this up. Where are you?'

'En route. Get there as quick as you can. I'll leave word at reception for you to be brought to the room. How long do you think you'll be?'

'I'll get a shift on, but at least an hour and a half.'

'OK. I'll keep in touch and let you know if anything changes. Just do your best.'

'I will. See you soon.'

Stacey hung up and dug out her kit bag. She left the cottage, backed the car out of the drive and took the steep lane up to the range road. She drove across the mountain as quickly as she dared, dropped down to Llywel, where Jack and Julie had their own cottage, then turned towards Brecon and picked up the A470, crossing through the Beacons to Merthyr Tydfil.

Good weather had encouraged late holidaymakers onto the road. Groups of middle-aged men riding sport motorbikes zoomed past her when the road allowed, only to congregate further along next to burger vans parked in lay-bys. The car parks close to the Cantref and Llwyn-on reservoirs were also packed with large motorhomes, owners sitting on folding chairs enjoying a cuppa in the sun. Stacey was impatient and considered cutting across country but there was no easy route through the tangle of small A-roads linking old mining communities. She gritted her teeth, kept her foot down and finally hit the M4 at junction 32. She sped up, keeping her eyes open for speed cameras.

Entering the services complex, she toured the car park at a more sedate pace and eventually spotted a sign advertising a motel. On the second trip past rows of parked cars, she spotted a space, pulled in, slung her bag across her shoulders and marched determinedly towards reception. Pushing through two sets of double doors, she found herself in a clean but sparsely furnished area, with thin red carpet, magnolia walls and an economically constructed front desk. The young woman behind the desk looked up as Stacey entered and flashed a mouthful of unrealistically white teeth.

'Good morning and welcome,' she said. 'How can I help you?'

‘Morning,’ Stacey said, puffing slightly from her march from the car. ‘I’m Stacey Logan, here to see DS Bevan. I believe you’re expecting me.’

The receptionist’s smile was replaced by a concerned frown. She leaned across the desk and lowered her voice, even though they were alone.

‘Can you tell me what’s going on?’ she asked. ‘I mean, I ought to know. I’m the closest thing to management on site.’

‘Sorry,’ Stacey said. ‘I don’t know anything myself yet. Can you tell me which room Sergeant Bevan is in?’

‘Number six. Let me show you the way.’

‘No need, thanks. You shouldn’t abandon your post. I’m sure I can find my own way.’

Stacey walked through another set of cheap, laminate doors and made her way along a quiet corridor, numbered rooms on each side. Number six was at the end and she tapped gently with her knuckles. It was opened almost immediately by Erica.

‘What took you so long?’ she hissed.

‘No blue light,’ Stacey hissed back.

Erica stepped to one side and Stacey entered the room which was depressingly similar to nearly every motel room she had ever stayed in. Sitting on one of the twin beds, feet on the bedspread, back resting against the headboard, was a woman, late teens or early twenties, wearing a short red dress splashed with silver sparkles. A pair of red heels lay on the floor, a crumpled, short leather jacket close by. She looked up with swollen, puffy eyes as Stacey walked closer.

‘Hello,’ the woman said. ‘I’m Lizzie. Are you Stacey, Erica’s friend?’

Stacey smiled. ‘Yes, that’s me. You know I’m a reporter don’t you?’

Lizzie nodded. ‘Erica told me.’ She dabbed her eyes. ‘I’m not sure I can tell you much. I don’t really know what has happened to me, can’t remember because of the drugs

I was given. I'm hoping if I talk to you about my experience, I might remember some more.'

'Must be very confusing having a gap in your memory.'

'A gap? It feels more like a bottomless void that I'm teetering on the edge of.' She blew her nose. 'Sorry, I'm rambling.'

Erica said, 'I'll go and round up some hot drinks. Can I get you anything to eat, Lizzie?'

'No thanks. Feel a bit pukey if I'm honest, but tea would be great.'

Erica smiled. 'Back soon.'

Stacey perched on the spare bed and put her bag next to her.

'You sure you're happy to talk to me?' she asked. 'If you've changed your mind, it's fine. I'm not going to force you. I'm not that sort of reporter.'

'I'm sure,' Lizzie said. 'I don't want this to happen to other women. Erica says she'll do everything she can to catch the guy who spiked me.' The flicker of a smile curled her lips. 'You have no idea how glad I was when she came on the phone. Didn't want to have to talk to some random guy.'

'You'll be well looked after, Erica is a great cop. Do you mind if I record our chat? I won't share it with anyone else.'

'OK with me.'

Stacey placed a small digital recorder on the bedside table and switched it on.

'Thank you,' she said. 'Now, take your time and just tell me what you remember.'

Lizzie took a deep breath then said, 'Me and three mates were on a girlie night out. We went to the Boston Bar, a club in Cardiff. We'd been before and had a lush time.'

Erica re-entered the room and handed out takeaway paper cups then sat on the only chair.

'Anyway,' Lizzie continued, 'I was at the bar and a guy offered me a drink.' She frowned. 'I don't usually take drinks from someone I don't know, but I was a bit low on funds like, so I said yes.'

'Tell me what he looked like,' Stacey said.

'Just a guy. About my age, bit taller, white, not fat or thin, an ordinary guy.'

'Did you talk about anything?'

'Not really, the music was too loud to actually have a conversation.'

'So, you accepted a drink. Then what?'

'Wasn't long before I felt awful – dizzy and sick. I fell off my heels and he put an arm around my waist, told me I needed some fresh air.' She dabbed her eyes again and looked up at Stacey. 'That was the last thing I remember, his arm around my waist, then I woke up here.' She snatched her tea, took a large gulp and a new rush of tears began to flow. 'I need to know what he did to me,' Lizzie said. 'I really need to know.'

Chapter nine

Jack pushed through the main door of the Wyeside Arts Centre and held it open for his boss. They walked past a ticket office and into an area with a small bar and a couple of groups of chairs surrounding low tables in the front windows. A young man looked up from behind the bar and smiled.

'Good morning, gentleman. Can I get you anything?'

'Couple of coffees would be great,' Jack said.

'Take a seat. I'll bring them over.'

'Is the manager in?' Ben asked.

'Upstairs in the office. May I ask why you want to see her?'

Ben showed his warrant card. 'DCI James and DS Trent. We just need a quick word.'

The bartender nodded, poured two mugs of coffee and delivered them to the table. 'I'll go and give her a shout.'

'Nice place this,' Jack said. 'Julie and I come to the cinema when we get time off, or a comedy night. The twins really enjoy the Christmas shows.'

They heard a door open and got to their feet as a pretty, middle-aged woman with long curly hair which hung around her face in tight spirals, entered the bar.

'Good morning,' she said and offered a graceful hand. 'I'm Corinne Ballinger, manager. What can I do for you?'

The officers introduced themselves, shook hands, and they all sat.

'We'd like to ask you about Kevin Townsend,' Ben said. 'We understand you are hosting an exhibition of his work.'

'That's right, we are. What would you like to know?'

'What's your impression of him?'

'Am I allowed to know the reason behind your question?'

'You may have heard about the murder in Llanwrtyd?' Jack asked.

Corinne nodded.

'Kevin is the younger brother of the victim.'

'Oh, God, how awful! Poor man. Is he OK?'

Ben nodded. 'We spoke with him and his older brother, Ian, yesterday. They're coping.'

'I met them both when they delivered Kevin's artwork. Seemed like a pleasant couple of chaps. Said they live in Tenby.'

'That's right,' Jack said.

'Must be dreadful to experience the murder of a family member.'

'Yes,' Ben agreed. 'So, what can you tell me about the brothers?'

'Not that much really. As I said, they were pleasant. Arrived mid-morning, unloaded the van and worked until after lunch hanging the pieces.' Corinne got to her feet. 'Come into the gallery and take a look.'

She led the way out of the bar area, past a flight of steps leading down to the theatre, and into a large, narrow room. A long table constructed from smaller ones took up the centre of the space, chairs tucked beneath.

'We sometimes hold courses in here,' Corinne explained. 'Creative writing, that sort of thing, and we also hire the room for conferences.'

Jack wandered slowly around the walls, gazing at a host of expansive canvases. They were all brightly coloured, a mixture of what looked like aerosol paint and thick black lines. Some appeared to be "tags", a series of letters and names, similar to graffiti painted on walls, bridges and old railway carriages. Others imitated the famous Bristolian street artist, Banksy, but didn't manage to reflect the satirical skill used by the original.

'Is this any good?' Jack asked. 'In your opinion?'

'Well,' Corinne said, 'it shows promise. Kevin obviously knows how to handle paint, has some skill, but I'm not sure he quite pulled off what he was after. His work isn't original enough, but he's young and will probably improve with time.'

'Did he seem OK to you?' Ben asked.

'What do you mean by "OK"?'

'When we spoke to him yesterday, he seemed – I don't know – moody. Up one minute, down the next.'

'Ah, I know what you mean. Must admit I wondered if he was a little bipolar or something similar, but moodiness isn't uncommon in creative types.'

'How about his brother, Ian?' Jack asked.

Corinne shrugged. 'Just an ordinary chap. Happy to help his brother with the exhibition. Seemed quite proud of him.'

Ben's mobile rang. He mumbled an apology, took it from his pocket and walked out of the room.

'DCI James.'

'Tegan here, sir. Where are you?'

'Builth, at The Wyeside. Why?'

'I'm in Llanwrtyd with a local woman who wants to talk to you. Looks like she has found the victim's clothes.'

'OK. Keep her with you. We'll leave now.'

'Yes, sir.'

Ben put his phone away and stuck his head inside the gallery.

'Sergeant. We need to be somewhere.' Ben smiled at Corinne. 'Thank you for your time. Sorry to be so abrupt, but we have to leave.'

'No problem,' she said. 'Hope I've been useful.' She hesitated. 'Are you asking about the Townsends because you think they were involved with the murder of their brother?'

'Just covering bases,' Ben said. 'Thanks again.'

The detectives left the building, crossed over the busy road and made their way to the car park on the banks of the river Wye.

'What's up, guv?' Jack asked.

'A woman in Llanwrtyd might have found Robin's clothes. Tegan is keeping her company until we get there.'

They got in the car and Jack manoeuvred it out of the space, threaded his way through the one-way system in town and as soon as he was out the other side, put his foot down. Fifteen minutes later they pulled up behind Tegan's squad car and Ben spotted her sitting on a bench next to the kite, an older woman by her side. Jack parked outside the cafe, they left the car and walked to The Square. Tegan got to her feet.

'Morning, sir,' she said. 'Come and meet Mrs Webb.'

Ben crossed the small patch of grass and sat next to the elderly woman.

'Good morning,' he said. 'I'm DCI James and my partner is DS Trent. Constable Hedges tells us you've found some clothes. Is that right?'

Mrs Webb nodded. 'Yes, that's right.' She held up dirty hands, nails caked with earth. 'I was planting bulbs in the containers under the statue. I'm a member of *Merched y Bont* and we take care of most of the planters in town.'

'*Merched y Bont*?' Ben queried.

Mrs Webb smiled. 'Women of the Bridge,' she explained. 'A splinter group of the WI.'

'Where are the clothes?'

Mrs Webb pointed a finger twisted with arthritis at the pots. 'In there,' she said. 'Buried in the compost. I haven't dug them out because I thought they might have something to do with the awful murder.'

'You did exactly the right thing,' Ben said.

He snapped on gloves and pulled out a biro which he used to prod into the soil. He heard footsteps and turned to see Denise Brumby walking towards him with a pair of mugs in her hands.

'Morning,' she said. 'I saw your officer and old Mrs Webb sitting out here. Thought they could do with a cuppa. What's going on?'

Jack intercepted her. 'Very kind of you,' he said, relieving her of the tea. 'Any chance of a couple more?'

'Suppose,' Denise said, 'but you didn't answer me. What's going on?'

'Sorry, I can't discuss the case.'

Denise shrugged. 'Fair enough. Tea or coffee?'

'Whatever's easiest,' Jack said. 'Two sugars in each. Thanks.'

Denise crossed back over the road and walked along the pavement towards her pub. Jack handed a mug to Mrs Webb.

'*Diolch.* I could do with that,' she said and slurped noisily.

Jack walked back to the planters and peered over Ben's shoulder as he poked about in the earth.

'I think there's a wallet in the trousers,' Ben said quietly.

Jack removed a plastic evidence bag from his pocket, carefully extricated the wallet and tapped off excess compost. He opened the wallet carefully.

'Well?' Ben asked.

'Belongs to our man.' Jack dropped it in the bag. 'I'll whistle up SOCO, although how they missed this first time around I'll never know.'

Denise reappeared with more tea.

'Oo,' she said. 'A wallet. Is it Robin's?'

Ben straightened up and took a mug. 'You need to step back please.'

Denise didn't move. 'Found anything else?'

Jack stepped closer. 'Thanks for the tea,' he said, helping himself to the remaining mug. 'The Chief Inspector is right, you really do need to move away. This is a crime scene and we don't want to run the risk of corrupting any evidence.'

'Well, that's bleeding nice I must say. I'll be on my way then. Make sure someone brings my mugs back.' Denise turned and stomped away.

Chapter ten

Ben let himself in through the front door of Noddfa, draped his jacket on the newel post and called for Stacey.

'In the office,' she answered. 'I'll be there in a minute.'

Ben smiled, walked into the kitchen and began to lay the table. Stacey appeared in the kitchen a few minutes later and brushed a kiss on her partner's cheek.

'How's your day been?' she asked and opened the Aga door to remove a chicken casserole.

'Busy,' Ben said. 'Yours?'

'The same. Erica rang first thing, another woman had reported being spiked in Cardiff. Her name is Lizzie Palmer and she woke up distressed and confused in a motel at Sarn Park just off the motorway.'

'Sounds as though you've met her.'

Stacey chuckled. 'No wonder you're a detective. Yes, I have. Erica arranged for me to interview Lizzie for the paper.'

'Not sure that was such a good idea.'

'I don't know why you'd say that.'

'Might affect a future court case.'

'If there is one,' Stacey said. 'Lizzie was happy to talk, anxious to warn other young women about what is going on. It's not like I'm planning to plaster her face across the front page.'

'Yeah, I guess.' Ben sighed and plonked himself on the carver. 'How was she?'

'As I said, very distressed and very confused. Losing a chunk of time from your memory is pretty unsettling.'

'I can see that.'

'So, tell me about your day,' Stacey said, lifting a tray of roast potatoes from the oven.

'Went to the Wyeside with Jack. Not sure we learned much but we managed to have a look at Kevin's exhibition.'

'Any good?'

'Didn't do much for me, to be honest, just like graffiti in frames. Didn't stay long. Tegan rang. An elderly resident of Llanwrtyd discovered a set of clothes buried in the planters beneath the statue. They belonged to the victim.'

'Gosh. That's progress.'

'Need to wait while FSS takes a look, but I'm hoping they'll find something to move the case forward.'

Stacey dished out supper while Ben poured chilled white wine into glasses. He took a sip, then turned his attention to the food, forked a large hunk of chicken into his mouth and chewed.

'This is delicious, Pumpkin, thanks.'

They ate in silence for a few minutes then Ben asked, 'Did you get your tyre fixed? I still can't believe you and Heidi went off-roading in your old banger.'

'Wouldn't have done if I knew how disgustingly awful the track to BB's farmhouse was. Heidi said we should have taken her truck.'

'You'd have been better off not going at all.'

Stacey topped up their glasses. 'Drink some more,' she said, 'you're grumpy, and yes, I did get the tyre fixed at Sammy's in Llandovery.'

Ben shovelled more food into his mouth. 'So, did BB tell you anything?'

'No. She helped us with the car but wouldn't let us in the house. How do people live so isolated? I didn't know she existed. I asked around town and very few residents knew about her either. I'm sure newcomers thought I was relaying some ancient Welsh myth.'

Ben nodded. 'There aren't many like her around anymore. Mind you, I reckon I could get used to it, living in the wilds. No twenty-first-century noise, just the sounds of nature, and of course the odd low-flying RAF jet.'

'I can see the appeal, but not sure I could handle it. I'm not built like BB.'

Ben grinned. 'Thankfully.'

'Tell you one thing though, she'd have no trouble tossing a body on top of the kite. She swung a pillar jack around as though it was a bag of feathers.'

'I know what you mean. I wouldn't want to upset her, but why would she kill Robin? We don't know they'd even met, apart from in the Stonecroft the evening he died. Murder requires a motive and I can't see one.'

* * *

The phone shook the couple awake a little after seven the next morning. Stacey fumbled on the bedside table for the handset and held it to her ear.

'Hello?'

'Sorry to wake you, Stace. Is Ben with you?'

'Hang on.' She dug her partner in the ribs. 'Jack for you.' She passed the phone over and snuggled back under the duvet.

'What's up, Sergeant?' Ben asked, his voice heavy with sleep.

'I'm on my way to you. A body's been found in Cilmery. I'll pick you up from Noddfa. Ten minutes away.'

'A body in Cilmery?' Ben asked, rubbing his eyes, but the weak connection had dropped out.

'Trouble?' Stacey asked from beneath the bedding.

'Looks like it. Jack's on his way.' Ben got out of bed and began pulling on clothes.

'Anything I might be interested in?'

'Undoubtedly, but before you ask, you can't come. Stay here and I'll ring you later.'

Ben finished dressing and splashed his face with cold water in the bathroom. He slipped out of the cottage and perched on the low, front wall. A few minutes later, Jack's vehicle appeared around the bend. Ben got into the car then Jack turned it around and headed through the lanes towards the main road at Garth.

'So, tell me,' Ben said.

'A sergeant at Builth station took the first call. He's already sent SOCO out with the white tent. Needed to get the body out of sight sharpish.'

'Why the urgency?'

'Because it's tied to the monument in Cilmery, right next to the road.'

'Man? Woman?'

'Man. No identity, no clothes. Sounds very similar to the previous killing.'

Jack hit the main road, switched on the blue lights but not the siren, and soon pulled into a small lay-by just past a cottage with red window frames.

'People in the cottage called this in about an hour and a half ago.'

Ben nodded. 'OK. Let's take a look, see what we're dealing with.'

The officers left the car and walked through a small pedestrian wooden gate. The monument, sitting on top of a low mound, was set in about two thirds of an acre of grass, surrounded by thirteen oak trees representing the thirteen historic counties of ancient Wales, and obscured by a white tent. Ben dipped his head to enter and was aware of a pale body which seemed to be hanging from the fifteen-foot-tall shard of Caernarvonshire granite, head and face in shadow. He spotted Carrie working behind the stone and wished her good morning.

'Fancy seeing you out here,' she said with a smile. 'And before you ask, I'll need to examine him before I can be any use to you. However' – she held up an evidence bag – 'there was a card in the victim's mouth... U2.'

'Guv,' Jack called. 'Come and look at this.'

Ben walked around the stone and Jack pointed a torch beam at the victim's face.

'Is that who I think it is?' he asked.

Ben looked up and stared into the sightless eyes of Ian Townsend. 'Bloody hell,' he muttered. 'Who found him?'

'Like I said, the couple in the cottage. Spotted him as soon as they opened their bedroom curtains just after five thirty. They dialled 999 immediately and spoke to Sergeant Biggs. They're a bit shaken. Tegan's with them making tea. Ollie is checking out the immediate area.'

Ben rubbed his face and groaned. 'What does this mean, Jack?' he asked.

'That someone has it in for the Townsend boys, or you-know-who fancies a full share of the parents' stash.'

Carrie joined them and removed her gloves.

'Time of death between midnight and three this morning. I don't know what caused his death, no injuries or defence wounds, but discovering the card convinces me I'll find date rape drugs in his system.'

'Same killer then?' Ben asked.

Carrie smiled. 'Not being a copper, I don't get to make pronouncements like that, but it would seem likely.'

'How was he strung up there?'

'Rope under his arms, wrists tied together and ropes from them crossed over the top of the stone and attached to the chest rope. Effectively hung him from his arms.'

'Any sign of his clothes?' Jack asked.

'Not so far. Ollie and a few uniforms are having a look.' She snapped a couple more photos. 'Do you need him longer, or shall I have him brought down?'

'Take him down,' Ben said.

The detectives vacated the tent so the body could be removed, and walked to the back of the site where Jack spotted a stone with chiselled letters on its face.

> *Ger y fan hon y lladdwyd Llywelyn ein llyw olaf 1282*

'What does that say, guv?' he asked.

'That it was near this place Llewelyn the Last was killed.'

'And he was a prince?'

Ben nodded. 'The English took his head to London where it was displayed for weeks. There's a small well at the back of the site where the head was washed.'

Jack snorted. 'I can see why some of the Welsh aren't keen on Englishmen although, having said that, I've never had any trouble, even with my upper-class accent.'

They turned back to the monument and watched as a stretcher was carried from beneath the tent and taken to a waiting ambulance. Ben spotted movement behind a large bush on the other side of the main road and sighed. Stacey hadn't gone back to sleep after all and this latest murder was sure to grace the front page of tomorrow's *Mid Wales Times*.

* * *

Stacey was in her office working on the new article. She smiled when she looked at the picture she'd taken of the stretcher being loaded into a dark van, with Ben and Jack standing side by side in the background. Knowing neither would be overjoyed at seeing their faces in the press, she hoped they didn't look too closely. An email from Sam Jenkins pinged in, demanding the article. Stacey uploaded the finished piece and was composing a reply when the doorbell rang. She got to her feet and discovered Heidi on the doorstep.

'Hey, you,' Stacey said. 'Come in. Coffee on the stove. I just need a couple of ticks to finish an email.'

'Knock yourself out,' Heidi said and headed for the kitchen.

By the time Stacey joined her, Heidi had poured two mugs of strong and black and was adding sugar to her own. Stacey sat opposite her friend.

'Are you bored again?' she asked.

'Far from it,' Heidi said. 'Anyway, look where we ended up last time I told you I was bored.'

Stacey grinned. 'Quite an experience, I agree. So, if you're not bored, what are you doing?'

'Research and lots of thinking.'

'What about?'

'Mainly this spiking business and I don't like what I've found.'

Stacey cut two slices of bara brith. Heidi began picking sultanas out of her slice with nimble fingers, before putting them in her mouth.

'So – spiking,' Stacey said. 'What did you find?'

'Way too many occurrences of this vile practice and a huge amount of under-reporting. Many victims feel stupid and don't come forward, and of course aren't keen to do so because everyone knows how police officers deal with them. Disbelieving, uncompassionate and incredulous seem to sum up their attitude.'

'All this was on the net, was it?'

'Not quite. I joined a Facebook group based around clubbing, under a false name, gathered "friends" and monitored what they talked about amongst themselves. As I said, there are many more victims than those which show up on the system.'

'Are they all in Cardiff?'

'Mainly, but not exclusively.'

'Any idea what to do about it?'

Heidi grinned. 'Funnily enough… fancy a trip to the capital?'

'What, today?'

'Why not? You are the investigative journalist after all.'

'What will we do when we get there?' Stacey asked.

'We can start by looking at the clubs. There are three that seem to have been particularly badly affected. I'd like a chat with the owners. Find out what, if anything, they are doing to try to prevent this sort of thing happening.'

'Sounds like a plan. Help yourself to another cuppa while I change, then we can get off.'

Chapter eleven

Jack tore along the A40 while Ben mentally thanked the inventor of seatbelts and clung to the grab rail above the passenger door.

'Kevin better be there,' Jack growled. 'If he's absent, in my mind that proves he's the killer.'

Playing devil's advocate Ben muttered, 'Unless he popped out for milk.'

'I'm sure it's him,' Jack said. 'If not for the money, then because he knew Robin was a killer and maybe also that Ian was involved. Who else would display the bodies like that other than an artist?'

'A psychopath perhaps? Relatives of the murdered woman? Honestly, Jack, you've been at this game long enough to know gut feelings aren't evidence. If you fixate on them, you'll run the risk of missing real clues.'

Jack snorted. 'Not like we've got many of those. How long is FSS gonna take examining the clothes we recovered?'

'Too long for you, obviously.'

'We should never have handed forensics to outside labs. Utter madness.'

'I agree, but it is what it is.'

Jack humphed, turned onto the A477 towards Tenby and a short while later pulled up in a car park at the top of the caravan site. A marked police car rested on the gravel, a couple of uniformed officers in the front seats. They left the vehicle as Ben opened his door.

'Morning, sir,' the driver said.

'Morning, Constable. Anything to tell us?'

'Yes, sir. We've tried to speak to Ian Townsend's wife, Anna, but she's not at home. The site manager, Bill Hill – nice chap, helpful – informed us she left with the children yesterday morning, said she was going to London to spend time with her folks.'

'Any sign of Kevin, the younger brother?'

'Not so far, sir. We checked his place and he doesn't seem to be around.'

'There's a bloody surprise,' Jack muttered under his breath.

Ben frowned at him and said, 'I'll take a walk down and make sure. Sergeant, with me.'

The detectives set off along the narrow strip of tarmac which circled the site. At the bottom, on the edge of a patch of woodland, Kevin's converted cottage came into sight, a second building next to it. Ben marched up to the cottage and pounded loudly on the door. Not receiving an answer, he repeated the exercise.

'Jack, check out the studio would you?'

Ben tried the door and was surprised when it swung open. Cautiously he pushed it wider and stuck his head into a small living room, its walls covered with garish artwork.

'Kevin Townsend?' he called. 'Police. Are you in here?'

Ben climbed the stairs, the bedrooms were empty, as was the bathroom, office and kitchen. He left the cottage and walked towards the studio. Stepping inside he was surprised to see Jack towering over Kevin, who was sitting on a chair, face in his hands. Jack moved closer to his boss.

'I've told him about Ian,' he said quietly. 'Lad was wearing earphones and working on a large canvas. Didn't hear anyone knocking at the cottage.'

Ben nodded, then sat on a chair next to the young man and asked, 'Are you alright? Can I get you something?'

Kevin shook his head, rubbed his face and then looked at Ben.

'Is it true?' he asked. 'Is Ian really dead?'

'I'm sorry, but yes it's true.'

'Was he... you know... killed like Robin?'

'We're not sure yet, but it's possible.'

'Someone caught up with him too then?'

'What do you mean?'

'First Robin, now Ian. Am I at risk? Is someone coming for me?'

'Why would you think that?' Ben asked.

Kevin shrugged, then he got to his feet and wandered out of the studio.

'Where are you going?'

'I need a cuppa,' Kevin said over his shoulder.

Ben and Jack followed Kevin into his cottage. He flopped on a chair and Jack put the kettle on and began a hunt for mugs and teabags.

Ben sat opposite and asked, 'Where were you last night, Kevin?'

'Here, working. Why? You can't think I killed Ian?'

'We have to ask. Anyone with you? Someone who can confirm you were at home?'

'No, I was alone. I can't paint with an audience.'

'We spoke to your site manager, Mr Hill, who told us Mrs Townsend went to London yesterday morning. Might he be able to confirm you were here last night?'

'I don't know. Ask him.'

Ben nodded. 'Yes, we will. Do you know why Ian's family went to London?'

'She said she was visiting her folks.'

'Leaving Ian at home?'

'Usually does. Her dad and my brother didn't get on in the slightest.'

'Why was that?'

'He was never very keen on Ian, but after he got arrested with Robin, he was upgraded to persona non grata. The man wouldn't have him in the house.'

'Did he think Ian was involved with the murder of Robin's girlfriend?'

'How would I know?' Kevin snapped. 'You'll have to ask him.'

Jack carried tea to the table, then he sat next to his boss and asked, 'Do you know where Ian went last night?'

'For fuck's sake! I'm not his keeper. Can't you see I'm hurting here? Lost both parents a couple of years ago and now two brothers within days of each other – bloody murdered – so go away and leave me alone. I need time to grieve.'

Ben leaned across the table and patted Kevin on his shoulder, then he got to his feet, walked outside and beckoned Jack to follow.

'We're not getting far with this,' Ben said. 'He's clearly distressed.'

'Actor as well as artist,' Jack hissed.

'I've already spoken to you about gut feelings.' Ben rubbed his face. 'OK. We'll arrange an FLO from the local nick to keep Kevin company. For all we know, Kevin might be the next on a hit list.'

'That's rubbish. We should interview him properly, under caution, in an interview room.'

'We still can if we think it's necessary, but at this moment in time we have no hard evidence against him. Nothing to warrant an arrest.'

Jack turned and began to walk away.

'Where are you going, Sergeant?'

'To arrange a bloody FLO.'

Ben opened his mouth to reprimand his partner, but knowing it wouldn't help matters, he closed it again and went back inside the cottage.

* * *

Heidi and Stacey were shown into a cramped office at the end of a long corridor leading to the rear of the building. The man behind the desk was the owner of Rascals, a club in the centre of Cardiff. He looked up as the women entered and his eyes widened as he spotted Heidi's tiny frame and her nearly white, very short hair. He looked away and smiled at Stacey.

'Ladies,' he said. 'Can I get you anything to drink?'

'Wouldn't mind some water,' Heidi said.

The man nodded and his long salt-and-pepper hair swung around his face.

'Owen, fetch some bottled water would you?'

A young man in jeans and a T-shirt nodded and left the room, and the club owner leaned back in his chair, lacing his fingers behind his head.

'My security officer said you wanted to talk to the owner about a serious issue. Well, here I am, Jonnie Jones at your service. Who are you and what is the serious issue you wanted to talk about?'

As agreed previously, Stacey began the discussion.

'Thank you for seeing us, Mr Jones.'

'Jonnie please.'

Stacey nodded. 'My name is Stacey Logan. I'm a reporter for *The Mid Wales Times*. My friend is Heidi Holtz, my... researcher.' Stacey saw Heidi twitch and could tell she hadn't appreciated the description.

'Good to meet you both,' Jonnie said.

The office door opened. Owen brought in a tray on which balanced three glasses and three bottles of spring water. Jonnie nodded his thanks and Owen left, closing the door behind him.

'Now then. This serious issue you mentioned.'

Stacey said, 'I'm investigating the practice of spiking which is on the increase; needles too it would seem.'

'It is a problem,' Jonnie admitted, 'and I'll be up for anything that can help.'

'Have you caught anyone at it?' Heidi asked.

'Not conclusively, but we run a tight ship and anyone looking dodgy is asked to leave.'

'Do you conduct searches on entry?'

'Yeah. The door staff are well trained. They sometimes turn up stuff, weed and pills maybe, but we've never found any syringes, on customers or discarded in the club.'

'Is there more you could do to keep clubbers safe?' Stacey asked.

Jonnie chuckled and began counting fingers.

'We pat down, conduct bag searches, there's a medical room on site if anyone needs it, and constant security in the club. I have two employees who dress like punters, mix with the kids and keep an eye out for anything suspicious.' He took a large swallow from his glass. 'All this nastiness spoils the world doesn't it? Each night we open, I stand by the door and talk to the clubbers, tell them who I am. I make sure the girls know they can come to me if they have a problem and ask the boys if they know what "no" means.' He chuckled. 'I tell them to remember it. If they don't, they'll see me again and I won't be smiling. So far, I haven't seen them twice. Just as well, wouldn't know what to do with them.'

'Whack their knuckles with rulers,' Heidi said. 'Teach them to keep their hands to themselves.'

'That's certainly one way of doing it,' Jonnie said and topped up his glass. 'I enjoy watching people having fun, dancing all night, but it's difficult to catch anyone actually tampering with a drink. Doesn't take long to tip powder into a glass.'

'Any ideas about suspects?' Stacey asked. 'Customers who frequent your place who you think are a bit... off?'

'Not really, they're just kids. There's the odd one who has too much to drink, but they're escorted out the second they begin annoying other people.'

'Seems as though you're doing all you can... as strip searches aren't allowed,' Heidi said.

'Funny,' Jonnie said. 'So why did you come to my place? Are you only talking to me?'

'No,' Stacey said. 'We made a list of local clubs suffering this sort of thing and pulled three names out of the hat, including yours.'

'Have you been to the Boston Bar? I've heard they've had problems.'

'On the list,' Heidi said and drained her water.

Stacey got to her feet. 'Thank you for seeing us,' she said. 'Are you happy if I mention you and your establishment in my article?'

Jonnie grinned. 'Depends what you're going to say.'

'That you're a responsible owner who takes his responsibilities to provide a safe space very seriously.' Stacey handed him her business card. 'My number's on there if you want to get in touch.'

Heidi got to her feet. 'And if you ever want a researcher...'

They were shown out and once on the pavement, Heidi giggled.

'Another one who didn't know what to make of me,' she said.

'Are you surprised? No one else looks like you, and you do play up to the image.'

'Of course, it amuses me. Right, we'll visit the Boston Bar then find some food. It's nearly teatime and I'm famished.'

Chapter twelve

Ben called the team to order and took his position at the head of the large table. Jack sat at the back of the incident room, knowing Ben wasn't very pleased with him, and still annoyed that Kevin hadn't been brought in for questioning.

'Right then, you lot,' Ben said. 'Anyone made any progress?'

'Yes, sir,' Tegan said. 'Elsa and I have finally managed to speak to the relatives of the murdered woman in London.'

'All of them?'

'A few had moved away, but I'm pretty sure we tracked down everyone. They all have alibis. None have been near Wales for months, never mind the nights in question. We have a list of friends of the deceased which we're working through, but nothing so far.'

'Have we discovered who the third man in the Stonecroft was the night Robin was killed?'

'No, sir,' Tegan said. 'Not a lot to go on. Pete is quite a common name and I'm not convinced he's a local.'

'Well, keep at it.'

'Carrie's report on Ian Townsend came in,' Ollie Langdon said. 'Large quantities of GHB in his system plus alcohol, also in large amounts. She says there's no doubt about what caused his death. No luck so far with finding his clothes.'

'Anything from FSS?' Jack asked.

'Not yet, Sarge.'

Ben took a seat. 'There are too many loose ends,' he said. 'We need to make more progress than this. CS Warren is getting very twitchy, especially now we have a second body.'

'I spoke to Carrie earlier,' Tegan said, 'and she thinks we should put out a warning.'

'What sort of warning?'

'The sort women are usually given. Don't go out alone, carry your keys in your hand, don't go out after dark...'

Ben snorted. 'Surely she wasn't serious?'

'I think she was, sir.'

'We can't possibly release a statement like that.'

'I don't know why not,' Tegan grumbled. 'It's the same advice women are given – over and over again – makes it look as though it is our fault when something bad happens, rather than the perpetrators.'

Ben nodded but didn't comment. 'As you know,' he said, 'Jack and I went to speak to Kevin Townsend. He seemed genuinely upset by his brother's death. Told us he had been working at home last night and the site manager, Bill Hill, confirms that.'

'So where do we go from here, sir?' Tegan asked.

'Top of the list is to uncover Ian Townsend's movements leading up to his death. Mr Hill told us that Ian's family left for London yesterday morning without him to visit family. Mr Hill saw Ian drive away from the site around lunchtime yesterday, but doesn't know where he went. We need to check ANPR, pick up his vehicle and try to work out where he was going.'

'We ought to be able to find his car,' Ollie said. 'If it wasn't outside his house, and isn't parked next to the memorial in Cilmery, it must be somewhere. I'll get in touch with the local stations and speak to Traffic.'

'Good plan,' Ben said. 'Add Kevin's registration number to the search. We need to prove he wasn't in the area.'

'What about BB?' Tegan asked. 'As far as we know, apart from the killer, she was the last person to speak to Robin Townsend. We need to find out if she knows anything about the second murder. Maybe she was in the area?'

Ben groaned and rubbed his eyes. 'You're right of course, but this time I'm taking the Land Rover. Stacey and Heidi made the trip recently and nearly didn't get back.' He paused, thinking. 'OK,' he said. 'Tegan and Elsa, tomorrow you'll be working on the ANPR images and we'll hope you can trace Ian's car. Jack and I will go to talk to BB. Ollie, take a couple of uniforms and ask around in Cilmery. Find out if anyone saw our latest victim before his death. Also, organise a second fingertip search around the monument for clues, in particular look for his clothes and widen the area.' Ben got to his feet. 'Anyone got anything else to say?' No one did. 'OK, we'll knock off now, back in first thing tomorrow.'

Ben slipped his jacket on, caught Jack's eye and nodded, then went upstairs to speak to CS Warren and provide an update on the investigation.

* * *

Heidi and Stacey wandered down the alley away from the Boston Bar.

'We should have forced our way in,' Heidi said.

Stacey laughed. 'Don't be daft. You aren't a cop anymore and I'm no match for a 6'5" thug-in-a-suit, even if you are. Anyway, he said the owner is only there when the club is open.'

'I'll bet he was upstairs. It's nearly six, he's bound to be in there.'

'We need food. You definitely do, you're crabby.'

'That's cos I haven't eaten since this morning.'

A hand suddenly shot out of the shadows between two large waste bins and fastened on Heidi's arm.

'Hey!' she yelled. Heidi peered into the dark and saw an older teenaged lad, just as his other hand made a clumsy grab for her breasts.

Heidi slapped the hand away and sent a backhander into the darkness where she judged her attacker's face to be. There was a yelp. The hand holding her relaxed and Heidi tore her arm away, as a second lad grabbed her from behind, pining both arms to her sides and lifting her feet clear off the ground. She wriggled and kicked out violently as Stacey ran closer. The first teenager suddenly emerged from between the bins and Stacey cannoned into him. She felt a heavy blow to her thigh, shoved hard and sent him flying backwards, his skull hitting the dirty tarmac of the alley with a loud crack.

Unable to free her arms, Heidi reached down with her right hand, grabbed hold of the young man's scrotum and squeezed with all her strength. A howl of pain filled the evening air. The lad let go, Heidi didn't. Stacey risked a quick glance at her tormentor. Satisfied he wasn't an immediate threat, she dialled 999.

'Police!' she told the operator. 'Alley behind the Boston Bar in Cardiff. Mugging in progress. Send help.'

She hung up and looked at Heidi. Her friend still held the transgressor tightly, but now he was kneeling on the ground, tears running down his face.

'Heidi,' Stacey said, limping closer. 'You need to let him go.'

'Why would you say that?' Heidi asked. 'He might take a swing at us, or try to run away.'

'He'll be lucky if he can walk.' Stacey removed the belt from her jacket and dangled it in front of Heidi's eyes.

'Restrain him rather than castrate him. Police are on their way.'

Heidi took a deep breath and glared at her captive. 'If you run,' she growled, 'you'll wish you hadn't. Got that?'

He nodded. Heidi niftily changed her grip to his wrists and bound them tightly as blue lights penetrated the darkness of the narrow alley.

'How's the other one doing?' she asked.

'Breathing but out cold,' Stacey said. 'He's cut his head.'

'He'll be fine. Lucky you were.'

'What do you mean?'

'I don't want you to freak out or anything,' Heidi said, 'but there's a short knife sticking out of your left thigh.'

'What?' Stacey glanced down and saw a dark wooden handle seemingly glued to her jeans, bright blood soaking the denim. 'I thought he'd punched me.' Her hands moved automatically towards the blade, ready to pull it out.

'No, don't,' Heidi warned. 'Paramedics will be here in seconds.'

A sudden thud of boots in the confined space of the alley sounded as though dozens of officers were running towards them. Heidi squinted into the dark as the lead officer passed beneath a weak overhead light and gasped. Erica! She watched her ex-lover draw closer and spotted the moment Erica recognised her. Heidi couldn't decide whether what she saw on Erica's face was surprise or horror.

'Heidi! What are you doing here?' she asked.

'Your job for you,' Heidi grouched and offered the end of Stacey's belt to Erica, as though passing her a dog's lead. She nodded at the kneeling man. 'This one,' Heidi said, 'grabbed me from behind, lifted me off the ground. The other' – she pointed to the prone teenager – 'tried to sexually assault me, pulled a knife and stabbed Stacey.' She looked back at Erica. 'You did bring paramedics with you?'

'On their way.'

Erica handcuffed the sniffling lad and recited the caution, before handing him to a uniformed constable who led him away. Erica walked closer to Stacey who was propped against a bin and examined the knife.

'You OK?' she asked.

Stacey gave a weak smile. 'Seem to be, so far. Not as painful as I thought being stabbed would be, not much blood either.'

'It'll hurt tomorrow, but the chances are he hasn't nicked anything vital.' Erica bent lower and peered at the fallen teenager as his eyelids flickered open.

He stared into Erica's face and blinked rapidly.

'Wha...?' he mumbled. 'What's happening?'

'I'm arresting you, sunshine, that's what's happening.'

She cautioned him as paramedics arrived, assessed their patients and removed them from the alley. Heidi and Erica listened to Stacey's protests about not needing hospital and that she was fine, until she was loaded into the ambulance and the doors were closed.

'So tell me,' Erica said as the vehicle pulled away. 'What are you two doing here?'

'Looking into the spiking problem you've got. You were the one who asked Stacey to get involved.'

'I meant from a distance. Are you OK? Any injuries?'

Heidi shrugged and cracked her knuckles. 'I'm fine. You know me.'

Erica nodded. 'Yes, I do. Now let's get to the hospital so when Stacey's released, we can take her home. No arguments, you're both staying at my place tonight.'

Chapter thirteen

Just after eight o'clock, Erica unlocked the door to her flat and showed her guests inside.

'Sorry about the muddle,' she said. 'Don't get much time for housework. Go into the living room. I'll open a bottle of wine then ring for a takeaway.'

'I'm on it,' Heidi said. 'If I don't eat soon, something might get broken. I'll phone the local curry house as soon as I've got Stacey comfy.'

Heidi wrapped an arm around her friend's waist and helped her to settle on the sofa, injured leg stretched out on the cushions.

'Are you warm enough? Need a pillow behind you or anything?'

'I'm fine,' Stacey said. 'Don't fuss.'

'You should have accepted a wheelchair,' Heidi said. 'You've got stitches in your muscle as well as the skin. Put too much weight on your leg and they might tear.'

Stacey smiled. 'I know, the nurse told me. I'll be careful.'

Heidi nodded, then she pulled out her mobile and began ordering supper just as Stacey's phone rang and her partner's number flashed on the screen.

'Hi, Sherlock,' she said.

'Where are you?' he asked, sounding irritated. 'I've been ringing but your phone was switched off.'

'I'm sorry. It's been a bit of a day. I'm in Cardiff with Heidi.'

'Well, are you planning to come home any time soon?'

'Uh... no... not really.' Stacey took a deep breath. 'I'm OK and don't want you to be worried, but I managed to get myself stabbed a couple of hours ago. The phone was off cos I was in the hospital.'

'Stabbed? Shit! I'll come and pick you up. Are you still at the hospital?'

'No, we're at Erica's place.'

'What happened?' Ben asked. 'Are you really OK?'

'Honestly I am, just tired. We bumped into a couple of likely lads in a dark alley and I got stabbed in my thigh. Just a few stitches.'

'Is it very painful?'

'It's sore now because the anaesthetic is wearing off, but they gave me painkillers. Erica was first on the scene after I called 999 and both dirtbags were arrested.'

'Give me Erica's address. I can be there before ten.'

'Really, Ben, there's no need. Stay where you are. You sound tired.' She chuckled. 'And grouchy.'

'Sorry, *cariad*. Been a long day and Jack and I aren't seeing eye to eye.'

'Oh?'

'It's nothing.' He sighed. 'Sure you don't want me to collect you?'

'I'm sure, but thanks for the offer.'

'OK then, remember I love you. Sleep well,' Ben said.

'You too.'

Erica entered the room juggling a bottle of wine, glasses, plates and cutlery.

'How long is supper going to be?' she asked.

'Twenty minutes,' Heidi said, helping herself to a glass of wine. She gazed around the room. 'Not a bad place you've got here, E. Better if it was tidy.' She removed a pile of cardboard files from an easy chair and flopped onto it.

'What did you order?' Erica asked, ignoring the jibe.

'Everyone's favourite with stuffed naan and poppadams. I can't remember being so hungry – not ever.'

* * *

After the takeaway had been demolished, and a second bottle of wine was breathing on the low table, the women relaxed.

'Heidi,' Stacey said, 'did you manage to carry out any research on BB?' She turned to Erica. 'Have you heard about the woman who lives in the hills?'

Erica nodded. 'Heidi told me about her... and your adventure, while we waited in the hospital.'

Heidi sipped her wine. 'I've been looking at her,' she said, 'or not looking at her, to be precise.'

'What do you mean?' Stacey asked.

'Well, according to Dyfed-Powys Police, her full name is Bronwen Llewelyn, her dad is Iolo. The police recorded her age as sixty-two. I guess that's what she told them when they visited.'

'And?'

'That's it. Neither are on the electoral roll, no record of any council tax paid or owed.'

'So the council don't know they are there?'

'I don't think anyone does,' Heidi said. She wiped her finger around a foil curry container, then put the finger in her mouth.

'What, no one?' Erica asked.

'When we were messing about with the puncture, BB told us her mother had died years ago and I can't find a record of that. No bills, no bank accounts, not even a birth certificate for BB and trust me – I've looked.'

'How is that possible?' Stacey asked. 'Surely these days everyone is recorded somewhere?'

'Seems not,' Heidi said. 'Think about it. If you didn't need anything from the state and managed to be completely self-sufficient, would you want to have anything to do with it?'

'Probably not,' Stacey agreed. 'I can't stand having to get involved with the council. Trying to get them to do anything useful is like trying to swim the Atlantic with bricks tied to your ankles.'

'Life would certainly be simpler,' Erica said. 'I wonder what it's like inside the cottage.'

Heidi shrugged. 'As you know, we didn't get in.'

'There must be a safeguarding issue here,' Erica said. 'It's not right, people living without proper services.'

Heidi chuckled. 'We all used to. My advice would be to leave them alone.'

Erica frowned. 'But if she did kill Robin Townsend...'

Heidi made a rude noise. 'You need a motive, E. Being big and strong isn't really a good enough reason for even being a suspect.'

Erica poured more wine.

'What about the two lads from this evening?' Stacey asked. 'What will happen to them?'

'They will be interviewed in the morning,' Erica said. 'A night cooling off in the cells won't hurt them. Looks like they match the description Eve Salmon gave us of the men who assaulted her. I'll see if I can arrange an identity parade. Be good if we could add a few more charges which end with a custodial sentence. They need a short, sharp shock.'

Stacey laughed. 'I think Heidi has already delivered one of those. How's Lizzie?'

'As well as can be expected. She insisted on an examination and like the other victims, no one had touched her. She's struggling a little mentally but she's being well cared for at home.'

'That's something to be thankful for.'

'Any useful CCTV from the Boston Bar?' Heidi asked.

Erica shook her head. 'Not really. There is one shot of a kid in a baseball cap standing right next to Lizzie at the bar, but no evidence he put anything in her drink, and zero chance of identifying him.'

'Do you think the same lad has been responsible for all the incidents in town?'

'Can't prove it, but a similar kid, in a similar hat, appears in over half of the available footage.'

'If it is one guy,' Heidi said, 'you need to nick him fast, before he graduates to actually doing worse things to the women he drugs.'

'My thoughts exactly.'

'What about CCTV at the motels the victims end up in?' Stacey asked.

'Crap quality and not much of it.' Erica yawned. 'Sorry, I'm not bored, just knackered.'

'Don't apologise,' Stacey said. 'I'm nodding. The painkillers are making me feel woozy.'

'That's cos you washed them down with two glasses of red,' Heidi said.

Erica hauled herself upright. 'Must be bedtime then,' she said. 'Stacey, you're in the spare room. Heidi's on the sofa, blankets in the airing cupboard.'

The women walked Stacey along the hall and into the spare room. Erica helped her wriggle out of one-legged jeans, shorn during treatment, and Heidi tucked her under the quilt.

'I'll find you some joggers for tomorrow,' Erica said. 'They'll be a bit short, but these are only good for the bin.'

'Thanks.'

'If you need anything in the night, just holler,' Heidi said.

'For goodness sake! Stop fussing the pair of you. I'll see you in the morning.'

'Night then.'

'Yeah, night. Sleep well.'

Erica pulled the door closed, leaving a two-inch gap. Stacey wriggled under the quilt, made sure the wound in her leg was uppermost, and was just about to drop off, when she spotted a pair of shadows glide pass the bedroom door. She smiled to herself in the darkness. It didn't seem as though Heidi was going to be sleeping on the sofa after all.

Chapter fourteen

Ben opened the door of Noddfa and waved Jack inside.

'Blimey, guv. Were you out on the town last night?'

Ben shook his head. 'Be useful, Sergeant. Make some coffee while I finish getting dressed.'

Jack went to the kitchen, switched on the coffee machine and removed a pair of mugs from an overhead cupboard. He glanced up when Ben entered.

'Where's Stacey?' Jack asked. 'Gone out for an early walk? Or seen sense and left you?' He smiled to show he wasn't serious and poured coffee.

'Worse than that,' Ben growled. 'She went to Cardiff with Heidi yesterday and ended up getting stabbed.'

'You're kidding! Is she OK? Shall I drive you over to the hospital? Tell me what I can do, guv.'

'No need for a mercy dash, but thanks. The knife went into her upper thigh, short blade, clean cut. Doc stitched her up, then her and Heidi stayed at DS Bevan's place last night.'

'Erica's place?' Jack grinned. 'Wow. How did that happen?'

'Stacey rang 999 and Erica was first on scene.'

'So how is Stacey this morning?'

'We haven't spoken. I don't want to wake her up.'

'Are we still off for a word with BB?'

Ben nodded. 'Land Rover's on the drive.'

'That shouldn't take all day.'

'Hopefully not, as long as you take the track slowly. After that we'll go and have another chat with the couple in the cottage in Cilmery. Living so close to the monument they must have heard something.'

'Sounds good.' Jack drained his mug. 'I owe you an apology, guv,' he said. 'When we were at Kevin's, I was a bit...'

'Insubordinate?' Ben smiled.

'Yeah... that.'

'Forget it. Right, let's get on. I'm not looking forward to the track and don't fancy having to walk back out to the main road if we get stuck.'

'We'll be fine.'

'I didn't get much sleep last night. Very odd being here without Stacey.'

Jack grinned. 'Don't worry, I won't tell the team what a softy you are. I'll go and fire up the truck.'

'Be there in two. Might as well put the rest of this coffee in a flask, just in case.'

They were soon on the road. Yellow autumn sunshine lit up the mountains, brown and gold rather than the green of summer. Kites and buzzards sailed through clear air beneath a blue sky, searching for a dead sheep or something similar for breakfast. A nye of pheasants galloped along the verge just outside Llanwrtyd and slowed the detectives down, then on the main road, Jack had to pull to one side to allow a convoy of logging lorries to squeeze over The White Bridge.

'I think I might buy a Landie,' Jack said as he passed through Abergwesyn village. 'They sit on the road like a brick. Very confidence-building if you're planning off-roading.'

'Not so good on the main roads though,' Ben said. 'Not really built for swooping around bends, heavy on fuel too.'

The landscape opened into a wide, steep-sided valley, crossed by small rivers. Jack drove carefully over the curiously low bridges.

'This is little better than driving over planks,' he grumbled.

'Locals call them Irish bridges,' Ben said, 'cos when the river is in spate, the water flows over the top.'

'Remind me not to come this way when it's doing that.'

The vehicle rattled over a cattle grid and Jack began the slow crawl up the one-in-four gradient, working the steering wheel hard around the series of hairpin bends. Not far from the top was the start of BB's drive and Jack turned onto the rutted surface with care. The detectives travelled in silence until Jack pulled up in the yard. He stepped out of the truck and massaged his rump.

'Better upholstery wouldn't go amiss,' he said and knocked loudly on the ancient front door.

'Ms Llewelyn?' he called. 'Police.'

He put his ear close to the door, shook his head and headed for the rear of the single-story building. Ben hammered on the door and tried to peer through a front window, only to discover the curtains were pulled tight. Jack reappeared.

'Any luck?' Ben asked.

'Nope. Door locked, curtains closed; the truck's not here either.'

'Bugger, all this way for nothing.'

'I could get us in, guv...'

'Better not, we haven't got a good enough excuse. We'll have a sniff around outside though, while we're here.'

The men walked through the garden and spent some time rummaging around in a low barn with walls two-feet thick. There was a stack of sheep hurdles at one end, a pile of newly harvested hay smelling of summer at the other.

At the back of the barn was a long, wide, lean-to workshop full of tools. A bench ran along one wall and was littered with spanners, screwdrivers, an old cleaver and tins full of rusty nuts and bolts. Bags of fleece and a few fifty-year-old wooden tea chests were crammed beneath the bench, garden forks, spades and hoes leaning against it. Between the house and the barn was a path which led to a vegetable patch, its crops harvested, ground turned over and bare.

At the far end of the kitchen garden, Jack noticed a small, grassy bump, tucked in the shadow of a crumbling, dry-stone wall. A large, spiky gorse bush leaned over the wall, branches shaped by the wind, sage-green leaves peppered with bright yellow flowers.

Jack moved closer, stretched out a hand and pushed away some rust-coloured bracken, exposing a medium-sized boulder. Letters had been added to the stone with white paint. Two words: "Myfanwy Llewelyn".

'What do you reckon this looks like, guv?'

'To be perfectly honest, "grave" springs to mind.'

'How long ago did BB say her mother had died?'

'She said "many years ago". How long do you think that grave – if that's what it is – has been there?'

'Couple at the most, maybe not even that.' Jack straightened up. 'I guess we've just discovered a reason to enter the property.'

'Guess we have.'

* * *

Stacey woke a few minutes after nine, stretched and squeaked as the wound in her leg pulled sharply. She took a deep breath, hauled herself up the bed and gently swung her legs from beneath the quilt, until her bare feet rested on the carpet. She was wondering whether she could make it to the loo, when there was a tap on the door and Heidi peeped in.

'Morning,' she said. 'Thought I heard you moving about. Bathroom?'

'Yes, please. Just as far as the door.'

'Lean on me and keep the weight off your leg. You could do with a crutch.'

'I think I've got one at home. Leftover from when Ben had his knee op.'

Heidi opened the bathroom door. 'I'll be in the kitchen,' she said. 'Shout if you need me.'

'I will, thanks.'

Ten minutes later, Stacey limped into the kitchen and perched on a high stool.

'How is it?' Heidi asked.

'Feels pretty much like a stab wound.'

'Funny. Here, coffee and painkillers.'

'You seem grumpy this morning. I thought you'd be in a better mood today.'

'Why would you think that?'

'Never mind,' Stacey said. 'Has Erica gone to work?'

'Yeah, she left early. She can't wait to get her hands on yesterday's scumbags, metaphorically speaking, but she's good in an interview room. Bet she makes them cry again.'

'Does she want statements from us?'

'Of course. She's coming over to your place for supper tonight. I'm planning to stay with you for a couple days, give you a hand until you're more mobile.'

'That's kind, but there's no need. I have Ben.'

'Who is working on a double murder investigation.'

'OK then, if you're sure.'

Heidi shrugged and cracked her knuckles. 'Erica has come up with an idea how to catch the spikers.'

'Did she? What's her plan?'

'Well,' Heidi said, 'we visit a few of the worst-affected clubs as punters, hang around the bar and watch what goes on.'

'Not much of a plan.'

'Maybe not, but worth a couple of runs at. She thought we'd all go, more pairs of eyes. Don't worry, we'll give you some recuperation time.'

'We don't need to wait. It's not like I'm going to be dancing. I'll be lounging about at the bar.'

'Let's see what the nurse says when your leg is redressed.'

Heidi rounded up dirty mugs and swilled them under the tap, then she made sure everything was switched off and put her leather jacket on.

'Ready?' she asked. 'Make sure you don't leave anything behind. Once I've shut the front door, we won't be able to get back in.'

'Erica hasn't given you a key then?'

'No. Now let's get going, I want to be home – well your home – I have work to do.'

Unable to help herself, Stacey asked, 'So... how was last night?'

'Useful. We talked.'

'Are you going to get back together?'

'I really have no idea, haven't thought about it. Now, home, so you can write up your shocking experience for the paper. I can see the headline now, "Brave reporter endures stabbing in pursuit of truth".'

'Haha, very funny.'

'So, are you ready?'

'Yep. We'll have to pop into the supermarket if I have supper guests tonight.'

'No problem.'

They let themselves out of the flat and Heidi helped Stacey down the single flight of stairs. Once on the pavement, Heidi hailed a taxi and directed it to the car park where she had left her truck. Ten minutes later, the driver pulled up behind the Land Rover. Heidi paid him and helped Stacey out.

'Bloody hell,' the driver said. 'You ladies must have had some party, both of you wearing last night's clothes.' He chuckled and pointed at Heidi's windscreen and the parking tickets plastered to the glass. 'Yeah, must have been a right old do. You could come back to my place for the after-party if you like. Three's never a crowd in my book.'

'Stay there, Stace,' Heidi said and marched back to the cab.

The driver opened his window further and Heidi stuck her face into his personal space.

'You, sir' – she snarled the title – 'are on a very sticky wicket. I'm going to make a complaint and if I find I'm not the first, it'll be best for you if you give up cabbing.'

'Why would I give up cabbing?'

'Cos one day, I'll be a passenger in your cab again and you won't enjoy the experience.'

The cabbie frowned. 'Just fuck off, freak!'

Heidi's hand zipped through the open window, caught hold of the man's nose between her thumb and fingers and pinched hard. The cabbie squealed and fumbled for the window button. Heidi removed her hand at the last moment and ran back to Stacey.

'You really don't take prisoners,' Stacey said.

Heidi grinned. 'Try not to.' She helped her friend into the truck and they set off for Llanagethin.

Chapter fifteen

After five minutes fiddling with his picklock, Jack managed to unlock the back door of the farmhouse and pushed it wide open.

'After you, guv.'

Ben ducked his head beneath the low lintel and walked into a room which was obviously used as a kitchen. An ancient wooden table sat in the middle of the flagstone floor, two chairs close by. A stone sink was fixed to the wall next to the open back door, and a conglomeration of outdated cupboards and dressers leaned against stone walls. Small, curtained windows shed little light inside the room and Ben removed a torch from his pocket.

'Feels as though I've stepped into a wormhole,' Jack said. 'Doesn't look like anything's changed in here for decades. Maybe longer.' He moved closer to the end of the room where a black, cast-iron stove hunkered beneath the wide chimney breast. He opened the door and peered inside. 'Stone cold. Looks like BB and her dad have been gone a while.'

Ben nodded, then left the kitchen and peered inside two further rooms which contained brass bedsteads, with lumpy, old-fashioned horsehair mattresses. A plain bedside table sat next to each, a candlestick resting on top of both. He pulled open one of the drawers of a simple wooden chest. Inside he found a small selection of men's clothing. Tucked beneath the clothes was a bible printed in Welsh and a larger, leather-bound book. Ben flipped through pages covered in handwriting which crawled across the paper like an arthritic spider. Jack stuck his head into the room.

'Find anything?' he asked.

Ben held up the book. 'This might be a journal. I can't read it, it's written in Welsh. How about you?'

'Nothing much, old photo of what I assume is a young BB sitting on her mother's lap. What do we do now?'

'We need a team, led by Carrie, to take a look out the back, but I can't ring from here, no chance of a signal.'

'I'll stay if you like,' Jack said. 'Protect the scene.'

Ben laughed. 'From what? No, we'll stick together. We've no idea how BB would react if she came home and found you here.' Ben returned the journal to the drawer in the bedroom. 'Lock the door on the way out, then if she does return, she won't know anyone's been inside.'

'Where would they have gone?' Jack asked.

'Your guess is as good as mine. We need to find out much more about the family. They could have relatives somewhere.' Ben rubbed his face. 'I've never come across anything like this before and don't really know where to start.'

'I'd have a chat with Heidi. She's good at thinking outside the box and if anyone can find something, it'll be her.' Jack grinned. 'Ask her nicely and she'll probably translate the journal for you.'

They walked back into the sunshine. Jack relocked the door, they climbed into the Land Rover and began the journey back to the main road. It wasn't until they reached the outskirts of Llanwrtyd that Ben's mobile finally picked up a signal. Jack pulled into a passing place as his boss dialled Carrie Salmon's number.

'Afternoon, Chief Inspector,' she said. 'What can I do for you today? Queries relating to my last report?'

'Hi, Carrie. No, something different.'

'I'm listening.'

'Did I mention a woman known locally as Big Bron?'

'Yes, lives in the mountains above Devil's Staircase?'

'That's the one. Jack and I have just been to her house. No one in, but we think we've discovered a grave in the back garden.'

'Not so uncommon in rural areas. There was a case last year, Brecon way. Old house sold, new owners began building an extension and the digger uncovered a body.' She chuckled. 'Well, more like body-soup. The bereaved widower wrapped his wife's body in bailing plastic.'

'Nice,' Ben said. 'That's put me off my lunch. I reckon this is something else.'

'Why?'

'Bronwen Llewelyn told us her mother had died a long time ago but the grave doesn't look that old.'

'Was her mother's death registered?'

'If it was, we're looking in the wrong places. I'd like you to come out.'

'No problem, but it'll make more sense to do this first thing tomorrow, more hours of daylight. It'll be dark in a few hours.'

'You're right. How about we meet up next to the kite in town at seven thirty tomorrow?'

'Fine by me. I'll assemble the kit and arrange an assistant.'

'Good. See you tomorrow.' Ben disconnected the call and his mobile rang immediately. 'DCI James.'

'Ben! I've been trying to call you for ages. Are you OK?' Stacey asked.

'I'm fine. Got Jack with me. Been out to BB's and didn't have a signal. How about you? Where are you?'

'Home. Heidi's here.'

'How's your leg?'

'Sore, but I'll live. Erica's coming over for supper this evening to take our statements. I thought you could bring Jack with you when you knock off.'

'Nice idea, but I haven't a clue when that will be.'

'Heidi's gonna make curry so it won't matter if you're late.'

'OK, I'll see what I can do. Gotta go, lots to do.'

'Take care, Sherlock.'

'You too.' Ben slipped the mobile back into his pocket.

'Where to now, guv?' Jack asked.

'Cilmery for a quiet chat with the cottage owners.'

* * *

It was nearly seven when Erica knocked on Noddfa's front door. Heidi pulled it open and Erica smiled.

'Hello, again,' she said.

'Hello,' Heidi said. 'We're in the kitchen.'

Erica walked along the hall and found Stacey sitting in the carver with her injured leg propped on a stool.

'Hi, you,' Stacey said. 'How's your day been?'

'Good,' Erica said, taking off her jacket and placing a bottle of wine on the table. 'Charged both lads. One with common assault, the other with unlawful wounding and sexual assault – so far.' She took a seat at the table. 'Eve Salmon is coming in tomorrow. I managed to convince the powers that be an ID parade is appropriate. If Eve can pick these two out of a line up, more charges are bound to follow.'

'Well done.'

'I was pleased. Probably wouldn't have caught them without you two. Thanks.' Erica uncorked the bottle and poured three glasses.

'Our pleasure,' Stacey said. 'Heidi told me about your surveillance plan in the clubs. I'm definitely up for it. Any idea when we might give it a go?'

'I thought about next weekend, if your leg isn't too bad. Most of the spiking occurs on a Friday or Saturday night.' She scented the air. 'Something smells amazing.'

'Jalfrezi,' Heidi said, stirring a large pan on the Aga. 'I could eat curry every day.'

Erica smiled. 'Yes, I know.'

The back door suddenly swung open and Ben and Jack walked in.

'Hi, gang,' Jack said. 'Great to see you all.' He peered at Stacey. 'How are you doing, Tank Girl?'

'I wish you wouldn't call me that,' Stacey said, 'but I'm doing OK thanks. Doesn't hurt much unless I knock my leg on something.'

Ben moved closer and placed a kiss on his partner's forehead.

'You sure you're OK?' he asked.

'Perfectly. I do wish everyone would stop fussing. Tell me how you got on at BB's this morning.'

Ben groaned and rubbed his face. 'Came away with more questions than answers.'

'We found what we believe to be a grave in the back garden,' Jack said.

'Really?' Stacey asked.

Jack nodded, then he slipped a mobile from his pocket, scrolled through the image folder and passed Stacey the device, as Ben described what they had found in the garden on the remote cottage.

'Can you tell me more about the grave?' Stacey asked.

'Only off the record.'

'Of course.'

Ben took a sip of wine. 'We haven't been able to find an official record of her mother's death, so we need to examine the body... if there is one of course.'

'Why would there be a headstone with no body?' Jack asked.

'Just a monument maybe?'

'Did you talk to the folks who found Ian's body?' Stacey asked.

'We did,' Ben said, 'but they had nothing new to say.'

'Found his car or his clothes yet?'

'No, and before you ask, Robin's clothes didn't give us any clues either. No DNA other than his own, and no trace evidence other than potting compost.'

'Meticulous and methodical,' Heidi said. 'The killer works hard at this – the posing, using risky body dumps, taking time to strip the victims – yet manages to do so without leaving any DNA behind. Whoever did this wants to make a point.'

'OK,' Ben said, 'so who would do this?'

'I'm not sure relatives of the dead woman in London could pull this off, unless' – Heidi smiled – 'one of them happens to be a psychopath. If pushed, I would lean towards a stranger killing. Someone who knows about the murder in London, knows the Townsend brothers were involved and wants to punish them.'

Heidi cleared the bowls and put the coffee machine on.

'Is Carrie going out to BB's tomorrow?' Stacey asked.

'That's the plan,' Ben said.

'Any chance I could tag along? Just as an observer, not as a reporter?'

'Let me think about it,' Ben said as Heidi took an apple pie from the Aga and a tub of ice cream from the freezer.

'Before we all get too comfy,' Erica said. 'I do have to take statements this evening.'

'We haven't forgotten,' Heidi said. 'Soon as we finish supper.'

Chapter sixteen

Jack navigated the rough track slowly. Carrie and her assistant travelled behind in a long-wheelbase Land Rover, driven by a member of the first response team. The warm sunshine of the last week had been obliterated by thick, low cloud cover and a chilly wind funnelled through the deep valley. Stacey, having convinced Ben she should be allowed to go with them, sat in the back, her sore leg stretched out on the bench seat. Heidi had remained at Noddfa to search cyberspace for Bronwen Llewelyn's history.

'Difficult to believe we're in the same place,' Jack said. 'Be bloody grim up here in the snow.'

'Better hope we don't get any,' Ben grouched, peering up at the sky. 'The next few hours will be difficult enough as it is.'

'Maybe BB will be home,' Stacey said. 'We'll be able to ask her what has happened and not do any digging.'

'That would certainly make things much easier,' Ben said.

Jack pulled into the yard and parked at the end of the cottage, Carrie's vehicle on his tail.

'No sign of BB's truck,' Jack said. 'Looks like Carrie will have to dig after all.'

The small team left the relative warmth of the Land Rovers. An icy gust of wind blew around them and Stacey shivered.

'Wow,' she said. 'That's really cold. Takes your breath away.'

'Stay in the truck,' Ben said. 'You don't need to stand around in this. You're supposed to be convalescing, not tramping about in the mountains.'

'I'll be fine,' Stacey said, tucking a crutch beneath her arm. 'No need to worry about me. I'll find somewhere sheltered to wait. I'm not missing this.'

Carrie unloaded her kit helped by her assistant, a young woman called Lucy who was studying forensic pathology. The first response driver lugged the crates and cases to the back of the dwelling and placed them at the end of the kitchen garden. The team stared at the grassy lump tucked in the shadow of an ancient, dry-stone wall, while Carrie took official photographs of the scene before beginning the excavations. Stacey took unofficial ones using a small point-and-shoot camera she had secreted in her pocket before leaving home. Luckily, no one noticed what she was up to.

'OK, then,' Carrie said. 'Let's make a start.'

She moved next to the mound, Lucy by her side. They knelt on the damp ground and using trowels and a small, narrow spade, began peeling away the peaty turf. Carrie described what she found as they worked, her words captured on a digital recorder resting on top of the painted boulder. Beneath the grass, the soil was peat-black and relatively loosely packed.

Carrie and Lucy carefully removed the earth and placed it inside large buckets, in case they needed to sift through it later for evidence. The rest of the team hovered close by, huddling in their coats and craning their necks as the excavation grew deeper. At about two feet down, both diggers leaned back on their heels.

'Found something?' Ben asked.

'We have,' Carrie said. She got to her feet and picked up the camera. 'You were right, this is most definitely a grave. First guess is that it has been here maybe eighteen months, couple of years at most.'

She took a series of photographs, then returned to the hole and, with Lucy's help, scraped away the remaining loose soil until a body-shaped lump, wrapped in an old blanket, was finally uncovered. Carrie gently peeled away one end of the woollen material to reveal a skull, with black strips of almost mummified flesh clinging to the bone. Lucy documented the find, snapping more pictures as Carrie held the blanket clear of the remains.

The camera was returned to its case and Carrie examined the skull, gently manipulating it with gloved hands. After a little while, she hauled herself upright and brushed damp earth from her protective white suit.

'Anyone think to bring a flask?' she asked. 'I could do with a hot drink, my bones are shivering.'

'I did,' Stacey said. 'There's a bag in the back of the Land Rover.'

'I'll get it,' Lucy said and set off up the path.

Ben walked closer to the grave and gingerly peered inside at the decomposed body. Carrie moved to stand by his side.

'What can you tell me?' Ben asked.

'Not as much as you'd like. I'll need to get the body back to town for a proper look, however...'

'What?'

'There is significant damage to the skull. A slice or cut, deep into the bone at the back.'

'Meaning what?'

'That this probably is a murder. The skull was hit with some force using a heavy, bladed weapon.' She took a deep breath and recited, "'Lizzie Borden took an axe and gave her mother forty whacks." You should search the house and outbuildings. You might get lucky and find the weapon. We need SOCO too. The victim would have bled heavily at the time of the injury and it would be good to discover where that happened.'

'Will you move the body now?'

Carrie nodded. 'Yes, we'll bag it and take it to town in the long-wheelbase truck. Not sure a standard ambulance would get here in one piece.'

'Any idea of the victim's sex?'

'From the shape and size of the skull, I'd guess female, but I'll confirm when I've had a proper look.'

Lucy returned and handed out plastic mugs. Once the drinks were finished, Carrie and her assistant gently lifted the wrapped body out of the grave and into a body bag. As soon as it was zipped closed, they carried it to the front of the cottage and, with the help of the first responder, loaded it inside the vehicle. Jack appeared from the lean-to workshop.

'Guv,' he called. 'Come and take a look at this.'

Ben followed him into the narrow building and Stacey tagged along at a distance, leaning heavily on her crutch. Jack pointed at the bench and Ben spotted a large, semi-rusted cleaver. He called for Carrie who appeared in the doorway. She removed a hand lens from her pocket and examined the blade closely without touching it.

'Anything?' Ben asked.

'Looks like there's dried blood crusted between the blade and its wooden handle.' She turned the implement over with gloved hands. 'I can't tell by looking how old the blood is, or even if it's human, but this certainly could have caused the damage to our victim's skull.'

Jack stepped forward holding open an evidence bag and Carrie placed the cleaver safely inside.

'I'll get off now,' she said, 'take this with me and have a closer look. Want me to contact SOCO?'

Ben nodded. 'If you wouldn't mind, tell them to hurry. Too cold to hang around for hours. Would you mind dropping Stacey at home for me?'

'I'm happy to wait with you,' Stacey said.

'You'll be better indoors by the fire. I'll be back as soon as I can.'

'OK,' she agreed reluctantly, 'but take this.' She handed over a small box.

'What's this?' Ben asked.

'Present from Heidi. A miniature outdoor camera. She thought if you set it up at the start of the track, you can see when BB arrives home.'

'Good idea. Tell her thanks. Now go with Carrie and I'll see you later.' He leaned close, brushed a kiss on her cheek, then turned away to help Jack search the rest of the workshop.

* * *

Stacey let herself in through the back door and called for Heidi, who emerged from the office.

'How did it go?' she asked. 'Find a body?'

Stacey nodded, removed her coat and dropped onto the carver. 'Carrie thinks the remains are probably female and discovered a deep gouge in the skull. Cleaver, she thinks. Jack found one in a workshop at the back of the cottage.'

'Seems I may have misjudged Big Bron,' Heidi said. 'Are the boys with you?'

'No. Carrie took the body to Brecon. Ben and Jack are waiting for SOCO to arrive. First response chap dropped me off. How have you got on today?'

'Not brilliantly,' Heidi grouched. 'As far as I can see, no one in authority knows the Llewelyns exist. Not an official record of anything. I'll be honest, I'm a bit stumped.'

Stacey smiled. 'That doesn't happen often.'

'No, it doesn't and I don't like a puzzle I can't solve.'

Heidi opened the Aga door and peered inside.

'Have you cooked again?' Stacey asked.

'Nothing special, sausage casserole.'

'So how do you think you can work out who BB actually is?'

'Need to search in the real world, cyberspace can't help. I'm planning to check out local historical societies and find some elderly local residents to talk to. Denise Brumby at the Stonecroft knew who BB was at least, but she hasn't lived here long enough to know much more than that.'

'She's run the pub for ten years or so.'

Heidi smiled. 'As I said, she hasn't been here long enough.'

'Talking to historical societies sounds good to me. I'll come with you.'

Heidi sat at the table. 'How is your spiking article progressing?'

'Slowly. Like you, I need to speak to more people. I've written up Lizzie's story, nice quotes and first-hand testimony. The interview with Jonnie Jones from Rascals was useful, but like all stories, I need a bit more middle and an ending.'

Heidi grinned. 'Might be able to help you there. My clubbing Facebook friends are very agitated about the problem. I have a couple of names you might be interested in. Seems one of them was spiked but chose not to report the matter to the police.'

'Marvellous, thanks,' Stacey said,

'Just don't ever call me a researcher again. I am way more than that.'

'Yes, I know and I'm sorry.'

Heidi cracked her knuckles. 'So, road trip tomorrow then?'

'Looks like it, as long as you don't mind driving.'

'Don't mind at all, as long as my next job description isn't chauffeur.'

Chapter seventeen

Ben and Jack stood on one side of a stainless-steel table and tried not to look at the remains lying on the shiny surface. Most, but not all, of the soft tissue had completely decomposed. Some black strips and patches clung to the skeleton; its bones were stained a deep brown by the peat in which they had been buried. Ben was grateful the only scent hanging above the corpse was one of damp earth, like the smell of new potting compost when a bag is first opened.

Carrie stood on the other side of the table and delivered her findings, like a show-and-tell for Halloween.

'Let's begin,' she said. 'Female, over seventy, mother. Pelvic striations present. Just over six feet tall. Teeth in remarkably good condition. All present – including the wisdoms – no fillings or other dental work and few caries. Suggests to me a diet low in sugar.'

'No chance of identifying her through dental records then?' Jack said.

'Correct, Sergeant, no chance.' Carrie picked up an LED pointer and used it to indicate a lesion in the skull which looked like a thin valley on a moonlike surface. 'This injury is the cause of death – catastrophic. The victim was more than likely dead before she hit the floor.

'Did you find blood on the cleaver?' Ben asked.

'Yes. Rabbit and human. I've collected a decent sample for DNA testing.'

'How long can blood sit on a blade and still contain DNA?'

'Depends on the conditions. Cool, dark and dry are ideal. UV light degrades DNA.' She pointed at the skull again. 'I've taken a sample from the petrous bone – big hard lump protecting the inner ear. We can check to see if the samples match.'

'Which will confirm, or not, that the cleaver was the weapon,' Jack said.

'Exactly. I've spoken to SOCO to make sure they collect samples from the house – toothbrushes, hairbrushes, that sort of thing. If the dead woman is Bronwen's mother, the DNA will tell us.'

'Do you still believe the grave is relatively recent?' Ben asked.

'I do. Even though the body wasn't found in a bog, the earth up there is acidic. There isn't enough bone degradation for the burial to be older than a couple of years.'

'Was she dressed?'

'No sign of any clothing, but SOCO will be back out today. They'll dig a bit deeper – literally. The clothes might be buried further down.'

'Bloody hell, guv,' Jack said. 'Another body found without clothes.'

'This can't possibly be connected to the others,' Ben said.

'They were all naked,' Jack pointed out, 'and all found within ten miles of each other.'

* * *

Heidi and Stacey were sitting at a table in the bar of the Neuadd Arms, an elderly resident sat opposite. Mrs Williams had recently celebrated her ninetieth birthday. Unsurprisingly she was a widow, her hill farmer husband had passed away nearly twenty years ago. She was a small woman, with a round, smiling face and lively blue eyes, dressed in a calf-length skirt and cream blouse beneath a natural brown jumper, hand-spun and knitted by herself.

'I made this before Evan died,' she said. 'As long as you keep the moths out, good wool will last forever.'

'How long have you lived in the area?' Heidi asked.

'I was born here,' Mrs Williams said. 'Well, up on the Epynt. I was a child when the army took over in the 1940s. Everyone up there had to move. Da found us a place near Llandovery, then I married Evan and moved to his family farm outside Llanwrtyd.' She sighed. 'Such a long time ago. The world was very different then.'

'I can imagine,' Stacey said. 'Being forced to move out of your home must have been very traumatic.'

Mrs Williams nodded. 'Yes, it was. Only time I saw Da cry was when we shut the front door of the farmhouse for the last time. He was never the same after.'

'We wondered if you knew the Llewelyns,' Heidi said. 'Got a place in one of the valleys on the far side of the Devil's Staircase.'

'I think I know who you mean.' Mrs Williams' face creased into a frown as she searched her memory. 'Iolo was the man's name, if I remember correctly.'

'That's right,' Heidi said. 'Married to Myfanwy, had a daughter called Bronwen.'

'Yes, that's them. They used to farm sheep and had a few hill ponies. Haven't seen any of them for years, so I guess they moved away.'

Stacey shook her head. 'They didn't. Heidi and I went to visit their place recently and met Bronwen. Still a shepherd apparently.'

'*Duw duw*. I can't remember when I last saw the girl. Are her parents still with us?'

'Her da is,' Heidi said, 'but she told us her mother passed away years ago.'

'Myfanwy was a big woman, tall, heavy-boned. She'd make you and me look like midgets.'

Heidi chuckled. 'We are – pretty much.'

Mrs Williams continued, 'They used to come into town occasionally, brought ponies down for the sales, sheep too. That was a long time ago. Amazing the family is still there.'

'Bronwen is tall too,' Stacey said. 'Seems locals call her Big Bron.'

Mrs Williams clapped a hand to her face. 'Oh my good God! Big Bron is little Bronwen? I never put the two together. Well I never, you learn something new every day.'

The door to the bar opened. Stacey glanced up, recognised Idris Jones and watched as he walked to the bar.

'Excuse me,' she said. 'I just need a word with that young man. Shall I order more tea?'

'Yes please,' Mrs Williams said. 'A couple of buttered Welsh cakes might be nice too.'

Stacey grinned, picked up her crutch and limped to the bar. 'Hi, Idris,' she said. 'How are you?'

He looked over his shoulder. 'Oh, it's you from the other night. Stacey, isn't it?'

'That's right. Are you here for lunch?'

'Sort of. Place does decent takeaways, curry, burgers, fish and chips. Cos I'm the new boy, I'm also the gopher.' He shrugged. 'Gets me out of the yard. Mud everywhere since last night's downpour. Not keen on mud like.' He nodded at the crutch. 'You didn't have that the other night, babes. What happened?'

'I got stabbed in the leg.'

'No shit! Who stabbed you?'

'I went to Cardiff with a mate. Couple of teenagers tried to mug us.'

'Don't like knives me, nor guns. Five-oh nick anyone?'

'Both were arrested. My friend' – Stacey nodded at Heidi – 'restrained one until the police turned up.'

'That little white-haired girl talking to Mrs Williams?'

'That's her.'

'How did she manage to hang onto a mugger?'

'Grabbed him by the balls,' Stacey said and chuckled when Idris flinched.

The landlord appeared behind the bar. Idris handed over his lunch list, paid for the meals and ordered a pint of cider to drink while he waited.

'Let me pay for your drink,' Stacey said. 'As a thank you for staying with me the night you found the body.'

'Oh, cheers.' He took a large swallow. 'Has your fella nicked the murderer yet?'

'Unfortunately not. Did you hear there was another murder down the road at Cilmery?'

'Yeah. Someone told me the dead guy was the first dead guy's brother. Is that right?'

'It is, yes.'

'Looks as though someone had it in for them.'

'Did you ever meet Robin's brothers?'

'He had another one did he? Christ, two brothers killed like that. I'd be shitting bricks if I was the last one standing. Does he live round here then?'

'No,' Stacey said, 'he's not local.'

Idris nodded and drained his pint as the landlord placed a large, paper carrier bag on the bar.

'Before you go,' Stacey said. 'The night you saw Robin in the pub, he was with his brothers and a friend of his called Pete. Short, non-descript chap in his twenties, stubbly beard and wore a flat cap. Know who he was?'

Idris picked up the bag and pushed out of the pub.

The landlord caught Stacey's eye. 'I reckon you might be talking about Pete the Pot,' he said.

'He's a potter?' Stacey asked.

The man's face split into a huge grin. 'Not to my knowledge. Work it out.' He turned away and began polishing glasses.

* * *

Ben's phone rang just before he got into the car outside the county morgue.

'DCI James.'

'Ollie Langdon, sir. Where are you?'

'Just about to leave Brecon. Why?'

'I've found Ian Townsend's car.'

'Well done. Where is it?'

'Tucked in a corner of the Co-op's car park at the back of Builth. Want me to give SOCO a ring?'

'Not yet, Constable. Stay there and don't let anyone near it. We're on our way.'

Ben hung up. 'Ian's car has been found,' he said, 'outside the Co-op in Builth. Ollie's standing guard until we arrive.'

Jack nodded, unlocked the car and started the engine. He pulled out of the car park, switched on the blue lights and shot along the bypass as though the devil was on his tail. Ben clung to the grab rail, his right foot twitching on an imaginary brake pedal, as other drivers pulled close to the verge to allow the unmarked vehicle to overtake.

Just over half an hour later, Jack turned left at the end of Builth's high street, another left opposite the tiny livestock market and Ben spotted DC Langdon sitting on the bonnet of his car. He raised a hand and Jack pulled up behind an elderly Ford Mondeo. Ollie walked closer.

'Morning, sir,' he said. 'Vehicle's locked. Looks like there's a bundle of clothes on the floor behind the driver's seat.'

Ben stepped out of the car. 'How did you find the car?' he asked.

'I didn't,' Ollie admitted, 'not really. Popped in for a sandwich and Karen – girl I used to go to school with and knows I'm a copper – told me the car had been here for a few days. Her boss thought it might have been dumped and was on the verge of calling us.' He grinned broadly. 'Couldn't believe my luck when I checked the reg number.'

Ben bent low and squinted through the windows. 'That does look like a pile of clothes on the floor,' he said. 'Can it really be possible the killer stripped Ian here then drove him naked to Cilmery?'

'Let's get it open,' Jack said, 'before we jump to conclusions.'

He removed a thin length of metal from the door pocket in his car and slipped it down between the driver's window and the bodywork. A quick tug and the central locking clicked open. Jack donned a pair of gloves and opened the back door. He lifted the bundle of clothes from the floor and spread them on the upholstery.

'Full set of kit, guv,' he said. 'Even socks and underwear.' He tucked the clothes inside an evidence bag and scribbled on the label.

Ben also snapped on gloves, then he opened the passenger door and searched the glove compartment and door pocket. He found nothing more interesting than a road atlas, an empty can of Coke and a selection of chocolate wrappers. He straightened up and shut the door.

'DC Langdon, get in touch with the nick and arrange transport,' he said. 'We'll get this vehicle to the police garage. SOCO can look over it there – without an audience.' He nodded at a small group of shoppers near the supermarket's entrance, trying their best not to be caught rubbernecking.

'Will do, sir,' Ollie said. 'How did it go with Carrie?'

'Well enough,' Ben said. 'Wait here for the transport, then come back to the station. We'll catch up there with the rest of the team.'

Chapter eighteen

Heidi perched on a saggy pouffe in Noddfa's cosy living room and added a log to the fire. Ben and Stacey were sitting together on the sofa, glasses of brandy in their hands.

'Supper was good, Heidi,' Ben said, 'thanks for cooking and keeping an eye on Stacey.'

'Hey,' Stacey said and jabbed her partner in his ribs. 'I don't need anyone keeping an eye on me.

'Did you have any luck tracking the Llewelyns online?' Ben asked.

'None at all,' Heidi said, then she told Ben about their conversations with Mrs Williams and Idris.

'She heard of any relatives around?' he asked.

'No.' Heidi stirred the embers with a long poker.

'I think I've discovered something about Robin's friend, Pete,' Stacey said.

Ben raised his eyebrows. 'Oh?'

'Not much, although Idris called him Pete the Pot, and not because he's a potter. Idris and his mates were smoking cannabis the night they found the first body, so I reckon Pete might be their dealer.'

'Is that all he said?' Ben asked.

'Yes, that was it, but Jack knows most of the dealers locally so maybe he'll have an address.'

'Let's hope so. This Pete character has been a loose end for far too long. Everyone we asked in Llanwrtyd claimed not to know who we were talking about.'

Heidi chuckled. 'More than likely cos he is a dealer.'

'After the pub,' Stacey said. 'Heidi drove us to Llandeilo.'

'Shopping trip?' Ben asked.

'Work,' Heidi said. 'A little while ago I joined a Facebook group dedicated to clubbers. I've been monitoring the chatter amongst them, specifically young women who knew of someone that, or themselves had been spiked.' She topped up her glass. 'I reached out to a couple in Llandeilo, Kim and Debbie. They'd been clubbing together at a place in Swansea a while back and Debbie was spiked. Stacey and I went over for a chat.'

'What did they tell you?'

'Pretty much the same MO as the cases in Cardiff. Debbie woke up in a cheap motel just off the motorway at Junction 47.'

'So, Debbie goes missing from a night club, and her friend Kim, just goes home?'

'Of course not!' Heidi snapped. 'She flagged down a passing patrol car outside the club and asked for help to find her friend.'

'Did she get any?'

'What do you think?' Heidi sipped brandy. 'The officer riding shotgun came onto her.'

'In what way?'

'He made inappropriate comments about Kim's appearance, what she was wearing. Suggested Debbie had "copped off". Said it was why girls went to clubs, "looking for a shag", as he charmingly put it.' Heidi got to her feet, paced angrily then glared at Ben. 'Whoever is in charge of recruitment these days is either scraping the bottom of the barrel or just shit at their job!'

'Please sit down,' Stacey said. 'You'll trip over my leg.'

Heidi cracked her knuckles and flopped on the easy chair.

'Unfortunately,' Ben said, 'policing does attract the odd bad apple, the macho image appeals.'

'The bad apples that spoil the barrel, don't forget.'

'I agree our vetting process should be more stringent, but we don't make the rules. The government does.'

'That's not quite right,' Heidi said. 'Forces do have some autonomy.'

'They do, but everything comes down to money. Not enough staff or time, bad communication between forces... it's a long list and allows the bad apples to stay under the radar.'

'Whatever,' Heidi said, 'but the issues women face every day must be taken seriously.'

'I agree and I am firmly on your side.' Ben smiled. 'First thing tomorrow, I promise I'll find out who Kim spoke to and make his – and his partner's – lives miserable.'

'Just bloody sack them!' Heidi said. She got to her feet, strode from the room and stomped up to the spare room.

* * *

The next morning, a sighting by a beat officer of Pete the Pot, shopping in Llandrindod Wells, prevented Ben from following up on Heidi's complaint. Jack parked in the railway station's car park and without too much difficulty, soon spotted their target ambling along the main street.

Pete paused often to peer through shop windows and nipped into a couple of charity shops. Ben and Jack did the same, anxious not to get too close and advertise their interest. At the end of the street, Pete turned left and walked past the bandstand, then he cut across a side street and took a right onto a steep hill leading towards the council offices. A short row of shops, many empty, included a Chinese takeaway and Ben and Jack watched from a distance as their man went inside. Ten minutes later he was back out on the pavement carrying a bag of food. The officers stared in disbelief as Pete took four steps away from the shopfront, slipped a key into the lock of a blue front door and let himself in.

Jack chuckled quietly. 'I love it when we get lucky. I checked, Pete is on probation and hasn't registered his new address with his PO. Perfect excuse to drop in.' He grinned. 'We'll give him long enough to start his lunch.'

'Drug dealers always bring out your cruel streak,' Ben said.

'Can't stand them, guv. I've been aware of Peter Butler for a while, but wasn't sure where he laid his head – until now.' Jack checked his watch. 'Let's go and say hello then, just as he puts the first forkful of chow mein in his mouth.'

The officers walked across the road. Next to the front door of the three-story building were six doorbells and Jack rang them all. After a short wait, the door buzzed. Ben pushed it open and they walked inside a damp, scruffy hall. A side table groaned under a mound of junk mail and unclaimed bills, the colourful, mosaic floor tiles thick with grime. Ben frowned, a mop once a week would have made them shine.

'Places like this always depress me,' he said. 'Which flat do you reckon?'

Jack scented the air. 'Top floor,' he said. 'I love the smell of soy sauce in the morning.'

On the third floor were two doors. Ben and Jack chose one each and knocked simultaneously. Ben's choice was opened by a middle-aged woman, dressed in a purple skirt and an obviously hand-knitted jumper which hung from her thin frame like a crooked rainbow. Her long hair was dyed a deep burgundy, blonde at the ends, and reached midway down her back in an unruly mass of curls. A pair of round, metal-framed glasses perched on the end of her upturned nose.

'Hello,' she said. 'Who are you?'

'Police, madam. We're looking for a man called Peter Butler. Does he live here?'

The woman shook her head, setting the curls in motion and Ben was reminded of Medusa.

'What do you want with him?' she asked.

'Just a chat. Does he live in the building?'

'Across the landing.'

Ben glanced over his shoulder in time to see the opposite door open briefly then slam shut. Jack didn't hesitate, he ploughed his bulk into the flimsy wood and burst the lock. The hippy woman looked on in horror.

'Some chat,' she said and closed her door.

Ben heard the chain rattle as he crossed the landing in three paces and entered the flat, just as his sergeant grabbed a young man by the front of his hoodie and propelled him up against the nearest wall.

'Don't ever slam the door on me, Petey boy,' Jack growled. 'Not ever.'

Pete wriggled like a rabbit in a snare. 'I thought you were someone else,' he gasped. 'I wouldn't slam a door on you, Mr Trent. Let me go, I can't breathe.'

Jack reluctantly released his grip and Pete rubbed his chest.

'Who did you think I was?' Jack asked.

'No one you know,' Pete said and went into the kitchen, back to his takeaway.

Jack followed and perched on a stool. 'Do you need reminding you're only useful if you keep me up to date with what's occurring in our drug-filled community?'

'I have,' Pete said. 'I do.'

'Not lately you don't. Didn't hear anything about what went on at the Stonecroft in Llanwrtyd. You were in there with Robin Townsend who was killed soon after he left. Why were you there?'

'No special reason. Robin is – uh, was – a mate of mine. He invited me over to meet his brothers, have a pint, few smokes maybe.'

'You mean weed?' Ben asked.

Pete nodded.

'So you admit giving weed to Robin?' Jack asked.

Pete snorted. 'I didn't give him anything. He paid.'

'Was he after anything else? GHB or something similar?'

Pete shrugged. 'Didn't say he was.'

'Did you spike his drink?' Ben asked.

'What the fuck? No, of course not! Not my style. I only deal weed.'

'I'm not convinced,' Jack said. 'I need to take a look around. I can do that with your permission, or I'll arrest you on the spot – on suspicion of murder. Your choice, Petey Boy.'

'Murder? Don't be bloody daft.'

'That's on top of supplying controlled substances. You've already got form, remember. This time the judge will throw the book at you – I'll make sure he does.'

Pete rolled his eyes. 'Get on with it, then you can sod off. I'll think twice next time I have any info.'

For the next twenty minutes, the detectives opened cupboards, riffled through drawers, felt along the tops and bottoms of curtains and hunted under the bed, in the bathroom, living room and kitchen. Jack was about to give up, when he removed the top of a biscuit barrel and from the corner of his eye, saw Pete twitch. Jack burrowed his hand to the bottom and when he removed it, a medium-sized plastic bag, full of smaller ones containing white powder, dangled from his fingers. Jack grinned and held up his find.

'So, Pete, you only sell weed? What's this? Baking powder?'

Pete didn't answer but his eyes dropped and he stared at the floor.

'Right then,' Ben said. 'Peter Butler, let's get you to the station. Sergeant, arrest him.'

Jack recited the caution, snapped handcuffs on Pete's wrists and they led him from the flat.

Chapter nineteen

At the station, Jack handed his prisoner over to the custody sergeant, then followed Ben upstairs to the squad room for a much-needed coffee. Constables Hedges and Duffin worked at the end of the room in front of a pair of computer screens. They were searching for digital clues: a single shot missed on CCTV, something a local resident had said during the investigation process which hadn't seemed important at the time, rechecking ANPR footage. Ben smiled at them as he walked in.

'How are you two getting on?' he asked.

'Slow. No bolts out of the blue,' Tegan said, 'although...'

'What?'

'The woman who found Robin's clothes, Mrs Webb, mentioned something to me while we waited for you, about Big Bron having a sister. She said there had been some gossip years ago but she was unwilling to pass it on as she didn't know how much of it was true.'

'What did she say?' Ben asked.

'That the sister, Gwen, had left the farm in disgrace, sent packing by her mother. There was talk that the girl was pregnant. Some said she'd been raped – maybe by her father – others that a young man Gwen met at the pony sales was responsible.' She sighed. 'Any or all of that could be true, or completely fictitious. Honestly, sir, I feel like I'm stuck in a historical novel. I find it difficult to believe people know so little about their neighbours, yet still make up gossip about them.'

Jack chuckled. 'They're not really neighbours and the Llewelyns obviously chose to live that way.' He put on a booming American accent. 'The land that time forgot.'

Tegan giggled. 'Did you see any dinosaurs or tiny horses?'

Ben grinned and said, 'Keep at it and call me immediately if you find anything. Heidi told me last night that she and Stacey had spoken to a Mrs Williams, who said she knew the Llewelyns years ago. Might be worth having another chat with her.'

'Yes, sir.'

'Also, pay particular attention to ANPR records. We need to know how Ian's car got to the Co-op in Builth.' He drained his mug. 'Right then, Sergeant, downstairs to talk to Pete the Pot. Bloody stupid handle.'

'Just carrying on local traditions,' Jack said. 'Mike the Coal, Huw the Milk, Eddie the Van.' He laughed and led the way down to the custody suite.

Pete was brought to the interview room by a uniformed officer. He looked angry and raised his cuffed wrists.

'I shouldn't be treated like this,' he said. 'I've helped you in the past, we had an arrangement.'

'Which you broke,' Jack said. 'By not telling us you were drinking with a man who was found dead a couple of hours later – murdered.'

Pete didn't say anything, but held up his wrists again.

'Sit,' Jack ordered.

The prisoner sat and rested his hands on the table. Jack switched on the recording device and noted those present, date and time.

'About the evening Robin died,' Jack said. 'Your friend's face was plastered on the front of the papers, you must have seen them. Why didn't you come forward when we appealed for witnesses?'

'I don't read the papers, Mr Trent. Come on, take the chains off, they're tight.'

Ben reached into a pocket, removed a key and unlocked the cuffs. Pete rubbed his skin.

Jack leaned back in his chair. 'OK then, Peter Butler, let's start with the easy stuff, get it out of the way. A possible class A substance was found in your flat, packed and seemingly ready for sale. Care to comment?'

Pete smirked. 'Not my flat. Not my class A.'

'Did you know it was there?'

'No, I didn't.'

'So who does the flat belong to... if it really isn't yours?'

'None of your business.'

'Everything's my business in a murder inquiry,' Jack said. He slammed his fist on the table inches from Pete's face, who flinched so violently he knocked his chair backwards and sprawled on the floor.

Jack watched as the prisoner righted his chair, then said, 'I'll try again. I want to know everything about the evening you spent in the Stonecroft. How did you get there? By car?'

'No, train from Llan'dod, got off in Llanwrtyd. Caught the last one back the same night.'

'Speak to anyone on the train?'

'Only the guy I bought the ticket from.'

'Did you go straight to the pub from the station?' Ben asked.

'No, I bought some sandwiches in the garage, sat by the river to eat, then went to the pub.'

'Were you the first to arrive?'

'No. Robin was already there, his brothers came later.'

'At the time of your arrest, you told us you sold cannabis to Robin,' Jack said. 'Did the others buy anything from you?'

'Nah. Robin asked for half an ounce, enough for all of them.'

'So tell me about the powder we found in your flat.'

Pete sighed heavily. 'I've already said, not my flat, not my drugs.'

Jack leaned on the table. 'Then give us the name of the flat's owner so at least some of us can get out of here.'

'He's away,' Pete muttered. 'Not contactable.'

'Where's he gone? Elon Musk flown him to the moon? Come on, Petey, this is your only chance. Give us a name, or you'll go down – again. Who is he?'

'Can't tell you.'

'Can't or won't?'

Pete glanced up. 'I expected better treatment from you, Mr Trent. We've been helping each other for a while now, yet we fall out like this. You know how it is, I have to pick my moment to pass stuff on. If I didn't do that, I'd be so much dead meat.'

'OK, have it your way,' Jack said. 'We'll bang you up, have the powder checked and then we'll speak again.'

'You can't keep me in here. I've places to be, stuff to do.'

'Anything we'd be interested in?' Ben asked.

Pete shrugged.

'Then we'll get you back to your cell and make sure the custody sergeant feeds you. Ask him nicely and he might pop to the chippy just down the road.'

'This is all wrong,' Pete complained. 'You're not playing the game.'

'Neither are you,' Jack snapped. 'Your probation officer didn't know you'd moved, consequently, we consider you to be a flight risk. We won't release if we can help it.'

Pete grinned. 'You'll have to let me go in the end.'

'You reckon, do you?'

Jack ended the interview and Pete was escorted back to his cell.

The interview room door closed and Ben asked, 'Do you reckon he knows more than he's saying?'

'Definitely and always.' Jack frowned. 'This meeting with Robin and his brothers – what exactly was that about? If Robin wanted to buy weed, there was no need to invite his dealer to join them for the evening. There had to be something else.'

'Pete said they were friends,' Ben said.

'People like him don't have friends.'

'He might be more forthcoming after a night in the cells. I'll apply for an extension and we'll question him again in the morning. The report on the powder will be back by then. If it is a class A, he'll be looking at a substantial prison sentence, being he's a repeat offender. The prospect of that might loosen his tongue.'

'We can but hope,' Jack said, 'just don't hold your breath.'

Chapter twenty

Stacey pulled herself up from her desk in the office and limped to the bottom of the stairs.

'I'm making lunch,' she called. 'Soup and sandwiches. Want some?'

'That'll be good,' Heidi said. 'I'll come down.'

Stacey filled the kettle, put it on the Aga to boil and rummaged in the fridge, noticing her leg wasn't as painful and that she no longer relied so heavily on the crutch. She began constructing ham and cheese sandwiches while the soup heated up.

Heidi appeared. 'Need a hand?' she asked.

'No thanks. I can do this, my leg is much better. Planning to give driving a go this afternoon. I'm concerned about taking up so much of your time.'

'And I've told you it's fine. How's the writing going?'

'Not bad, but I've run out of material. We need to arrange that night out with Erica before I can write much more.' She smiled. 'Been a while since I've been clubbing. No way will I be able to blend in.'

'You'll be surprised,' Heidi said.

Stacey passed her friend a mug of coffee and asked, 'What have you been up to?'

'Ben sent me a copy of BB's journal, asked if I'd have a go at translating it – as he's so short-staffed.'

'Did she write every day?'

Heidi shook her head. 'Not even every month, just when something worth recording happened. The journal covers over thirty years. Nothing like prose either, just short factual statements rather than sentences. I've been working backwards, newer stuff first.'

'What have you found?'

'Well...' Heidi shuffled sheets of paper. 'How about this, the last entry she wrote, "Need help with Da, can't cope."'

'Maybe that's a clue as to where they went. She might have taken her dad to a doctor.'

'Possible,' Heidi said and turned pages. 'The next entry was probably written a couple of years ago.'

'How do you know that if BB didn't record the date?'

'She always recorded spring lambing, how many were born, how many ewes she lost. There were two lambings mentioned between the entries.'

Stacey nodded. 'I get it. Read the second one.'

'"Mam hurt Da – again. I hit her, she died. Buried in the garden."' Heidi glanced up and grinned. 'Close your mouth, Stace. Goldfish impersonations do nothing for me and aren't attractive.'

'Shit!' Stacey said. 'BB really wrote that?'

'You really think I'd make it up?'

'No, sorry. Have you told Ben?'

'Not yet. He has one of his staff working through the journal, but I'm banking on them starting at the beginning. I just need some time before they get to this part.'

'Why?' Stacey asked.

Heidi shrugged. 'Most of the entries are disturbing, no happy events, just a catalogue of dreadful ones.'

'Such as?'

'Seems to me Myfanwy was an abuser,' Heidi said. 'I've discovered countless entries relating to her hurting people, mainly her husband and her daughters.'

Stacey gasped. 'Daughters? BB had a sister?'

'According to the journal she did. Her name was Gwen and BB wrote that her sister was driven out by Myfanwy over thirty years ago. That was recorded in one of the earliest entries.'

'Any clues about why?'

'Nothing definite. Referred to briefly as, "the trouble". Pregnancy would be my guess, but it could have been something else entirely.'

Heidi got to her feet and filled two bowls with creamy leek and potato soup.

'This smells fab,' she said. 'Veg from your garden?'

'Of course.' Stacey carried a plate of sandwiches to the table. 'Any chance the journal will provide enough information to find Gwen?'

'Not on its own, but now I have more data and certain knowledge the internet can't help me. It'd be a change to investigate something in the real world.' She dunked a sandwich in her soup and took a large bite. 'This is great.' She wiped her lips. 'I've a few places to visit tomorrow, including Brecon library to take a look at their collection of old newspapers. After that, the chairman of one of the local historical groups has agreed I can riffle through their old photos and documents. Great places to meet amateur historians and older residents.'

'So, basically,' Stacey said, 'you've discovered the Llewelyns were not a happy family. After years of abuse, BB snapped and killed her mother, and you need to verify that somehow. Find her sister and maybe other family?'

'That's about the size of it, but there's a lot more work to do. Want a lift to Brecon in the morning?'

'Yes please. Sam's been on the phone, he wants an update on the spiking story.'

'OK, we'll leave at nine. Lots to do.'

'Having studied the journal,' Stacey said, 'do you think BB had anything to do with the deaths of the Townsends? Killed one abuser and thought she'd get rid of a couple more?'

'If she did, she didn't write about it, but she seems to have written about everything else worth noting.'

'I'd love to know where she's gone,' Stacey said. 'Why would she up and leave having lived in the valley her entire life?'

'I reckon because she suddenly had visitors, Ben and Jack followed by us. People knew she was there. That could frighten someone away, especially someone who was used to living like a hermit and had something to hide.'

'So you do think it's possible she could be the murderer?'

'I didn't say that, but killing your mother with a cleaver is a pretty enormous secret, wouldn't you agree?'

* * *

During the hours of darkness, a heavy frost had settled on the Epynt, the air so dry and cold it might shatter. Stacey opened the back door and stood shivering on the step, feet swathed in thick bed socks, a fluffy bathrobe wrapped tightly around her body.

The sun was just rising above the forestry plantations, casting a weak, lemon-tinted glow over trees and mountains. The gentle light shone into the back garden and illuminated tiny ice crystals until it seemed every twig and blade of grass had been sprinkled with diamond dust. A male blackbird, its jet-black feathers stark against white sparkles, fluffed up against the cold, a sooty snowball balanced on the edge of the cinder path. A pair of fieldfares, perched in a leafless sallow, looked just as cold and hungry.

Stacey collected a couple of withered apples from the fruit bowl, cut them in half and threw pieces onto the grass. She shut the door and shivered. After a fortnight of mild autumn days, such a hard frost had shocked her system. Through the window above the sink, she watched the blackbird hop across the frosty lawn and attack the fruit, swallowing large chunks before the fieldfares spotted the feast. A small group of hungry-looking starlings swooshed in, sunshine reflecting on their feathers like spilt oil in puddles.

Stacey poured coffee, propped her wool-clad feet on the base of the Aga and switched on her laptop to proofread yesterday's work. Half an hour later Heidi entered the kitchen, her small body completely swathed in a fleecy blanket, only her face exposed.

'Morning,' she said and helped herself to coffee. 'It's bloody cold,' she complained.

'That's cos winter is nearly here and I live on a mountain. Always colder up here than at lower levels.'

Heidi sat at the table and wrapped her pale hands around the hot mug. 'We'll take my Land Rover again today,' she said. 'If it's icy here it'll be worse on the top.'

'I'll make some porridge. Full stomachs will help keep us warm.'

'I'm only eating it if you have honey and cream. Plain porridge tastes like sticky sawdust.'

Stacey smiled. 'I've got both.'

'Good. You cook and I'll get dressed.'

Shortly after nine, having packed a couple of flasks of coffee, some energy bars, a couple of blankets and a shovel for spreading road salt if they got stuck, Stacey followed Heidi out to the truck. The lane shone as weak sunbeams brushed across the surface of the tarmac; the ice was nearly half a centimetre thick.

'Blimey,' Heidi said. 'Must have rained last night, landed and frozen solid on contact. Careful you don't slip. A fall won't do your leg any good.'

'Maybe we should leave it until later, or tomorrow?' Stacey suggested.

'No, time is of the essence.'

'Why is it?'

'If the police read BB's confession in the journal – and manage to track her down before I do – she'll be arrested for murder and that'll be her life done.'

'What else do you expect the police to do? She did kill her mother.'

'You know things aren't as black and white,' Heidi said. 'I want to find her before the police, ask about her life. If her mother was an abuser and had attacked her husband so violently BB thought to note it down, a case for self-defence could be made.' She opened the door of her vehicle and helped Stacey inside. 'BB should have a chance.'

Heidi closed the passenger door, slipped behind the steering wheel and fired up the engine. She turned on the heating fan, then stepped back out to scrape the windscreen clear of ice. Five minutes later, when she could see through the glass, she drove past Llanagethin village and headed up the steep lane to the start of the ranges. Heidi was right, the frost was even harsher on the mountaintop.

With such clear, frigid air, Pen-y-Fan loomed into the pale sky, its flanks streaked with white where rivulets of water had solidified when the temperature dropped. About halfway along the army road, a group of ravens caught Stacey's eye. Heidi slowed to a stop and the women watched a small unkindness of the birds worry at a sheep's carcass, hammering at the frozen meat with strong, thick beaks, so desperate for a meal they took little notice of the vehicle parked a few feet away.

'You were right,' Heidi said, 'you don't need Welsh vultures.'

Stacey pointed at the sky where three red kites sailed ever lower, also hungry. 'There won't be much left of this when we drive back.' She frowned. 'Lots of farmers hate ravens and spout utter rubbish about them, but the birds do a good job cleaning up. Probably my favourite bird, the raven.'

'You surprise me,' Heidi said. 'I'd have put you down as a kingfisher sort of woman.'

'Well...'

Heidi put the truck into gear. 'Fascinating as ornithology is, we have lots to achieve today.' She checked her mirror, pulled away and left the corvids to their feast.

* * *

Ben slammed down the office phone. He put his face in his hands, rubbed vigorously and groaned. After a long and difficult conversation with an inspector at Swansea's main police station, he knew he'd achieved very little, if anything.

The inspector had told him no complaints had been made, no record of any spikings or abductions from the local clubs on the night in question, that it was difficult to be completely sure which officers had been asked for assistance and consequently, impossible to verify if anyone had been inappropriate. Ben knew he'd been fed a string of excuses – that no one at Swansea nick would be spoken to and nothing was likely to change. He scribbled a note on a pad next to the phone, a reminder to speak to CS Warren. A call from her might shake things up. His phone rang and he picked up the receiver.

'DCI James.'

'Morning, sir. Front desk. A young man is here asking to see you.' The desk sergeant lowered his voice. 'He's in a bit of a state, distracted you might say.'

'Has he got a name?'

'Yes, sir, Kevin Townsend, brother of...'

'Yes, I know. Keep him there. I'll round up DS Trent and we'll be down. Any idea what he wants?'

'Just to talk to you, sir.'

Chapter twenty-one

Ben collected Kevin from reception and showed him into an interview room where Jack waited, three vending machine teas on the table. Kevin entered warily, like a mouse about to break cover, and looked around the room.

'Not very nice in here,' he said. 'Put some pictures on the wall for God's sake. All this neutral, earthy colour stuff isn't good for anyone.'

'Take a seat,' Ben said, 'and tell us what we can do for you.'

Kevin perched on the edge of a plastic chair. 'I need help,' he said. 'I'm fairly sure someone is following me.'

'Really?' Jack asked. 'Why do you think that?'

'I wonder, let me see... oh, yes, because someone killed both my brothers?' His face crumpled. 'I know I'm next.'

'How do you know that?'

'I can feel death coming, deep inside my guts, feel someone behind me. I know he's there but when I turn around, I can't spot him. He hides.'

'So it's a man doing the following?' Ben asked.

Kevin nodded. 'Follows me when I'm driving too, uses lots of different cars. Makes it difficult for me to keep tabs on him. You have to do something about this or I'll be found tied up, naked and dead.'

Jack caught Ben's eye and sent him an "is-this-for-real?" look. Ben sent half a shrug in response.

'Have you received any direct threats?' Ben asked. 'Phone calls, social media, anything?'

'You mean apart from having two dead brothers on my hands?' Kevin asked, his mood changing quickly from frightened to angry and his hands on the table forming fists, knuckles white.

Jack tensed, ready for trouble. 'You still have an FLO with you,' he said. 'You're not on your own. Have you talked to him about this?'

'Yes, but I can tell he isn't taking me seriously – same as you. I'm telling you; I need witness protection or a bodyguard.'

'I'm sorry,' Ben said, 'that isn't possible. What I can do is speak to your local police, request extra patrols and a security check of your home.'

Disturbingly, Kevin began to cry. Great rushes of tears ran down his cheeks and he sobbed loudly, struggling to breathe as what appeared to be a mixture of misery and terror threatened to drown him. Even Jack was moved and patted the young man on his arm. Ben pushed a box of tissues across the table. Kevin grabbed a handful and wiped his face. He looked up at the officers.

'I don't miss them you know,' he said.

'Don't miss who?' Ben asked.

'My brothers. They weren't very nice people, either of them.'

'Why do you say they weren't nice?'

Kevin snorted. 'Bloody incredible! You're the police! You know what happened in London. Robin killed his girlfriend and Ian helped him. Ian was arrested and released. Robin stood trial. You couldn't prove what they'd done, could you? Both guilty as sin and both got away with it.'

'How do you know all this?' Jack asked.

'Heard them talking the night it happened.' Kevin sniffed and wiped his nose. 'They didn't know I was listening.'

'Did you come forward at the time? Speak to the detectives running the investigation?'

'How could I? They'd have killed me too.' Kevin began sobbing again.

'Kevin,' Ben said, 'did you kill your brothers?'

Kevin's eyes opened wide, his mood shifted again and he laughed. 'Kill my brothers? Are you mad? Do I look like a killer?'

'What does a killer look like?' Jack asked.

'Anyone who doesn't look like me!' Kevin got to his feet. 'I'm wasting my time here,' he said, kicking at the chair. 'Maybe I should just get myself a gun then I can look after myself. It's obvious you're not going to help.'

'Sit down, Kevin,' Ben said. 'I think we need a break.' He got to his feet. 'Wait here. I'll have someone sit with you while Jack and I fetch tea we could all do with one. Will you stay and talk this through? Buying a gun is a very bad idea.'

Kevin nodded. He tore more tissues from the box and scrubbed at his face. The detectives left the room, a uniformed officer took their place and closed the door.

Jack whistled. 'Blimey, guv, he's in a proper state. Should we have the doc look him over?'

'Not a bad idea. Do you still think the lad killed his brothers?'

'Wouldn't surprise me. No love lost between him and the other two. He's obviously distressed but something else is definitely going on. Might be guilt.'

'What about his story of being followed? Do you think that's real?'

'Who knows, sounds paranoid to me. Let's see what the doc says before we have another run at him. Kevin isn't the only one who could do with a break.'

* * *

Heidi found Stacey and Sam Jenkins in the back of Sam's favourite lunchtime pub. Much to his surprise, Heidi dropped on a chair next to him and smiled.

'So,' Sam said, 'Heidi Holtz, we meet at last. I have to ask, are you a carnivore?'

Heidi nodded. 'Enthusiastically so,' she said.

'You surprise me, you look... undernourished.'

'I have small bones.'

'Wine?' Sam peered at his new guest. 'You are old enough to drink?'

'Sam!' Stacey said. 'Are you being purposely rude?'

'What? No, I'm not being rude at all. Thought I was being polite.' He turned back to Heidi. 'Working lunches are always steak when the paper is paying. Is that OK with you?'

'I enjoy a good steak,' Heidi said. 'As long as it's well done and smothered in honey and mustard sauce.'

Sam waved the waiter over, confirmed his order and requested a second bottle of wine.

'Heidi, how did you get on at the library?' Stacey asked.

Heidi cracked her knuckles and Sam winced. 'Not as well as I'd hoped,' she said. 'Discovered some old editions of newspapers which had recorded sheep prices at local markets. The Llewelyns consistently sold animals up until about five years ago.'

'Nothing since then?' Stacey asked.

'Nope, not that I can find and can't think she'd use markets miles away. It is possible, I suppose, that she sells animals on to other farmers, but I'm not sure how I could prove that. Bound to be cash transactions.'

The waiter reappeared, plates balancing on his forearms, a large steak sitting on top of each.

'Goodness,' Stacey said. 'Not sure I'll be able to eat all this.'

'They'll do a doggy bag.' Sam hacked a chunk from his slab of meat and stuffed it into his mouth. He chewed, swallowed then asked, 'Tell me Stacey, how is your, "thoughtful exposé" coming along?'

'Progressing well and experiencing slight mission creep.'

'How so?' Sam asked.

'There's the spiking, the way police handle reports and an unsurprising lack of arrests. We spoke to a woman whose friend went missing from a club and was treated to sleazy behaviour by uniformed officers.'

Sam glanced up. 'That's put more meat on the bones. I trust you will pursue that aspect in your feature?'

'Of course, together with the fact that the few women who are brave enough to report bad behaviour aren't treated very sympathetically either.'

'It's all abuse,' Heidi said, 'low- to high-level abuse and it must stop. The fact some of it is dished out by serving police officers appals me. Instead of working to make the country a safe place for women, they spout numerous, ridiculous safety rules. Then, if anything happens, women can be blamed for not sticking to them. Utterly scandalous.'

Sam grinned. 'I like passionate people,' he said. 'Fancy an opinion column in the paper?'

'Not a good idea, Mr Jenkins. I have some very extreme opinions on all sorts of topics. You wouldn't keep me on, and to be honest, I don't need the money.'

Sam looked shocked, his eyebrows vanishing beneath what was left of his hair.

'Back to the feature,' Stacey said. 'Heidi and me, plus a friend of ours, have planned a night out in one of the Cardiff clubs, this weekend maybe, see if we can spot anything going on.'

'Why are you telling me this? I'm not handing over expenses, not for three of you.'

'Did I even ask?'

'Not much of a plan if you ask me,' Sam said. 'Not sure how well your undercover thing will work either. You'll be at least fifteen years older than the other patrons and leaning on a crutch.' He laughed.

'I knew you were grumpy, a friend of mine warned me about you,' Heidi said, 'but she didn't say you were unkind.' She leaned closer. 'You won't recognise your top reporter once Erica gets her hands on her. I'll send you a photo and if you can't pick Stacey out, I'll expect you to eat it.'

'It's a wager,' Sam said. 'I could pick her out anywhere, but I'd prefer a cash bet.'

'No money,' Heidi said. 'Just the photo.'

Sam stretched out a flabby hand and they sealed the bet. He changed the subject. 'Nice piece about your brush with death the other evening, Stacey. How is your injury?'

'Healing well. Thank God the kid only had a penknife with a short blade.'

'Quite,' Sam said and posted another forkful of meat into his mouth. 'Make sure you take care when you go clubbing. I don't fancy having to look for a replacement.'

* * *

Jack strode into the squad room, door bouncing off the plaster. Ben looked up from a pile of reports.

'How did it go?' he asked.

Jack dropped onto a nearby chair. 'Kevin's on his way back to Tenby. The only way I could get him to leave was if one of ours followed on behind and kept an eye out for the stalker.'

'Who did you send?'

'Ollie Langdon.'

'Waste of manpower,' Ben said, 'not like we have any spare capacity as it is. Did the doc manage to take a look at the lad?'

Jack nodded. 'Said he was suffering from shock. He spoke to Kevin's GP. There isn't any record of mental health issues but she's agreed to make a house call.' Jack peered across the table. 'What have you got there?'

'The DNA results came back. Blood on the cleaver belongs to the body in the garden so we definitely have the murder weapon.' Ben turned a page. 'Also says that DNA recovered from hair follicles trapped in a brush, proves that whoever shed them was the daughter of the victim.'

'That's bound to be BB. Just need to find her and take a swab to prove it. How is Tegan getting on with translating the journal?'

'Not as well as I'd like.' Ben sighed. 'We're spread so thin, then Ollie gets sent on a fool's errand.'

Jack nodded. 'Only way to get rid of Kevin,' he said. 'At one point he said he'd stay in one of the cells where he'd be safe.'

'Do you think anyone is actually following him?'

'I can see why he might think there is, given the circumstances.' Jack got to his feet and headed for the coffee machine. 'Anything back on Ian Townsend's car or clothes?'

'Nothing useful. Tegan managed to pick up the vehicle using ANPR on the A40, driving east. Last shot captured early afternoon on the outskirts of Llandovery.'

'So Ian turned off onto smaller roads with no cameras?'

'Looks like it,' Ben said. 'He could have crossed over the mountains to Builth, but why was he there?'

'Did he go inside the Co-op?'

'No CCTV to prove that he did and none of the staff recognised his photo.'

Jack carried a pair of mugs to the table and sat. 'What about Peter Butler?' he asked. 'I trust we still have him in the cells?'

'His solicitor arrived first thing, spoke to his client for about an hour and reported back that Pete the Pot would be giving no-comment interviews from now on.'

'So we charge him, take him to court and hope he's remanded?' Jack asked.

'That's the size of it. At least we'll know where he is. Do you think it's possible he is involved with the murders?'

'He's never been nicked for anything other than drug offenses,' Jack said, 'so I can't see he'd suddenly turn killer.'

'The drugs you found in the flat were confirmed to be GHB.'

'OK, so maybe Pete the Pot supplied the drug, but we need to be able to prove it. We can't even prove he knew Ian or Kevin before they met at the Stonecroft.'

Ben frowned while Jack sifted through the pile of reports.

'I'm missing something,' Ben said. 'We all are, but I've no idea where to look next.'

'Unknown unknowns, guv, always tricky. Any word from Erica Bevan and her spiking cases?'

'Stacey, Heidi and Erica are planning a trip to one of the clubs in Cardiff where there have been recent incidents.' Ben laughed. '"Undercover" was how Stacey put it.'

'What are they going to do there?'

'Surveillance. See if they can catch anyone at it, or spot the kid with the baseball cap who has been captured on film. They're going to stay over in Cardiff and come back the next day.'

'When's that happening?'

'This weekend I think.'

Jack nodded. 'What now then?'

Ben got to his feet and put on his jacket.

'Let's have another wander around Builth. Until we can find someone or something that can tell us Ian was actually in town, we can't even prove he drove himself to the Co-op. We must uncover more about his movements before he died. Without that, we're spinning our wheels.'

* * *

Ben pulled up in the lane outside Noddfa, turned off the engine and peered into the darkness on the far side of the windscreen. He rubbed his eyes and groaned. He was so tired, too tired to open the car door and walk up the path to the cottage. He and Jack had wasted an entire afternoon.

He walked inside the cottage, removed his jacket, went to the kitchen and dropped on the carver. 'Something smells good,' he said.

Stacey smiled. 'Lasagne this evening.'

'Marvellous, I'm starving.'

Heidi appeared in the doorway. 'Evening,' she said and took a place at the table. 'Did you manage to track down those useless coppers in Swansea?'

'Not yet. I was fed a load of bunkum by an inspector at the main station, but I've spoken to CS Warren. She's as angry as you are and is on the case. It's difficult to ignore a chief superintendent, so she should have more luck.'

Heidi nodded and helped herself to a large piece of garlic bread.

'Are you still planning to go dancing this weekend?' Ben asked.

Stacey nodded. 'Yes, this weekend. You're off on Saturday aren't you?'

Ben nodded. 'Yes and a late shift on Sunday. Are you sure you're up to dancing? How's your leg?'

'Much better and I'm not planning on dancing.'

'Just be careful – all of you.'

'Safety in numbers,' Heidi said, wiping bread around her plate. 'We'll keep an eye on each other.'

'I don't want anyone else stabbed.'

'Neither do I,' Heidi said. 'I had a chat with Erica earlier. Seems her ID parade went well. The lads Stacey and I locked horns with were successfully picked out by Eve Salmon. Court for them in the morning. Both pleading guilty apparently, so no need for me and Stacey to get involved. Erica reckons they'll both go down. At least they'll be off the streets for a while.'

'That's good news,' Ben said. 'Peter Butler, aka Pete the Pot, has been remanded. He's not intending to plead so he'll go to Crown.'

'I don't suppose anyone thought to check if the drugs found at Pete's flat matched those found in the victims?'

'We did, but we found nothing conclusive. GHB metabolises too quickly once it has been ingested.'

Heidi nodded, collected empty plates and carried them to the sink. Stacey removed an apple and blackberry crumble from the oven and took a tub of ice cream from the freezer. As she cut into the dessert, the warm scent of fruit and cinnamon escaped from beneath the crust and hung above the table.

Ben breathed deeply. 'Nothing says autumn like blackberry and apple.'

'Make the most of it,' Stacey said. 'Winter isn't far away.'

Chapter twenty-two

The next morning Ben was working through mounds of statements the investigation had generated, hunting for any missing clues, when his phone rang.

'DCI James.'

'Good morning, Chief Inspector.'

Ben recognised CS Warren's voice.

'Good morning, ma'am. What can I do for you?'

'More the other way around,' she said. 'I've been talking to an inspector in Swansea and he has been able to put names to the officers on patrol the night the young clubber asked for help.'

'Gosh, that's a long way from him telling me it would be impossible to identify them.'

'It helps if you've got more clout. The pair have been transferred to prisoner transport duties while the matter is being investigated.' She chuckled quietly. 'Just so happens they are currently in the station and have been told you'd like a word. I'm hoping you will be able to get to the bottom of what actually went on and I expect an update before the end of your shift. We need to clean up our act and this is a good a place to start.'

'Yes, ma'am, and I agree. Thanks for engineering this.'

'Just doing my job. Make sure you do yours.'

Ben put down the phone then rounded up Jack and together they went downstairs to the interview rooms, where two uniformed officers waited. They stood as the detectives entered. Ben waved them to their seats and introduced himself. The out-of-towners informed him they were PC Martin Stein and PC Joey Matthews. Both in their twenties, they reluctantly confirmed they were the officers who had spoken to a distressed young woman outside a club in Swansea. Ben listened as they delivered their accounts, his face darkening with anger.

'Well,' he said, when the pair fell silent. 'I suppose I have to give you some credit for admitting your part in this sorry affair, but I struggle to understand why you acted the way you did.' He frowned and took a deep breath. 'A young woman tells you her friend is missing, asks for help and you chat her up? You told her women only went to clubs because they were "looking for a shag"? What on earth possessed you?'

'I was trying to make her realise how unsafe the clubs are,' Martin Stein said, 'especially now there's an increase in spiking. Women shouldn't go to these places on their own.'

'I don't accept that!' Ben snapped. 'She was trying to report her friend missing. Turns out she was right to be concerned. Her friend regained consciousness in a motel room off the M4 having been drugged. You'll have to do better, Constable.'

'Easy with hindsight,' Stein muttered. 'The way I see it, if the girls stay home, they'll be less likely to end up as victims.'

'Gold star for the bleeding obvious, but why should they stay home? Maybe you think they should wear chastity belts?'

'Look, Inspector, I...'

'Chief Inspector.'

'Yes sir, Chief Inspector.' Stein took a breath. 'I want them safe and not on the streets after dark. I don't want to be chasing scumbags who can't keep it in their pants – even worse, what if one of them actually kills a woman. If we do manage to nick anyone and get them into court, they often walk out because of a technicality.' He sighed. 'We know they are guilty, did our jobs but it makes no difference.'

'So, your reason for refusing to help a teenager in distress, and telling her that her friend had more than likely "copped off", was your way of keeping her safe?'

Jack, leaning on the tiled wall of the interview room, snorted incredulously.

'Why not?' Stein asked. 'Nothing else works. We issue warnings, plaster posters everywhere and still girls go out on their own at night, wearing short skirts, revealing tops and heels they can't walk in, never mind run. They're asking for it, just so much easy meat.'

'So,' Jack said, 'if you see women out on their own in similar circumstances, do you roll down the window and shout "slag" at them?'

'No... not in a work car.'

Jack spluttered. 'You do that in your own car? Are you bloody serious?'

Stein looked at the floor and kept his mouth shut.

Jack glared at Joey Matthews who shrank lower in his chair. 'Do you pull stunts like that too?'

'Not really,' Matthews said, 'not the shouting. I just try to spook them off the streets to keep them safe like Martin says. Made sense to me.' He glanced up at Jack. 'What will happen now? To us I mean.'

'Lucky for you I don't get to make that decision, but you can bet there'll be an inquiry.'

'Have either of you had sex with any of these women – or any woman while on duty?' Ben asked.

Both constables' heads swivelled in his direction, eyes shocked wide.

'Why are you asking that?' Stein said.

'Best to get everything out in the open, know what we're dealing with.'

Jack leaned on the table and glared at the younger officers. 'Easy enough question, lads,' he snarled. 'Did either of you get your leg over while on duty? Favours from young women you've kept "safe"?'

The officers shook their heads.

'No, Sergeant,' Stein said. 'We never did.'

'We must have saved heaps of girls,' Matthews said. 'A verbal jolt usually sends them scurrying home so we can concentrate on more serious crimes. I reckon we're doing a good job.'

Jack laughed out loud. 'Bloody hell, guv,' he said. 'A verbal jolt? Do you reckon this initiative for crime prevention will catch on?' He looked back at the officers. 'Don't you idiots realise you are part of the problem? You verbally abuse women while in uniform, never mind refusing assistance to a member of the public who asked for it. Disgusting!'

'Better that,' Stein said, 'than wasting hours trying to get justice for victims, only to see the guilty walk.'

* * *

Erica leaned across the dressing table and tugged away a towel draped over the large mirror.

'Bloody hell!' Stacey said. 'What on earth have you done to me?'

Erica chuckled. 'Took fifteen years off and made you unrecognisable. Like it?'

'Not keen if I'm honest. I never wear as much make-up as this, and my hair? I look like Boy George. All I need is a bowler hat.'

Heidi laughed and plonked one on top of Stacey's new hairdo.

'Now you're having a laugh,' Stacey said. 'I can't do this, I look awful.'

'I think you look fab,' Heidi said. 'Better than that, you'll be able to watch your grumpy boss eat a photograph. He'll never recognise you.'

'Not sure about the skirt either,' Stacey said, tugging at the hem. 'Is this really what bright young things wear to clubs these days?'

'Of course,' Erica said. 'Now, let's go before your cold feet freeze solid.' She sighed. 'I've sent undercover officers in here a few times, but they've failed to spot anything, hence our night out. Fingers crossed, eh? We might get lucky.'

The women left the flat, stepped into a waiting taxi and the driver headed towards the Boston Bar. The weather had suddenly turned mild as strong westerlies blew rain fronts over South Wales. The driver battled through and pulled up at the end of the alley leading to the club. Heidi settled the bill then the women scurried through heavy rain to the entrance, Stacey hanging onto the bowler.

They'd arrived early, before the pubs kicked out, and consequently the place was only half full. Small groups of clubbers congregated in nooks containing sofas and low tables, a few little cliques at the bar. Stacey felt very self-conscious in her disguise but soon realised no one was staring and relaxed a touch. She laid claim to a sofa tucked in one of the darkest corners, while Erica and Heidi went to the bar. A DJ on a rostrum overlooking the dancing area played loud, fast-tempo dance music, but so far had failed to encourage anyone onto their feet. Stacey glanced up as her friends arrived in the corner, glasses of elaborate cocktails decorated with slices of fruit in their hands.

'Wow,' Stacey said. 'I thought we weren't drinking.'

'We're not,' Erica said. 'Fruit juice only but we have to look the part.'

Stacey took a cautious sip. 'This is gorgeous,' she said. She scooped a slice of what looked like mango from the glass and put it in her mouth. 'Maybe I should go alcohol-free at Noddfa.'

'I hope not,' Heidi said. 'Don't make drastic changes like that until I've gone home.'

'You're still staying with Stacey?' Erica asked.

Heidi nodded. 'Just until her leg is completely healed. I'll have to go back to the flat eventually.' She grinned at her ex-partner. 'Fancy moving back in with me?'

Erica looked away and Stacey changed the subject.

'Tell me again about the lad we're keeping an eye out for,' she said.

'Early twenties, medium height and build, white, wears a baseball cap.'

'Not much of a description.'

Erica shrugged. 'Not much in the way of decent CCTV.'

More young people entered the club, followed by a group of three older men. They all wore suits, skirted the dance floor and vanished through a door marked "Private" to the right of the mixing desk.

'Bet the guy in the middle with the ponytail is the owner,' Heidi said. 'Mustn't forget to talk to him before we leave.'

Ten o'clock came and went and the club began to fill. The DJ upped his game and managed to encourage groups of dancers off the sofas. Stacey smiled.

'Jonnie Jones at Rascals was right,' she said. 'Watching people have fun is great, and the outfits? Amazing.'

'Said you'd blend in,' Erica said. She pulled a mobile from her pocket and began snapping pictures, including a selfie of the three of them, drinks in their hands. She put the phone away and caught Heidi's eye. 'Fancy a bop?'

'You know dancing isn't my thing,' Heidi said.

'Aw, come on. Can't sit here all night, we need to circulate.'

'One of us should be staking out the bar. We won't spot any dodgy stuff happening tucked away here.'

'I'll do it,' Stacey said. 'Not like I can dance, although, that's a shame. I always enjoyed a wiggle on a dance floor.'

She smiled at her friends. 'Off you go, my lovelies, and strut your stuff. You know where to find me.'

'Just make sure you keep an eye on your drink,' Heidi said.

Chapter twenty-three

Ben poured himself another whisky, threw a log on the fire and looked back at the statements collected during the ongoing murder investigation. The usually quiet living room was anything but as a late autumn gale blew around the cottage driving on hailstones which rattled loudly against the windows, as though someone had flung a handful of pebbles at the glass.

Strong gusts tore across the open ranges like an oncoming express train and hurled themselves at the old building. The place was filled with knocks and bangs, as though a drummer had taken up residence in the attic, and rushing wind in the pipes sounded like a trumpeter in an Indian wedding band. Ben sighed heavily and struggled to concentrate on his work.

Checking his watch, he saw it was nearly midnight and wondered how the club night was working out for Stacey and her friends. He hoped they were having a good time if nothing else. He wasn't sure their evening of surveillance would produce anything useful, but he supposed it was worth a go. He drained the last dregs of his drink and hauled himself off the sofa, then he padded into the kitchen and put the kettle on for a last cuppa before bedtime. He opened the back door and stood on the step, and listened to the roaring storm and heavy rain pounding in the slate roof.

The kettle whistled, Ben shut and locked the door, made tea then went to the living room to put the fire guard in the grate. Returning to the kitchen, he picked up his mug, turned off the light and went upstairs to the front bedroom tucked beneath the eaves and got into bed. Hours later he was still awake, tossing and turning, listening to the gale and worrying about the murder case.

* * *

Stacey had settled herself at one end of the bar, stuck to fruity cocktails and watched the crowd on the dance floor. She refused all offers of drinks from strangers, but scrutinised each one carefully, searching for the lad in the baseball cap. Every now and again she spotted Heidi's white hair, as she and Erica danced in the middle of the crowd and Stacey smiled to herself. The pair seemed to be getting on well and she hoped they would soon be back together, where they belonged.

She got to her feet, used the crutch to make sure no one knocked her over, and made her way to the toilet. There was a queue, so she leaned against the wall and watched the clientele reapplying make-up, chatting and laughing with their friends, adjusting their outfits and fiddling with their hair. A few glanced her way and commented on how cool her hat looked. Ten minutes later, Stacey left the warm damp space and returned to the club. As she walked through the door, Heidi appeared at her side, clearly agitated.

'Is Erica in there?' she asked.

'No, just me. What's up?'

'I can't find her,' Heidi said. 'We were dancing, she said she was going to fetch more drinks but didn't return and I don't know where she is. Help me look?'

'Of course.'

The women began a circuit of the club in opposite directions and met up again at the bar.

'Any luck?' Heidi asked.

Stacey shook her head. 'Not a sign.'

'Right then,' Heidi said and turned away.

She stormed through the busy throng using her sharp elbows, a contemporary Moses parting the waves, and headed for the door marked "Private", situated next to the mixing desk. Putting her shoulder to the door, she burst into a medium-sized office, Stacey close behind. At one end a security guard stared at a bank of monitors displaying the inside and main entrance of the premises. At the other the ponytailed man sat behind a desk, his suit jacket draped on the back of his chair.

He looked up in surprise. 'Can't you read?' he snapped. 'This is private.'

Heidi took no notice, she marched up to the desk, swivelled his laptop away from him and began bashing keys, fingers blurring. The man behind the desk got to his feet as the security guard belatedly realised that maybe he should be doing something.

'Ladies,' he said. 'You need to leave Mr Johnson's office right now.'

'You need to shut up,' Heidi said, unblinking eyes fixed on the screen.

Stacey removed a press pass from her pocket and waved it at the owner.

'Please,' she said, 'don't stop her. We think our friend has been removed from the club against her will. Heidi is trying to find out where she went.'

'Come again?' Johnson asked.

'Our friend might have been spiked,' Stacey said. 'She's a cop, for God's sake.'

Johnson dropped onto his chair. 'A cop?'

'I'll explain, but I have to make a call first.'

Stacey speed-dialled Ben's number but couldn't get his phone to ring. She tried her landline but that was the same.

Maybe the gale had brought down the lines. She returned the phone to her pocket and asked, 'Any luck, Heidi?'

Heidi nodded. 'Found a CCTV shot of her being loaded into a white Transit Connect. Two lads, early twenties. Number plate light is out. Went south but I'm struggling to pick it up again.'

'Are you all cops?' Johnson asked.

'No,' Stacey said, 'I'm press. I showed you my pass.'

'What about her?' He nodded at Heidi.

'She used to be a copper, a detective.'

Johnson burst out laughing. 'Her? A copper? When was this, when she was ten?' He laughed some more. 'This is all a bloody wind-up. Well, ladies, you've had your fun. Security will escort you out.'

Heidi raised her eyes from the screen and glared at the laughing man.

'Shut up, can't you? I need to think.' She hammered at the keyboard then announced, 'Got her! Traffic camera image, van heading towards the M4. Still can't read the number plate. Let's go, Stacey.' Heidi slapped the laptop closed, tucked it under her arm and headed for the door.

'Hey,' the man said, 'you can't run off with my laptop. Stop!'

Stacey followed Heidi as she cleared a path through the clubbers. Within minutes they were outside.

'Where are we going?' Stacey asked.

'To rescue Erica.' Heidi squinted down the street. 'There!' she said. 'Taxi.'

She waved an urgent arm. The driver spotted her and pulled across the road. They slipped into the back seat and Heidi told the driver to get moving. Stacey looked though the back window and saw Johnson barrel out of the main door, scanning the pavement with frantic eyes.

'Where to, ladies?' the cabbie asked.

'M4,' Heidi said, eyes glued to the computer screen. 'As fast as you can drive.'

The driver laughed. ‘Can’t do that, love, unless it’s a matter of life and death.’

‘It could well be, so put your bloody foot down.’

Chapter twenty-four

Loud hammering shook Ben awake. He stared up at the ceiling and tried to work out whether the gale had caused the racket, or something else. He peered at his watch and reckoned he'd been asleep for less than an hour. He gave his pillow a couple of thumps and was about to close his eyes when he heard more hammering, louder this time. He got out of bed, opened the window and peered into the dark.

'Hello,' he called. 'Is someone there?'

'Yes, guv, it's me. Get the door open, it's bloody horrid out here.'

Ben pulled on a towelling robe and padded downstairs. He opened the door and Jack stepped in.

'Wild night,' Jack said.

'What are you doing here?'

'I tried calling but couldn't get through.'

'Everything OK at home?'

'Fine.' Jack took a deep breath. 'We've got another one.'

'Another what?'

'Naked bloke, tied to the Builth Bull, with a U2 card in his mouth.'

'Shit,' Ben said. 'Tell me it isn't Kevin Townsend.'

'It isn't Kevin Townsend and... he isn't quite dead.'

'You're kidding?'

'He's in Llandrindod Hospital. Paramedics discovered the card.'

'Right,' Ben said. 'Make us coffee to go while I get dressed and we'll head over.'

They were on the road five minutes later, Jack at the wheel.

'Not the weather for this,' Jack said. 'Bloody crazy coming over the ranges. That road is about the only one around here that gives me the willies. Like the end of the world after dark, sheep wandering about on the tarmac like ghosts.'

'Do we know the name of the victim?' Ben asked.

'Patrick Ryan. One of the first coppers on the scene recognised him. Nasty piece of work as it turns out.'

'Oh? What's he been up to?'

'Tried about eighteen months ago for assaulting his partner, domestic abuse with knobs on. Jury found him not guilty and he moved back in with his mother in Rhayader.'

'Who found him?'

'Couple of blokes in a van. They spotted him plonked on the statue, pulled over to take photos for their Facebook page and realised something was wrong.'

'Good job they did. How is he?'

'Poorly.'

'We've gotta catch this killer, Jack. He's getting a taste for it.'

Jack hit the main road and put his foot down. At Builth he pulled into the bus stop next to the bronze statue of a life-size Welsh Black bull. A group of SOCOs were trying to protect the scene but the tent wouldn't stay put as gusts of wind tore it from their hands. A uniformed constable approached the car. He bent to peer in the side window.

'Can I help you?' he asked.

Ben held up his warrant card. 'Anything to tell me, Constable?'

'No, sir,' he glanced over his shoulder. 'As you can see the conditions aren't helping. Are you off to the hospital?'

'We are. We'll call back on the return journey. Tell SOCO to do their best.'

'Yes, sir.'

Jack rejoined the road and drove over the Wye River Bridge, past the Royal Welsh Showground and up the hill towards Llandrindod and the hospital. Due to the hour, there were no vehicles outside the building and Jack parked in a space next to the main entrance. They left the car. Ben shoved the glass door and found it locked. He stabbed a thumb on the red emergency button and twitched with impatience until a tired-looking nurse finally appeared.

'Can I help you, gentlemen?' she asked.

Ben and Jack flashed their warrant cards and she allowed them inside.

'We're looking for Patrick Ryan,' Ben said. 'Discovered in Builth tied on the back of the bull.'

The nurse nodded. 'He's in ICU but I can't allow you in to see him. He's very unwell.'

'I understand,' Ben said, 'but is there a chance I can speak to his doctor?'

'I'll see what I can do. Wait here.'

The woman strode away, rubber-soled shoes squeaking on the tiles. Ben and Jack chose a couple of chairs and sat. The hospital was quiet, lights dimmed, a very different place from the hurly-burly during the day. The corridor smelt of cleaning fluid and was overly warm. The men removed their coats and Ben glanced at his watch.

'How long do you think we'll be stuck in here?' he asked.

Jack shrugged. 'No idea. I hope Ryan makes it though. He should be able to tell us who doped him up and tied him to the statue. The killer is methodical and meticulous and hasn't left any clues so far. We really need to hear what Ryan has to say.'

A door next to the lifts opened and a doctor in a white coat, stethoscope stuffed into a top pocket, walked quickly towards them. The detectives got to their feet.

'Good morning,' the man said. 'I'm Dr Sunderland. I understand you'd like a word about Patrick Ryan.'

'That's right,' Ben said. 'What can you tell me?'

'Nothing good I'm afraid.' The doctor sat and the officers followed suit. 'As you know the patient is in ICU. He's suffered a GHB overdose and I'll be honest, there isn't much we can do. There is no antidote.'

'What can you do?' Jack asked.

'Well, the drug causes severe respiratory depression – bradycardia. There is a risk of aspiration so he's been intubated. We're providing supportive management and monitoring vital signs. So far, his kidneys seem to be holding up, but if that changes we'll have to start dialysis.'

'Doesn't sound good,' Ben said. 'What are his chances?'

'Not great. Frankly, most of these patients die, but we're doing our best.' He got to his feet. 'Now, I'm sorry, but I need to get back.'

'Yes, of course.' Ben handed the man a card. 'Anything changes, please get in touch.'

'I will.' The doctor slipped the card in his pocket and walked away.

'Where to now, guv?' Jack asked.

'Back to Builth, check in with SOCO. The killer has made a mistake with Ryan. Let's hope he's made more than one.'

'Yes,' Jack said. 'Let's hope.'

* * *

The taxi driver did as Heidi asked and drove as fast as the road allowed. At junction 32, Heidi directed him to the eastbound carriageway, eyes not leaving the screen balanced on the back seat.

'Why did you nick his laptop?' Stacey asked.

'Easier than trying to do this on a phone's screen. I've just tethered to its internet connection,' Heidi said.

Stacey peered over her friend's shoulder, but her eyes couldn't keep up with the fast-changing images gleaned from traffic cameras. They covered a few miles in silence before the cabbie cleared his throat.

'Is there a final destination?' he asked.

'Keep going and I'll let you know,' Heidi said.

Another few minutes of awkward silence followed before she said, 'Next exit, services, not the forecourt, round the back.'

The driver nodded, turned onto the slip road, navigated the large roundabout and pulled into an enormous parking area ringed by fast food outlets, amusement arcades and away to the left, a medium-sized motel.

'This is perfect,' Heidi said. 'Thanks.'

The taxi stopped close to the entrance. Stacey handed over her emergency fifty-pound note and they stepped out. The driver sketched a salute and pulled away. Heidi climbed on top of a rubbish bin and scanned the car park. Her eyes settled on a small white van parked close to the motel beneath a stand of silver birch.

'There!' she said and jumped down from the bin. 'Let's go.'

'Ten seconds,' Stacey said. 'I'll let Ben know where we are, get him to send some help.'

'Catch me up,' Heidi said and began running towards the van.

Ben answered his phone.

'It's me,' Stacey said. 'Erica was taken from the club, driven away in a Transit Connect.'

'Where are you?' he asked.

'Junction 32, M4 eastbound. We've just found the van outside the Travelodge.'

'Where's Heidi?'

'Checking out the van.'

'OK, I'll arrange reinforcements. Wait outside for back-up. No storming motels. Neither of you have any authority and you have no idea what you'll find. Wait in the car park.'

'Sounds like great advice,' Stacey said, 'but it's too late. Tell the back-up not to hang about.'

She clicked off the phone and glanced over at the van. Heidi had left the side of the vehicle and was dashing towards the motel's entrance. Stacey gritted her teeth against the pain in her thigh and set off after her. By the time she caught up, Heidi was locking horns with the young receptionist.

'You need to calm down,' he told her. 'I've only just come on shift and have to check the records. What is your friend's name?'

'For crying out loud,' Heidi yelled. 'I told you she has been taken against her will, so it's highly unlikely she booked in. I need to look at your CCTV.' She put the laptop down and pushed her way behind the desk.

'Hey!' the man said. 'You're not allowed back here. Move away or I'm calling the police.'

'They're already on their way,' Stacey said. 'Please, show my friend the footage. The woman we're searching for is a police sergeant and we believe she's in real danger.'

The lad's eyes widened, but he didn't move.

'Please,' Stacey implored, 'run the footage, I beg you.'

Heidi ran out of patience, she shoved the man away from his terminal and searched for the recording herself.

'You can't do that,' he said and took a step forward. Heidi glared at him and he stopped moving. 'You'll lose me my job.'

'No,' Stacey said, 'she won't. I've told you, the police are on their way, so please, keep out of the way.'

He huffed and moved out from behind the desk.

'Room seventeen,' Heidi said, opening drawers, searching for the pass key.

Finding it, she snatched up the card and set off along the main corridor.

'Tell the police where we are,' Stacey said and followed her friend. Heidi was soon standing outside a door marked seventeen, slipped the pass key into the slot and kicked open the door. Stacey heard a woman scream, high-pitched, laden with shock, and entered the room in time to see Heidi barge into a young woman who was standing over a double bed. Erica was lying on the bedspread and the woman had a camera in her hand. She stumbled under Heidi's assault, hit the carpet and screamed again. Heidi dropped to her knees and got in the woman's face.

'What have you done?' she hissed dangerously. 'Tell me!' She raised a hand, preparing to deliver a slap.

'Don't,' Stacey said. 'That won't help. Check Erica. I'll deal with this one.' She looked down at the woman. 'Get up,' she ordered, 'and sit on the chair. If you try to run, I won't stop my friend hitting you.'

The woman slowly got to her feet and sat on the chair. Heidi bent over Erica, checking vital signs, while simultaneously tapping 999 into her phone to call an ambulance.

'Is she OK?' Stacey asked.

'So far,' Heidi muttered.

Stacey moved closer to the young woman who was sobbing, thick ladders of black mascara lining her cheeks, and removed the camera from the woman's hands.

'Who are you?' she asked. 'Don't spin me a story because I'll know and my friend will slap you.'

'Emily Ansell,' the woman sobbed. 'Who are you?'

'Doesn't matter. What have you done to our friend?'

'Me? Nothing. I haven't done anything to her.'

'Rubbish. You're here and you have a camera. Tell me why.'

'It's what I do, take photos. I'm studying at college to be a fashion photographer.'

Stacey snorted. 'So you're telling me that taking pictures of unconscious, drugged women is your homework?' Stacey felt her temper rise and forced her hands into her jacket pockets in case she was tempted. 'Well?'

'No! It's a gig, a job. I've done it before. I get paid and everything. What are you talking about drugged?'

'Slow down, you're gibbering. If this is a job, tell me who you work for.'

Emily slipped a hand into the back pocket of her jeans and removed a piece of folded paper. She offered it to Stacey with a trembling hand.

'It's the order,' Emily said. 'I get sent it via email then print it out.'

Stacey began unfolding the paper as the door suddenly burst in. She stepped back as paramedics rushed inside, followed by a CID officer and a couple of uniforms.

'Here,' Heidi said. 'Oxygen needed here. She's been spiked, more than likely with gamma-hydroxybutyrate.'

'OK, miss, move away now.'

Heidi snatched up Erica's hand, delivered a hot, urgent kiss on the palm and backed off. The CID officer walked closer and introduced himself.

'DS Willis,' he said. 'I know DS Bevan.' He nodded at Erica as she was transferred to a stretcher. 'Who are you?'

'I'm Stacey Logan, local reporter.' Stacey offered her press card. 'My friend is Heidi Holtz... ex-DC,' she added in case it made a difference.

'And the girl?' he asked.

'Says her name is Emily Ansell.' Stacey rubbed her eyes. 'Uh... I'm sorry... I need...' She nodded towards the bathroom, hand over her mouth, and Willis stood back.

Stacey shot past him, into the small room and locked the door. She quickly removed her mobile from her pocket, flattened the paper Emily had given her on the counter, and snapped a couple of shots. Tucking the phone away, she pulled the flush and went back to the main room in time to see a uniformed officer lead Emily away.

'You OK?' Willis asked, sounding genuinely concerned.

'Fine.' Stacey held out the paper and the camera. 'I took these off Emily.' She looked around. 'Where's Heidi?'

'She went in the ambulance with DS Bevan. Can I ask, are you DCI James's partner?'

Stacey nodded. 'I am, yes.'

'OK then. Let's take you to Cardiff nick. He can't get here yet, told me to look after you.'

'You need to search the room. It's a crime scene. There's a small white van in the car park, Erica was transported in it.'

Willis smiled. 'Yes, love, I know. Don't worry, we'll do our jobs. DS Bevan is one of ours.'

'Sorry,' Stacey said. 'I'm just a bit...'

'I know. Stuff like this can be very distressing. Hot, sweet tea is what you need. Come on now, my car's outside.'

'What will happen to Emily?'

'Same thing that happens to everyone who has been arrested.' He held the door wide. 'After you,' he said. 'I really like your hat. Suits you.'

Chapter twenty-five

The team in Builth had finally managed to erect a tent over the 1.5-ton bronze statue, but even so had failed to find any evidence. Ben instructed Jack to drive him to Noddfa so he could collect his own car then drive to Cardiff and pick up Stacey. Jack would go on to the station, update the team and begin the usual checks: suspects' alibis, talk to Builth residents, and start the endless trawl through CCTV.

Jack turned into the lanes and dodged deep expanses of floodwater and the odd branch torn down by the gale. Just outside Llanagethin he rounded a sharp bend, spotted a figure in the lane and stood on the brakes. The figure, clad in a long waxed-cotton coat, matching wide-brimmed hat and wellies, walked closer and revealed itself as a dumpy woman in her mid-seventies. Jack wound down the window.

Without preamble, the woman said, 'There's a tree down, boy.' She waved a hand behind her.

Jack saw an open-backed Land Rover blocking the lane on the far side of a thick ash pole resting on the tops of the hedges. Two more elderly women were gazing up at it. One of them held a chainsaw.

'Bugger!' Jack said. 'We're in a bit of a hurry.'

'Don't fret, won't be long. Ena is just about to slice it up. Good firewood ash.'

Jack's eyes widened. 'Would Ena like a hand?'

'No, you're alright, boy. Not dressed for it are you? Give us five minutes and you can get on, unless...'

'What?'

'There's enough clearance, you could creep under.'

'We'll wait thanks,' Jack said and watched as the behatted woman, looking not dissimilar to a dark green mushroom, stomped back to her friends.

Jack chuckled. 'Perfect example of why I love living here. Never met anyone like that in London.'

Ben nodded. 'Farmer's wives. Tough as old boots and not to be argued with.'

Jack flipped on the hazard lights and turned off the engine, as Ena climbed into the back of the truck, yanked on the chainsaw's ripcord and cut off the top of the tree. With a loud crack, the ash's roots gave away and the trunk dropped neatly onto the lane. Ena turned off the chainsaw while the others wrapped a length of chain around the smooth bark. Ena climbed into the driver's seat, revved the engine and dragged the obstruction clear. The short woman in the hat smiled and waved Jack on. He slowed and opened the window.

'Well done, ladies,' he said. 'Cracking job.'

She smiled. 'No use waiting for the council, we'll be here until Christmas. Useless buggers.'

Jack laughed and closed the window, and a few minutes later, he pulled up outside Noddfa.

'Sure you don't want me to drive you to Cardiff?' he asked.

'Sure thanks. Go on to the station like we said. Bit of luck I'll be there by lunchtime.'

'Any news how Erica is?'

'No. Stacey sent a text saying she was taken to hospital and Heidi went with her.'

'Let me know when you know?'

'I will.' Ben left the car, slammed the door, slapped on the roof and headed to the front door of the cottage.

* * *

Heidi sat in the family room at the end of ICU with the laptop she'd liberated from the owner of the Boston Bar open on the sofa next to her. She'd made up her mind early on to do something useful rather than fret and pace, and had discovered a file on the machine's hard drive marked, "CCTV". A few clicks had displayed a long list of dates and times relating to recorded footage. She opened the last on the list – captured a few hours ago. Within seconds she spotted Stacey at the bar, her bowler hat hard to miss. Frustratingly there wasn't any footage of the dance floor, so Heidi concentrated on the cameras covering the bar area and searched frame by frame, one click at a time.

Twenty minutes later, she picked out a kid in a baseball cap, and she watched as he propped himself on the bar at the opposite end to Stacey, who obviously hadn't seen him. Customers waiting to be served were three deep in places and Heidi examined every face, one by one, then – Erica! Heidi watched her ex-partner wriggle through the crowd and order drinks. Saw her look left and right, checking out the clubbers as a bar worker filled the order. She saw Erica wave at Stacey – who didn't notice her – and Heidi forgot to breathe as Baseball Cap Boy approached and stretched his hand briefly above the drinks. Erica paid and while she waited for change, drank deeply from her glass, thirsty from dancing, face glowing.

The screen suddenly went blank as the recording came to an abrupt end. Heidi swore and renewed her onslaught of the keyboard. Eventually, the footage flickered back. Erica and the kid were nowhere in sight. Heidi took a gulp of air. The door to the room opened and a serious-looking doctor entered then closed the door behind him and moved closer.

Heidi got to her feet, cracked her knuckles and said, 'Don't sugar-coat anything, Doc. Tell me straight – how is she?'

* * *

Ben strode into the staff canteen on the top floor of Cardiff's main police station and spotted Stacey sitting on her own at a table near the end of the room, a half-empty mug in front of her, mobile in her hand.

'Hey, you,' he called.

Stacey looked up from her phone and smiled.

'Hey, Sherlock.'

'Shush,' Ben said and walked closer. 'Not in here. How are you doing?'

'Exhausted, but OK I guess.'

'Any news from Heidi?'

'No. I can't work out whether that's a good sign or not.'

'I've always believed that no news is good news. You ready to go? I must get back, there have been developments.'

Stacey raised her eyebrows. 'Oh?'

Ben chuckled. 'Again, not in here. Wait until we're in the car at least.'

'OK, so let's go.'

On the journey back to Llanagethin, Ben and Stacey swapped reports of their evenings and promises to get in touch if either received news of Erica. Ben pulled up in the lane.

'Sorry I can't stay, Pumpkin,' he said, 'but I really do have to get to the station.'

'Don't worry, it's fine. I'll take the phone upstairs and try to grab an hour's sleep. Too old now to stay up all night and get away with it. Ring me if you hear anything.'

'I already promised I would. Bit of luck I'll be back by suppertime with a takeaway. If that changes for any reason,

I'll call.' He leaned across and kissed her. 'Go and sleep. You're very pale.'

Stacey nodded then she slipped out of her seat, slammed the door and waved as Ben drove around the bend and out of sight.

* * *

Stacey stirred as the door of her bedroom cracked open. Expecting Ben, she was surprised when Heidi peered through the gap.

'Are you awake?' Heidi asked.

'Yeah, sort of. What are you doing here? Is Erica OK?'

'Come downstairs and I'll update you. I've made coffee.'

'What time is it?'

'Just gone four – teatime.'

Heidi went downstairs. Stacey hauled herself out of bed and pulled on her fluffy dressing gown. Her head felt fuzzy, so she went to the bathroom and splashed cold water on her face, then down to the kitchen. Heidi was at the table, the stolen laptop open in front of her.

Stacey poured coffee and said, 'Tell me how Erica is.'

Heidi took a deep breath. 'Conscious and thankfully out of danger. Should be discharged tomorrow.'

'Oh, my,' Stacey said. 'Thank God for that.'

'Yes, great news. I'm going down to Cardiff tomorrow to pick up my truck, collect Erica and take her to my place in Brecon.' She glanced up. 'You can manage now can't you?'

'Of course, and Erica needs you more. I'm pleased she's agreed to stay with you.'

'She hasn't yet. I haven't got around to mentioning it.'

'Oh,' Stacey said. 'Really glad she's OK though. Any lasting effects likely?'

'Only the gap in her memory.'

'What are you working on?'

'This and that while I have the time. Checking hours of CCTV with the facial recognition program, while at the same time looking for Gwen, BB's sister.' Heidi topped up her mug and huffed. 'I still can't believe you handed over all the evidence to Willis. Did you even read whatever it was Emily Ansell gave you?'

Stacey grinned. 'Better than that.' She opened the images file on her phone, called up the pictures she'd taken at the motel, and handed the device to Heidi who returned the grin.

'Should have known you wouldn't have been that daft,' she said and tapped the screen to send the shots to the laptop.

The message pinged in and Heidi peered at the screen, then turned the computer sideways so Stacey could see the document which did appear to be an order. It was addressed to Emily Ansell and helpfully included her email address and mobile number. The room number and address of the motel was clearly stated, together with a small map, and date and time of the booking. The order had been placed by a company called Perfect Portraits.

'Blimey,' Stacey said. 'This is weird, what on earth is this about?'

'Too soon to tell,' Heidi said, 'but give me time. The email addresses and the mobile will be easy to hack and once I'm in...'

Stacey finished her sentence, '...nothing is sacred.'

'You've got it.'

Stacey stood. 'Ben should be here later, says he'll bring takeaways.'

Heidi's eyes left the screen. 'Don't tell him what we've got,' she said.

'I won't. I'm off for a quick shower and I'll get dressed.' She yawned. 'I'm too old for clubbing these days.'

'Rubbish, we weren't clubbing. We were doing way more than that.'

'You said you were looking for Gwen Llewelyn. Any closer to finding her?'

'Not yet, but I've finally worked out where to look. That reminds me, I need to disable the camera at the end of BB's track.' Her fingers returned to the keyboard.

'Oh? Why's that?'

'So if she does return the police don't go charging over to arrest her, they must have translated the journal by now. Like I said, she could do with a chance to explain what happened. I'm not sure she'll get that once she's been arrested.' Heidi flapped a hand. 'Go and attend to your ablutions. Give me some quiet time with this.'

'Sure.' Stacey picked up her mobile and went upstairs. She sent Ben a text.

Erica OK – phew! Heidi here. ETA? Sx

She went to the bathroom, showered and washed her hair, then dressed in warm baggy trousers and a fleecy top. She was untangling her long curls when her phone chirped.

Just leaving town. C U soon Bx

Chapter twenty-six

The team gathered in the squad room early the next morning to compare notes and plan their next move. As usual Ben sat beneath the incident board and waited until they all had drinks before he began.

'Morning,' he said. 'As of five minutes ago, Patrick Ryan is still with us but not capable of being interviewed. We may get the chance to speak to him, but best to assume that could be unlikely.' He took a deep breath. 'Extremely unusual for Mid Wales but, after a discussion with the brass, we are now officially looking for a serial killer and must find him before more die.' He glanced at Tegan and Elsa. 'How have you two got on?'

'There's not many cameras in Builth,' Tegan said, 'they only really cover the High Street. Some of the pubs have their own CCTV, inside and on the door. There's another in the post office and one on the last remaining cash machine. Nothing near the Builth Bull. Ollie rounded up a fair amount of footage yesterday, but no hits so far.'

Ben nodded and looked at Elsa. 'How about you? Any luck?'

'I've been checking our suspects' alibis.'

'Who made it onto your list?'

'Kevin Townsend, Bronwen Llewelyn, Pete the Pot and Idris Jones.'

'Why Idris?'

Elsa shrugged. 'Finder of the body, it's tradition.'

Jack chuckled quietly.

'Anyway,' Elsa continued, 'Idris was confirmed to be at his flat, Pete's banged up and BB is still missing. The camera on the track hasn't picked up anything other than sheep moving about and now seems to have gone offline. Kevin says he was working in his studio all night, but no one has been able to confirm that.'

'Does Patrick Ryan's ex-wife have any angry relatives?' Jack asked. 'Maybe a sixteen-stone brother who is up for a spot of revenge?'

'No, sir. She was brought up by her mother, no father or siblings.'

'Where is she living these days?' Ben asked.

'I'm working on that. Seems mother and daughter changed their names and moved away.' Elsa took a deep breath. 'I looked up Ryan's case, sir. He nearly killed his wife, left her in a terrible state. Managed to convince a jury he had experienced extreme provocation when he returned home to find his wife drinking a cuppa with a man he didn't know.'

'In bed?' Jack asked.

'No, sir, in the kitchen. He really should have gone down.'

Ben nodded. 'I agree. I also reviewed the case. Dreadful.' He drank from his mug. 'We need to tackle this in a different way. We now have four victims – if we include BB's mother – all discovered locally. To me, that suggests our killer also lives in the area, so we should try to construct a profile for him – or her.'

'Do you really think a woman did this?' Ollie asked. 'OK, BB might have been able to flip a body on the back of the kite, but could she really hoist a body up on the Cilmery monument? Surely that had to be two people?'

'It's a fair point,' Ben said, 'and proves we need to keep open minds. For example, if BB did kill her mother, maybe she got a taste for ridding the world of abusers.'

'I must admit I'm leaning towards a vigilante,' Jack said. 'The victims all had pasts linked to the abuse of women – and they all got away with it.'

'Yeah, maybe, but finding the killer without any physical evidence will be challenging to say the least.'

'I asked the computer to compile a list of all locals with criminal records,' Elsa said, 'then weeded out those who had only come to our notice because of unpaid council tax, stuff like that.'

'Why would that help?' Jack asked.

'I now have a list of all those convicted of violent offences. I can't believe the murderer hasn't been convicted of violence in the past.'

'Perhaps someone the killer knows was attacked,' Ollie said. 'Spiked maybe? Doesn't make sense otherwise. Why would he suddenly start killing?'

'Again, I agree,' Ben said, 'even though the victim's deaths were "gentle".'

'How do you mean, sir?' Ollie asked.

'Something Heidi Holtz said. If you were in the business of retribution, surely you'd want your victims to suffer, not just sleep themselves away? Just a thought.'

'How is Erica Bevan, sir?' Tegan asked.

Ben smiled. 'She'll be discharged today. Bit of luck she'll be back at work in a couple of days.'

'Any closer to knowing who is responsible for the spikings?'

'Cardiff's case, but I'll check in with them later. Now then, on with it.'

* * *

Stacey had been reading through the feature she'd promised Sam and realised the story was growing. Even though her editor was pressing her to hand in the work, she knew the piece wasn't anywhere near ready. Discovering Erica unconscious in a motel room, a woman with a camera looming over her, had been shocking and Stacey tried to work out what exactly had been going on. She called up pictures of the order form she'd snapped in the bathroom, but still couldn't fathom what the endgame of the scheme was. Her landline rang and she picked up the handset.

'Hi, Stace,' Heidi said.

'Hi, you. How's Erica? Are you both in Brecon?'

'We are,' Heidi said and Stacey heard a smile in her friend's voice. 'She's doing well. I've tucked her up in bed, she needs a couple of days to get the drugs out of her system. I'm insisting she takes things easy.'

'That's good news and lovely that she's with you. I wasn't sure...'

'Me neither. Anyway, I thought you would be interested to know that Emily Ansell has been released on police bail. Might be an idea for you to pay her a visit. It's possible she may say more to you than the police.'

'Wow, I didn't think they'd release her so quickly.'

'I was surprised, but I'm not sure what she could have been charged with. Seems as though the police had the same problem. That's why I think a visit from you is a good idea.'

'Do you know where she lives?' Stacey asked and picked up a pen.

'Of course.' Heidi rattled off an address in Penarth, four miles outside Cardiff on the coast. 'Looks like she shares a student house with a couple of women. Any chance you could get over there? I'd go but...'

'Not a problem,' Stacey said. 'Thanks for the tip-off. I'll drive over today.'

'Marvellous.'

'Has Erica been able to tell you anything about what happened at the club?'

'Not much and she has no memory of the journey to the motel. GHB is the perfect drug for scumbags to use. Can't always be detected and wipes the victim's brain so they're useless as witnesses.' Heidi sighed heavily. 'Erica could have died,' she said. 'Easy to add too much to a drink and not much is required for a fatal overdose.'

'OK, I'm on it. I'll ring if I discover anything.'

'Good, I'll be in. I'm dipping my toes into the dark web today. If I'm gonna find out anything about this scam, I'm sure that's where it will be. Talk later.'

Heidi hung up. Stacey switched off her computer, checked her kitbag contained the essentials, then carried her empty mug to the kitchen. She packed a second bag with a bottle of water and a flask of coffee, then laced on her boots and went out to the car.

Quieter weather had returned to the mountains. The odd beam of bright sunshine slipped through breaks in the clouds to illuminate the landscape; the sky was full of carrion eaters, searching the open ground with steely gazes. At Merthyr Tydfil, Stacey remained on the A470 towards Cardiff. Penarth, a pretty coastal town, was just a few miles from the capital and Stacey navigated carefully through the busy tangle of roads.

After a couple of wrong turns, she finally pulled up outside a medium-sized Victorian terraced house, with a small front garden and low privet hedge. She slung her kitbag across her shoulders and left the car, locking the doors behind her, then walked through a low wrought-iron gate and rang the doorbell. The downstairs curtains were closed and Stacey was just beginning to wonder if anyone was in, when the door opened and Emily Ansell, pale-faced, dressed in pyjamas, peered out. She recognised Stacey and took a step back as though she was going to close the door. Stacey moved closer and quickly plonked her boot firmly on the doormat to prevent that happening.

'Wait,' Stacey said. 'Please don't shut me out. I'd like to talk to you about what happened on Saturday.'

'Well I don't want to,' Emily said and tried to shut the door, but Stacey's boot stayed where it was.

'I want to make sure you're OK,' Stacey said. 'I'm not here to give you a hard time, just an opportunity to tell me your side of things. Please, give me a little of your time. I won't stay for hours, honest.'

Emily nodded, reluctantly swung the door wider and Stacey stepped inside quickly before the young woman changed her mind.

'Go to the kitchen,' Emily said quietly. 'The others aren't up yet and I don't want to wake them.'

'Thanks,' Stacey said and walked along the hall.

Emily followed, she filled the kettle, switched it on and sat at the table.

'Tell me,' Stacey said, 'how are you?'

Emily's eyes immediately filled with tears which trickled down her cheeks and dripped off her chin.

'Not great,' she said. 'I was held at the police station all day before they let me go. I've never been arrested before and they want me to go back in three weeks. I'm so scared.' More tears fell and she dabbed her face with a piece of kitchen roll. She glanced back at her guest. 'Is your friend OK?' she asked.

'She's back at home recuperating. She'll be fine.'

'I'm very glad. Honestly, I didn't know that she had been drugged, really I didn't.' She blew her nose. 'They told me at the station she's a cop. Is that true?'

'It is yes. A detective sergeant. The three of us went to the Boston Bar to try to catch whoever has been spiking women. We're not exactly sure what happened yet which is why I'm here, to find out what you know.'

The kettle clicked off. Emily got to her feet, made two mugs of tea and handed one to her guest.

'Thanks,' Stacey said. 'So tell me, what do you know about this?'

'Not much. I told you – and the police – I was on a job. You saw the order.'

'I did but it didn't tell us much. Who placed it?'

'A guy on the internet. Said his name was Tom, but I never met him.'

'How did he know you took photos?'

'I put an ad on Facebook offering my services at weddings and parties, that sort of stuff.' She sighed. 'I need to earn some money to pay for my tuition. I didn't realise everything would be so expensive and don't want to work in a bar with everyone looking at me.'

'Didn't you think it was strange that Tom wanted you to take pictures of sleeping women?'

'Not really. People relax properly when they sleep. All the worry and stress leaves their faces. A woman never looks more natural or beautiful than when she's sleeping and shows you her real self.'

'Did the women know you were photographing them?'

'I don't know. None of them ever spoke to me. Tom told me at the start that the doors to the rooms would be unlocked and just to creep in, not to disturb them, take the pictures then leave, and that's what I did.'

'Didn't you think it was odd?'

Emily shrugged. 'A bit I suppose, but there's lots of odd stuff on the net, and like I said, I needed the money.'

'How many jobs like this have you done before?'

'I don't know, a few.'

'A few as in three or four?'

'No, more like twenty.'

'Wow. Did you keep copies of the photographs you took?'

'Tom told me not to, but yes, I have copies.'

Stacey held up a memory stick. 'Be great if you'd put them on here. Maybe I can work out who the victims are, check they are OK.'

Emily nodded, took the offered flash drive, plugged it into her laptop and began the download.

Chapter twenty-seven

Stacey carefully negotiated the stone steps leading to the basement flat and rang the bell. After a short wait, Heidi opened the door and smiled.

'What are you doing here?' she asked.

'On my way home after speaking to Emily Ansell. Thought I'd pop in, find out how Erica is and beg a cuppa.' Stacey leaned closer and lowered her voice. 'How's it going with you two?'

Heidi shrugged and shut the door. Stacey entered the main room and saw Erica lying on the sofa beneath a feather duvet. She grinned at Stacey and patted the end of her daybed.

Stacey perched and asked, 'How are you feeling today?'

'Much better thanks,' Erica said. 'Just very tired, and pretty foolish for getting myself into this situation.'

'You shouldn't think like that. It's not your fault. I see Heidi's looking after you.'

'She is yes, but boy, can she fuss.'

'I heard that,' Heidi said.

'She's worried about you,' Stacey said.

'Yes, I know. She told me you went to talk to the woman you discovered in the room with me. What did she have to say?'

Heidi carried mugs of coffee, together with a plate of thickly buttered Welsh cakes, and put everything on the low table next to the sofa.

'Did she even let you in?' Heidi asked.

Stacey nodded. 'She wasn't keen at first, but I managed to talk her round. Doorstepping is an essential journalistic skill.'

In between mouthfuls of griddle cakes, Stacey brought her friends up to date before removing the memory stick from her pocket and handing it to Heidi.

'What's this?' Heidi asked.

'Photos of Emily's previous... clients? Models? Not sure what to call them.'

'Victims,' Heidi growled and took the stick.

She crossed the room to her desk, slipped the drive into her computer and within seconds was scrolling through pictures of women, lying on a bed, eyes closed.

'Little Emily has been busy,' Heidi said, 'there are over a dozen women here. How can young people be so naïve and get involved with schemes like this? Common sense seems to have gone out of the window these days.'

'I really don't understand any of this,' Erica said. 'Why pay someone to take these photos? And why drug the women? What does "Tom" do with the pictures?'

'I can't work it out either,' Stacey said, helping herself to another cake. 'Money is bound to be involved, but how could anyone make money from these portraits? Such a large risk for presumably little return. There are plenty of stock photos just like those online.'

'No idea,' Erica said. 'It even sounds mad. Do you think Tom was the person who spiked my drink?'

'Doubt it,' Heidi said. 'If it was him, surely he'd have taken these photos himself. No, whoever is behind whatever this is will have made sure he can't be traced.'

She glanced up from her screen. 'Well done getting hold of these, Stacey. I'll run my facial recognition program. If we can identify these women, we will surely stand a better chance of getting close to Tom.'

'What about the van that delivered Erica to the motel?'

'I haven't forgotten and I'm looking,' Heidi said. 'By the time the cops arrived it had gone. In the panic, I didn't note down the registration number so finding it is more difficult than it should be.'

'And BB, or her sister?'

'Well…' Heidi said and moved to the easy chair. 'I lifted the DNA results from police records and am trying to match them with others already online.'

'What, from other police reports?'

'No point. If there was a match there, I'd have seen it and so would they. No, I'm trawling the records of private companies who offer to read your DNA and tell you where your ancestors originated.'

Stacey nodded. 'I've seen the adverts. Tracing your roots is big business these days. Hope no one gives me a kit for my birthday.'

Heidi chuckled. 'Nor me. They can cause all sorts of strife and upset within families, especially if a member works out that "dad" isn't anything of the sort. Either of you heard of Bertold Wiesner?'

Stacey and Erica shook their heads.

'He was an Austrian Jewish physiologist. He and his wife, Mary Barton, ran a fertility clinic in Harley Street, from the late forties until the early seventies. Mary performed artificial insemination for women whose husbands couldn't father children.'

'What has that to do with finding BB's sister?' Stacey asked.

'Nothing. I'm proving a point. Without the ancestry sites, it would never have come to light that Bertold provided the sperm. Over 600 half-siblings have already been discovered.

'You'd think that doctor guy would have had more sense,' Erica said. 'Imagine meeting your ideal life partner, then discovering you are half-siblings.'

'Or not,' Heidi said, 'and having children.'

* * *

Ben and Jack were working together reviewing criminal records of local residents, trying to determine which – if any – were worth interviewing in connection with the recent murders.

'Blimey, guv,' Jack said. 'You'd never think there'd be so many crims in a rural area like this with such a low population.'

'Depressing isn't it? Discovered any likely candidates?'

'Not really. A couple might be worth checking in with, but as far as I can tell they haven't any female relatives who have suffered any form of abuse.'

'Put a list together and we'll make some visits – just in case.'

The phone rang and Ben picked it up.

'DCI James.'

'Good afternoon, Chief Inspector. Dr Sunderland here from Llandrindod Hospital.'

'Hello, Doctor. Not bad news I hope?'

'The opposite. Looks like Patrick Ryan will pull through. He's off the ventilator and managing to breathe for himself.'

'That is good news.' Ben said. 'Is he talking? Can he be interviewed?'

'Touch too soon for that, give it a couple of days. He's not going anywhere.' The doctor took a deep breath. 'I'm surprised he made it, incredibly lucky.'

'Testament to your care, I'm sure,' Ben said. 'Will you call me when we can visit?'

'Of course. Sorry, I've got to get on. Busy here.'

'No problem, and thanks again.' Ben put the phone down and glanced at Jack. 'Seems Ryan is out of the woods.'

Jack grinned. 'Can we speak to him?'

'Not yet. What we can do is visit his mother – now he isn't in imminent danger of dying. She might know if he was meeting anyone in town.'

Jack got to his feet and put on his jacket.

'I'll meet you out front in five,' he said and left the room.

Ben stood as Tegan suddenly exclaimed, 'Oh – my – God!'

'What is it, Constable?' Ben asked.

'BB did kill her mother! She wrote about it in the journal.'

'Really?' Ben walked closer.

'Yes, listen. This comes from one of the last entries, "Ma hurt Da – again. I hit her, she died. Buried in the garden".'

'Are you sure you've translated that correctly?'

'Yes, sir. That's what it says.'

Ben ran a hand over his short hair. 'Christ. Are we any closer to finding her sister?'

'No, sir, but Elsa is working on it. Having read through the journal, it seems to me that Myfanwy was quick to dish out physical violence, mainly to her family. It's possible BB was defending her father. What do you think?'

'That we need to redouble efforts to find Bronwen and her sister, ask them what happened.' He groaned. 'I can't believe we haven't found BB yet. Where could she hide? She took her dad with her and he wasn't at all well when we saw him. Having to stay hidden while caring for a man in a wheelchair can't be easy. Certainly cuts down their choice of a bolt-hole. Did we manage to find out what was wrong with him?'

'No. He doesn't appear to be registered with any of the local surgeries. It could be that he was always disabled,' Tegan said. 'Couldn't walk but otherwise healthy.'

'I'm not convinced, keep at it. I'm off to have a chat with Mrs Ryan now, but you should have another chat with Mrs Webb... and the other one. Heidi and Stacey spoke to her.'

'I know who you mean. Mrs Williams.'

'Yes, Mrs Williams. They both knew of the Llewelyns. See if you can jog their memories.'

'Yes, sir. I'll do my best.'

Ben ran down the stairs to the ground floor and as promised, Jack was waiting in the car outside the main entrance. Ben got into the passenger seat and put his seatbelt on.

'What kept you, guv?' Jack asked.

'Tegan has finished translating the journal. Found a passage relating to Myfanwy's death. Seems BB did kill her.'

'Good to know one of our investigations is progressing at least. All we have to do now is find her.'

'But where to look?' Ben sighed. 'OK, one thing at a time. Let's chat to Ryan's mother and hope she can tell us something useful.'

Jack nodded, pulled out and took the main road to Builth, where he turned onto the A470.

'Do the Ryans live in Rhayader?'

'No,' Ben said, 'the other side. The satnav says their place is about eight miles further on. Left turn just before Dolfach.'

Ben's phone chirped. He took it from his pocket, peered at the screen and saw a text from Stacey.

> *Hi, Sherlock. In Brecon with H and E. I'm gonna stay over. Plenty of food in the freezer. See you tomorrow. Love Sx*

He tapped a brief reply and tucked his phone away.

'Looks like I'm home alone again,' he said. 'Stacey's going to stay in Brecon tonight.'

'Fancy supper at mine?' Jack asked. 'Julie will be pleased to see you and the twins will be in bed.'

'Might take you up on that, thanks.' He peered through the windscreen at the road. 'Next left.'

Jack turned into a very narrow lane, even for Wales. Undergrowth on the verges brushed the vehicle's paintwork and tufts of grass grew in the centre of the tarmac. After a couple of miles, they reached what appeared to be a large turning circle with a couple of ramshackle garages, tucked beneath a group of Scots pines.

'Is this the place?' Jack asked, looking around for a house.

'Satnav says to keep going.' Ben peered through the windscreen and pointed at a stony track. 'Down there apparently.'

'Are you sure? That's barely a road.'

'We could leave the car and walk.'

'I'm not wrecking another pair of shoes. Should have brought the Land Rover.'

'Just take it steady,' Ben said and took firm hold of the grab rail.

Chapter twenty-eight

After fifteen minutes of some very uncomfortable driving, Jack pulled up at a wooden five-bar gate.

'Leave the car here,' Ben said and got out. 'Glad it isn't pouring with rain.'

The detectives walked through the gate and as it clicked shut, a large pack of dogs appeared and galloped along the track at full tilt, barking madly. Jack hesitated. Ben noticed and chuckled.

'What's up?' he asked. 'Not scared of a few dogs are you?'

'Not usually, but unruly gangs of terriers aren't my favourite. Unpredictable. Nippy little buggers.'

Ben rummaged in his jacket pocket and removed a handful of dog treats. 'Here,' he said offering some to Jack. 'Feed them, they'll be fine.'

Ben was right, the pack calmed, then they followed the men along the track and into a scruffy-looking yard. An old farmhouse stood on one side, a conglomeration of sheds, barns and henhouses opposite. A crumbling Morris Traveller was parked in the shadow of one of the sheds, an elder tree grew through the roof and a male peacock perched on the bonnet. It spotted the intruders and fanned its tail feathers, threw back its head back and let fly a deafening screech which set the dogs off again. The door of the house opened and a thin, grey-haired woman looked out nervously.

'Who's there?' she called.

Jack stepped forward and held up his warrant card. 'Police, madam.' He nodded at Ben. 'DCI James and I'm Sergeant Trent.'

The woman's face crumpled and a hand flew to her face. 'God, no,' she said. 'Has my Patrick died? Is that why you're here?'

'No, he's doing much better. Don't distress yourself.'

Mrs Ryan's knees sagged and she clung to the door jamb. 'Thank the Lord,' she gasped. 'You shouldn't just turn up like that, not with my boy so ill in hospital.'

Ben moved closer. 'Yes, I'm sorry, we should have rung. Let's go in. My sergeant will make some tea and we can have a chat.' He took her arm and gently guided her inside.

The house was as cluttered as the yard. Half the dogs made it inside before Jack closed the door and the pack spooked a glaring of cats upstairs. Ben picked his way along the hall and into a similarly disordered kitchen. Mrs Ryan settled at the table. Ben sat opposite, while Jack filled a kettle and swilled out three mugs.

'So,' Mrs Ryan said. 'Tell me why you're here.'

'We're the detectives in charge of your son's case,' Ben said. 'We want to talk to you about the evening he was found on the Builth Bull.'

'What about it?'

'We wondered if your son told you where he was going. Whether he was meeting anyone and if he told you who?'

Mrs Ryan snorted. 'Of course you are! You're trying to stitch him up again. Like you did last time.'

'Last time?' Ben queried.

'When you tried to lock him up for beating his wife. Everyone knew she fell down the stairs.'

'Is that what Patrick told you?'

'Didn't have to. I know my boy and he wouldn't beat a woman. Brought up better than that.' Her mouth twisted into a smile. 'Seems the jury agreed with me.'

Jack opened his mouth to contradict her, but Ben shook his head.

'Mrs Ryan,' Ben said, 'we're not here to discuss the past. We're here to ask you about the evening Patrick was found in Builth.'

'He didn't say who he was going to meet. He went out every Saturday night, used to stay over with one of his friends. Always home in time for Sunday lunch.'

Jack poured tea and asked, 'Do you know the names of his friends?'

'He's a popular boy, Sergeant. Always meeting new people.'

'How does he make his living?'

'He's my carer. I have mental health issues and can't be left on my own for long.' She spotted Jack's raised eyebrows. 'It's legitimate,' she snapped. 'Gets carer's allowance and everything.' She glared at Ben. 'It's your fault I'm ill. The false accusations against my son gave me a nervous breakdown. I never leave the house now and couldn't manage without Patrick. Do you know when he'll be coming home? I need him.'

'I spoke with the doctor earlier,' Ben said. 'He told me Patrick is on the mend, but it'll be a little while before he's home. Would you like me to contact social services? They might be able to provide some assistance.'

Mrs Ryan held up her hands. 'No thanks. I don't want strangers poking around in my house. I'll cope.'

'Do you know of anyone who has a problem with Patrick?' Jack asked. 'Has anyone threatened him?'

'Not so much these days.'

'What do you mean?'

She snorted. 'Think about it. You accuse him of beating his wife, nearly killed her was what you lot said. He goes to court, papers put him on the front page and people started sending hate mail, spitting at him in the street, so no, not so much these days.'

Ben removed a business card from his inside pocket, placed it on the table and got to his feet.

'If you need anything,' he said, 'my number's on the card. As your son has been the victim of a crime, you could call Victim Support. They are very good.'

Mrs Ryan nodded, but didn't look up.

'We'll be off then, leave you in peace, but please, if you think of anything, call us. We'll see ourselves out.'

Ben walked down the hall, Jack at his back, opened the front door and stepped into the daylight. They didn't speak until they had left the yard.

'When we get back to the station,' Ben said, 'make sure I ring social services. They should at least check that Mrs Ryan can manage on her own. I'm not convinced she can.'

'I always feel sorry for the mothers of scumbags,' Jack said, 'unless of course they mistreated their children and created monsters. True she's angry and has been fed a crock of shit by Patrick, which she believes, but she doesn't strike me as a bad person.'

They walked through the gate. Ben made sure it was properly fastened, while Jack worked hard at getting the car to point in the right direction.

'So,' he said when Ben got in, 'supper at mine?'

'Yeah, go on then. It'll be good to see everyone, stop this case churning around and around in my head.'

Jack laughed. 'The twins will definitely cure you of that. Rational thought is often impossible at home. Julie will be delighted to see you.'

* * *

Stacey sprawled on an easy chair, rubbed her belly and groaned. 'Beef Wellington,' she said. 'Can't remember when I last had Beef Wellington. That was great, thanks, Heidi. Why did I think you couldn't cook?'

'Why did you think there was anything I couldn't do?' Heidi asked.

Erica laughed. 'You haven't changed.'

'Hope not. I'm quite content with how I turned out.'

'This is great,' Stacey said, 'all of us back together.' She held up a black plastic bracelet. 'I didn't know you had one of these, Erica? Are they any good?'

Erica peered at the object. 'That's not mine.'

'Nor mine,' Heidi said. 'Where did you find it?'

'On the counter next to the bag of Erica's stuff from the hospital,' Stacey said. 'That's why I thought it was hers.'

Heidi took the band from Stacey's fingers. 'It's one of those Fitbit things, records you how far you've walked, monitors your heartbeat and doubles as a watch. Erica, are you sure this isn't yours?'

'I'm sure,' Erica said. 'I don't need a bit of plastic to tell me I walk too far every day on the job. I wonder how it got in the bag with my other belongings.'

Heidi shrugged. 'Busy nurses trying to do half a dozen things at once. I'll pop it back tomorrow when I go to your place for clean clothes.'

'No need for that,' Erica said. 'I'm well enough to go home now.'

'Do you want to go home?' Heidi asked quietly.

Erica didn't answer.

'You've got this week off,' Heidi said. 'Why not stay for a few days and I'll run you home at the weekend. It really is no trouble to collect what you need from the flat.'

'Well... if you're sure,' Erica said and yawned.

'Bedtime for you,' Heidi said. 'Go on. I'll make up Stacey's bed and join you soon.'

Erica got to her feet and yawned again. 'You're right. Sleep well, Stacey, see you in the morning.'

Stacey blew a kiss and Erica shuffled into the bedroom and closed the door.

Heidi lowered her voice. 'Are you busy tomorrow, Stace?'

'Not especially, why?'

'Can't get into it now.' She nodded towards the bedroom door. 'I want you to come to Cardiff with me. We have a lot to accomplish.'

Chapter twenty-nine

Stacey and Heidi prepared to leave the basement flat early the next morning. Erica was still asleep, so Heidi left a note.

Stacey rounded up her belongings, climbed the stone steps and unlocked the car. Heidi made sure the front door was locked, then slipped into the passenger seat. Stacey started the engine and smiled at her friend.

'So, hospital first?' she asked, pulling away from the kerb.

'No. Room seventeen at the Travelodge off junction 32.'

'Oh? Why are we going there?'

Heidi held up the smartwatch. 'When do nurses ever make mistakes with personal property?'

'I don't know. Wouldn't have thought they'd do that very often.'

'Nor me,' Heidi said. 'This Fitbit thingy was definitely in the bag with Erica's stuff – as it should be. She was wearing it when we found her, but I don't remember seeing it on her wrist at the club, and she confirmed last night it didn't belong to her.'

'So you think someone put it on her?'

'That's the only explanation.'

'But why? Those things aren't cheap.'

'Some are,' Heidi said, 'but not this one. It has a sleep tracker, oximeter – measures the amount of oxygen in the blood – heart rate monitor, and the usual steps walked and calories burnt.'

'Who do you think put it on Erica?'

'It could only have been Baseball Cap Boy or his driver.'

'Which brings me back to my earlier question. Why?'

Heidi shrugged and cracked her knuckles. 'That's why we need to take a look at the room. More data required.'

She removed her phone from a pocket and tapped the screen.

'Who are you calling?' Stacey asked.

'Do you remember my friend Angus?'

'The rock climber who works at GCHQ?'

Heidi nodded then said, 'Hi, Angus. How's tricks?' She switched on the mobile's speaker.

'Ms Holtz. Well, well. Don't tell me, you're throwing a party at the family seat and I'm top of the guest list.'

'No, not today. I could do with an extra hacker and who better than you?'

'No one... and it's a bloody good job I'm on a secure line. My boss gets very twitchy when he hears the word "hacker".'

'Will you help?'

Angus sighed. 'Never been able to say no to you – even if you only ring when you want something.'

'I do not.'

'Uh, yes, you do. Last time we spoke, you wanted help to break into the commune belonging to the Church of New Eden. We nearly died.'

'We did not, and I rang you on your birthday.'

Angus chuckled. 'Whatever. Now, what do you need?'

Heidi told her friend what had happened to Erica – and other young women – and that a smartwatch had been found.

'I don't know that much about them,' she said, 'I'm too busy to play with toys, but I understand they link to the internet.'

'Yep, you're right, they do. Information gathered on the devices ends up in the cloud, together with rubbish collected from anything deemed "smart". Fridges, tellies, computer games, you get the picture.'

'So if I gave you the serial number of one, could you retrieve the data?'

'It's possible, but could take a while. Users can protect their information if they know how, but few bother so I might get lucky.'

'Could you also check if anyone else has accessed it and if so, who they are?'

'Again, theoretically possible. You could do all this yourself I'm sure.'

'Yeah, I probably could, but time is my problem, and of course Erica is recuperating in my flat. I don't want to worry her.'

'Erica's at yours? Oh wow! Tell me she's forgiven you for skipping out on her and that you're back together.'

Heidi snorted. 'Why is everyone so bloody interested in my private life?'

Angus laughed. 'Cos we love you and well... your private life is usually interesting.'

Heidi frowned. 'Will you help me or not?'

'Of course I'll help. Give me the serial number and I'll get on with it.'

Heidi peered at the back of the watch and recited a sequence of letters and numbers.

'Got it,' Angus said. 'I'll be as quick as I can but obviously can't use the kit at the office.'

'Just do your best and ring when you find something.' Heidi disconnected the call and slipped the mobile back in her pocket.

'What is it you think has been going on?' Stacey asked.

'I'll have a better idea when I've had a look at the room. Did you bring your camera?'

'Never leave home without it.'

* * *

As Jack approached the outskirts of Llandrindod, Ben told him to call in at the Memorial Hospital.

'I want a chat with the doctor,' he said. 'Just to make sure we're not missing something. I'm still struggling to understand how it is possible for the killer not to leave a single clue at the sites of his attacks.'

'Criminals watch too much *CSI*,' Jack grumbled. 'Everyone knows about DNA and takes care not to leave any.'

'We do find some at crime scenes though, quite regularly in fact.'

'Yes, we do, but those crimes come under the headings of "spur of the moment" and "crime of passion". These murders were planned way in advance, must have been. They were complicated. Drugging, kidnapping, stripping, transporting and posing. What I'd like to know is how the killer picks his victims. It's not like he's taking out innocent bystanders. He kills bad men.'

'Yeah, I've wondered about that too. Ryan's case was covered at length by the local press – didn't make the nationals. The Townsend brothers moved here after being written about in their local press in London. If the killer does live nearby, how did he find out about them?'

'Must have a link to the city,' Jack said. 'He might work there, or have friends and family he visits regularly. Everyone I spoke to in Llanwrtyd was very shocked when they learned Robin Townsend had stood trial... and for what.'

Jack pulled up in the car park at the rear of the hospital. The detectives left the car and walked back to the main entrance. Jack went to reception, flashed his warrant card and asked if it was possible to speak to Dr Sunderland. Ben waited in the wide entrance hall and stared at the roll of honour, fixed high on the wall, crafted from polished wood and inscribed with the many names of the fallen, some from villages which no longer existed. Jack joined him.

'We got lucky,' he said. 'Doc's on his break. He'll see us in his office.' He followed Ben's gaze. 'The wars were hard. Seems the local area paid a heavy price.'

'Yes, Mid Wales lost many sons,' Ben said. 'Right then, where's Sunderland's office?'

'Top floor.'

The officers squeezed into a lift with a porter who was in charge of a wheeled bed, a young boy beneath the sheets. Jack smiled at the lad who looked away. Dr Sunderland's office was on the north side of the building and provided a sweeping view of the mountains surrounding the town. The doctor stood as they entered and waved them to seats. Ben noticed an open sandwich box on the desk.

'I'm sorry to disturb your lunch,' Ben said, 'but thank you for seeing us.'

'No problem. You want to talk about Patrick Ryan?'

'Yes, that's right. I wanted to ask if there were any signs of injury. Bruising maybe where Ryan tried to defend himself. Rope marks on the wrists, anything.'

'Nothing like that at all. He had a single rope burn across his back where he had been secured to the statue, but nothing else that I could find.'

'And you were able to detect traces of gamma-hydroxybutyrate in his system?'

The doctor nodded. 'Yes, certainly enough to be dangerous. It's difficult to be precise as to how much he'd been given because the drug metabolises so quickly. As I said, he was fortunate.'

'Do you know Ryan's mother?' Jack asked.

'Yes, she's a patient here.'

'Can you tell me why?'

Sunderland smiled. 'You know I can't.'

'OK,' Jack said, 'I'll do the talking. We've just been out to visit her and she told us she has mental health issues. That Ryan is her carer.'

The doctor offered a brief nod.

Jack continued, 'She told us she'd had a breakdown. We're concerned she might not be able to manage on her own.'

'I hear you, Sergeant. I'll speak to the mental health team… and thank you.'

'Is Ryan still improving?' Ben asked.

'He is. Check in with me tomorrow. Bit of luck he'll be talking by then.'

The detectives got to their feet.

Ben shook Sunderland's hand. 'I'll be in touch, thanks.'

Ben and Jack made their way out of the hospital and were halfway across the car park when Ben suddenly stopped dead and muttered, 'Brumbys.'

'You what, guv?'

'The Brumbys. Landlords of the Stonecroft. They both knew Robin Townsend – who was last seen alive in their pub – and moved here from London.'

Chapter thirty

The female receptionist at the Travelodge had been more than happy to open room seventeen after Stacey presented her press pass and explained the situation.

'I can't tell you who booked the room. The guy paid cash. He said his girlfriend had drunk too much. I'm not sure you'll find anything inside,' the receptionist said as she pushed open the door. 'The police gave it a good going-over, left black dust everywhere trying to find fingerprints.' She sighed. 'We haven't been able to get it cleaned yet.'

'All the better,' Heidi said and smiled at the woman. 'We shouldn't be long and we'll check in with you when we leave.'

Heidi shut the door and turned back to the room.

'What are we looking for?' Stacey asked.

'Any form of digital surveillance. Microphones, webcams, that sort of stuff.'

'Do you think Erica was being watched?'

'It's the only thing that makes sense. Someone was not only watching her, but her heartbeat was being recorded and sent to the cloud.'

'Why would anyone do that?'

'No idea, which is why we need to catch the guilty party and ask them. Now start looking. Remember the kit will be very small, easy to tuck away.'

Stacey nodded, then she moved the chair and placed it beneath a TV monitor hanging from a bracket on the wall facing the bed. Standing on the chair, she peered at the screen, ran her hands along the edges, shone a torch at the back and examined the bracket closely. Finding nothing, she worked her way along the wall, checking pictures, the curtain rail, the windowsill. Heidi hunted at a lower level, removed the shades from a pair of bedside lamps, felt around the bottoms, swept her hands along the headboard, then glanced up at the ceiling.

'Smoke detector,' she said. 'Put some gloves on, Stacey, and take the cover off. I can't reach.'

Stacey pulled on a pair of gloves, stood on the bed and stretched her long frame up towards the ceiling. Her fingers brushed the plastic cover and after some frantic fiddling, she popped the cover free and pointed her torch at the innards.

'There!' Heidi said. 'Right in the middle.'

Stacey reached out.

'No!' Heidi said. 'Leave it where it is. I can't get up there, so take some photos and let me look before we try to remove it.'

Stacey snapped a couple of pictures with her phone and handed it to Heidi who scrutinised them carefully.

'What is it?' Stacey asked.

'A webcam with its own power supply so images can be beamed to the cloud.'

'Shall I take it down?'

'Yes, but unscrew the detector from the ceiling and bring it down in one piece. Here.' Heidi held out a multi-tool which had a flip-out Phillips screwdriver.

'We should give this to the police,' Stacey said as she removed the device.

'And we will,' Heidi said. 'I just want a chance to look at it first. Check the headboard. I'm sure there's a microphone somewhere.'

Heidi tapped a number into Stacey's phone while peering at the tiny webcam.

'Angus... yes, I know. I'm gonna send you some photos of something discovered in the room where Erica was found.' She tapped the phone again and sent the pictures. 'There's another serial number for you... what? … No not yet, we're looking. I'll send you anything we find.' Heidi hung up.

Stacey wriggled out from under the bed, a small brass, button-like device in her gloved fingers. 'Is this what you're looking for?'

Heidi nodded, went to the bathroom and emerged with two new, pedal bin liners. She tucked their finds safely inside the bags and knotted the necks.

'OK then,' she said. 'Let's get over to Erica's place and I'll have a proper look at these while you pack some of her clothes. On the way back to Brecon, we'll drop into Cardiff nick and hand everything over to Sergeant Willis. He can lift fingerprints, I can't. You never know, he might get lucky. Please don't mention any of this to Erica. I don't want her to worry until we've got the whole story.'

* * *

Stacey dropped Heidi off at her basement flat, said hello to Erica and drank a swift coffee then headed towards the ranges and home. By the time she reached the start of the army road the sun had begun its descent, slipped below a thick covering of goose-grey clouds, and blazed through a chink beneath. Stacey pulled up in a lay-by, turned off the engine and got out of the car.

She leaned against the warm metal of the bonnet and gazed across the expanse of the ranges. A stiff, chilly breeze blew across the tops, rustling the dying bracken and carrying the noise of a fox screaming for a mate. Stacey shuddered. The discordant call always sounded like a woman in distress. A robin perched on the top of a gorse bush to sing down the day, bright yellow flowers radiating the last of the sun. She got into the driver's seat and fired up the engine. Ten minutes later, she crossed the cattle grid, dropped down the steep hill, drove past Llanagethin and pulled into the drive at Noddfa, smiling when she saw Ben's car parked on the lane. She walked up the path and unlocked the front door.

'Hey, Sherlock,' Stacey called as she removed her boots and stepped into slippers. She found him sitting in the carver next to the Aga and smiled as she entered.

'Hello, *cariad*,' he said. 'I was beginning to think you'd deserted me.' He got to his feet, wrapped long arms around her and delivered a kiss.

'Wow,' Stacey said. 'That's a proper welcome. I should stay away more often.'

'No, you shouldn't. That's a bad idea. What have you been up to? How is Erica doing?'

Stacey sat and told him what had been found in the motel room, but she didn't mention Heidi's theories, or the involvement of her friend, Angus.

'We've been trying to work up a profile of the killer,' Ben said.

'Good idea. How's that going?'

Ben groaned. 'Not great. Jack and I were talking today and reckoned the killer might live on the same patch he has used to display the victims.'

'Makes sense.'

'Then,' Ben said, 'we wondered how he picks his victims. If he is local, he'd have read about Patrick Ryan in the local press, but how would he hear about the misdeeds of the Townsends?'

'Knows someone in London, or visits the city regularly. Only way if their story didn't make the nationals.'

Ben laughed. 'You're wasted as a hack. That's exactly what we decided. He, or she, must have a link to London, which is why we're going to talk to the Brumbys in the morning.'

'Ah, clever. I'd forgotten they came from London. Do you think they were in it together?'

Ben chuckled. 'Now you're jumping the gun, although, two people working together would make the posing much easier. I still think one person on their own couldn't haul the victims into place.'

'Does that mean BB is off the hook?'

'I can't see these murders were her work, but we do need to talk to her about the death of her mother.' Ben sighed heavily. 'Where on earth can the woman have got to? I'm reluctant to put her face in the paper, but if she doesn't come home soon, I'll have to.'

Stacey smiled. '*The Mid Wales Times* will of course be happy to help. Heidi had a look at the copy of the journal you sent her. She told me that BB had written about abuse dished out by her mother.'

'Yes, Tegan said the same.'

'Is it possible then that BB acted in self-defence?'

'Anything's possible, but the evidence so far is clear. I need to speak with her, hear her side of life at home, but I can't do that if I can't find her.'

Chapter thirty-one

Ben left before seven the next morning leaving Stacey in bed and suggesting she had a lie in. She didn't need telling twice. She turned over, tucked the duvet around her shoulders and was asleep before Ben finished getting dressed. He crept from the room, didn't bother with coffee, got into his car and headed for the station.

Stacey slept on and when she next glanced at the bedside clock was surprised to see it was after ten. She slipped out of bed, threw on her fluffy robe and walked downstairs to the kitchen.

She flipped the kettle on as she walked by and opened the back door. Even though it was late, the day was gloomy and dismal. Feathers of fine drizzle floated out of thick, grey clouds and drenched everything it touched. She shivered and shut the door. Turning back to the kitchen, she opened the Aga door, stirred the embers and posted a log inside. She left the fire door open, made coffee, then perched on the carver and watched as bright flames crawled busily around the fresh wood. A few minutes later the phone rang and she picked it up.

'Good morning, Stacey Logan.'

'Is it good?' Sam Jenkins said. 'I'm not convinced. Disgusting weather, and even though your two weeks' leave was over a while ago, I still haven't received anything from you.'

'It was hardly leave, Sam. I've been working the whole time, not stuck on the sofa eating junk and watching crap on the telly. You'll get your feature.'

'But when, Stace? Nothing on the murders either.'

'That's because there isn't anything to write about. The investigation has stalled. You shouldn't fret, I like an exclusive as much as you, but a little patience wouldn't come amiss.'

'I'm not a patient man, you know that.'

Stacey smiled into the phone. 'Yes, I do.'

'So have you anything for me at all?'

'I could send over what I've written so far – just to give you an idea – but it's not to be published. It's not ready, or finished. Tell you one thing though.'

'Oh? What?'

'When it is ready, it'll be one hell of a story.'

Sam chuckled. 'That's what I like to hear. OK, send what you've got and I promise I won't print it. If the story will be as good as you think, take as long as you need.'

'Thanks, boss. You won't be disappointed.'

Stacey hung up, took a shower, dressed warmly and returned to the kitchen as the phone rang again. She recognised Heidi's number and picked up.

'Hi, you. Didn't expect to hear from you again so soon.'

'Are you grumbling?' Heidi asked.

'Of course not. Haven't been up long, still a bit dozy that's all.'

'Well give yourself a shake. I'm just about to leave home and drive to you. I've found Gwen Llewelyn.'

* * *

Ben and Jack sat at a table in the bar of the Stonecroft, Derek and Denise Brumby on chairs opposite. Derek seemed content to allow his wife to do the talking, and she seemed happy to be the appointed spokesperson.

'I heard there'd been an attempted killing,' Denise said. 'Sounds to me the lad had a lucky escape.'

'You're not wrong,' Ben said. 'Do you know Patrick Ryan? Lives the other side of Rhayader with his mother.'

'I know of him. Read about what he'd been up to in the paper. Never met him though and he ain't been in here, not to my knowledge.' She chuckled. 'He was the main subject of conversation among the punters when his trial was going on.' She huffed. 'Did you see the picture of his poor wife in the paper? Anyone who does that to a woman is a bleeding animal. Don't know how he got found innocent. Jury couldn't have been listening.'

'You sound angry,' Ben said.

'That's cos I am! Aren't you? Every time I hear about another woman suffering abuse like that, my blood boils.' She glared at the detectives. 'Once you get these bastards in a court, seems to me you don't try hard enough to get them sent down.'

'With respect, Mrs Brumby, we arrest and investigate. We're not responsible for what goes on in court.'

'Let's talk about Robin Townsend,' Jack said. 'You knew him, didn't you?'

'He was a regular. Often popped in at weekends.'

'Did you know why he had moved here from London?'

'Said he'd inherited some dosh from his folks. I know now he left cos he'd been to court, for killing his girlfriend no less.'

'If you'd known what he'd been accused of, would he have been welcome in your pub?' Ben asked.

Denise folded her arms across her ample breasts. 'He certainly would not have been welcome. I try to keep scum out of here.'

'You said you didn't know about his past,' Jack said, 'but you must have friends in London and friends talk. Did no one mention the murder case to you?'

Denise chuckled. 'London's a big place, Sergeant. These sorts of things happen more often there, one of the reasons we moved out. No, I didn't know and don't think any of the locals did either. Like I said, I only found out his history after he was dead. Good thing he's gone, if you ask me. That sort never change their spots, and I'm not keen on breathing the same air.'

'How about you, Mr Brumby?' Jack asked.

'Same as the wife,' Derek said. 'Never heard a whisper and it's difficult to keep secrets here.'

'The guy who was in here with Robin that evening,' Ben said, 'Peter Butler. Know anything about him?'

'Nah,' Denise said. 'Not a regular.'

'We arrested him recently,' Jack said. 'Charged him with supplying drugs. Did you see anything going on when he was drinking with Robin and his brothers?'

'I spot anything like that in here and the guilty party is swiftly shown the door.'

'Do you report dealers to us?' Ben asked.

'Not unless they try it a second time.' Denise grinned. 'Very few come back for another go. I make it plain they ain't welcome.' She got to her feet. 'Now then, gents, if that's all, I've got a pub to run. Can't sit around all day yacking.'

'Just before we go,' Ben said. 'Big Bron still hasn't returned home. I don't suppose you know where she might have gone?'

'No, Chief Inspector, not a clue. I told you before. She calls in once in a blue moon for a couple of pints to take home, and I know she lives somewhere above the Devil's Staircase, other than that...' She shrugged.

'Well, thanks for your time, and the tea,' Ben said.

'Next time, pop in when we're open, have a drink maybe, but no more bleeding daft questions I don't know the answers to.'

Chapter thirty-two

Stacey was lacing on her boots when she heard a car horn outside the cottage. She grabbed her kitbag, left through the front door, opened the door of Heidi's truck and settled in the passenger seat. Heidi turned the vehicle around and drove past Llanagethin and on towards the main road at Garth.

'Where are we headed?' Stacey asked.

'Place called Monkton, just this side of Leominster on the A44.'

'Your search of the ancestry sites struck gold then?'

'It did, yes. Found me Gwen. Nuclear DNA of her sample displays a 50% match with that collected from the farmhouse. No doubt whatsoever that this woman is the full sister of BB.'

'Amazing. You're very good at lateral thinking.'

'I know,' Heidi said.

At Builth they took the twisty A481 through Hundred House and slipped between the mountains. At the T-junction, they turned right onto the main road and an hour or so later, pulled up outside a pub called the Monkton Arms.

'Does Gwen live in the pub?' Stacey asked.

'No.' Heidi pointed across the road at an estate of newly built, detached homes. 'According to council tax records, number nineteen. Alone it would seem, she claims a 25% discount for single occupancy. We'll leave the truck here.'

Stacey picked up her bag and stepped out of the vehicle. Heidi locked the doors and joined her as they crossed the busy road and walked into the estate.

'Have you heard anything from Angus?' Stacey asked.

'Not yet. Like he said, he needs time to search the cloud.'

'I never use it,' Stacey said. 'I keep all my stuff backed up an on external hard drive.'

Heidi laughed. 'We all use it, all the time. The cloud is just the name given to the server farms that capture and store everything that goes on online. Without it you wouldn't be able to log on to another computer to access your emails. Proves they aren't only stored on your machine – if you take a moment to think about it.'

'That's my trouble,' Stacey said. 'I use the internet, but I don't know how it works and don't give it much thought, if any.'

'You and most of humanity, which gives people who do understand it – like me – a way in.'

They stopped outside number nineteen, a well-presented, modern house, with a shiny red door and a large area of yellow gravel in the neat front garden, a small water feature bubbling in the centre.

'We need to do this gently,' Stacey said. 'It's all very well knowing the woman who lives here is BB's sister, but we don't know her history. Domestic abuse is a dreadful thing and even though it happened years ago, Gwen might still be fragile.'

'I know,' Heidi said, 'and I can do "gentle" with the best of you.'

Stacey nodded and pushed open the garden gate then walked up to the door and rang the bell. She spotted one of the net curtains shiver, then a few moments later, the door opened and a woman in her early fifties appeared in the gap. Her deep green eyes were bright with something akin to fear.

'Hello,' the woman said. 'Can I help?'

Stacey stepped forward. 'I'm a journalist,' she said and showed her ID. 'My name is Stacey Logan and my friend, Heidi Holtz, is a retired police detective. Could we come inside and talk to you please?'

'What about?'

'You're Gwen Llewelyn, aren't you?'

'Yes, I am.'

'We're trying to find your father, Iolo, and your sister Bronwen.' Stacey smiled her best smile. 'We're here to help, not to cause trouble. Please let us in, it's pretty cold out here.'

'I've got CCTV,' Gwen warned, 'so if you aren't who you say, or try to sell me anything, I will report you.' She rattled the door chain, opened the door wider, waved her callers inside and shut the door behind them.

'Go into the front room,' she said. 'I'll make some tea.'

Stacey walked into the parlour, perched on a chair and gratefully took the weight off her sore leg.

'Told you to hang onto the crutch for a couple of days longer,' Heidi said.

'Whatever. It was getting in the way. Gain a crutch and effectively lose a hand.'

Heidi wandered around the tidy room, picking up ornaments, taking a look, then returning them to their shelf or nook. She leaned closer to the walls and examined a collection of family photographs. Nearly every picture contained a large woman, dark hair twisted into a severe bun on the top of her head, oversized bosom held in place by a three-inch-thick leather belt. She wore a white, loose-fitting blouse, and a voluminous, full-length skirt. Her husband was a good eight inches shorter and stood by her side. He was a wiry man, looked strong and fit like most hill farmers, wore a three-piece suit, and had slicked back hair and a broad friendly smile.

The only sign in the pictures that time had moved forward were the children, both girls, shown at around four through to sixteen. Heidi peered closer at the youngsters, one large in stature like her mother, the other a more normal size, with long hair woven into a thick plait. The door opened and Gwen entered, a tea tray in her hands. Heidi quickly removed a pile of magazines from a table in the window and Gwen put the tray down.

'Thank you,' she said. 'Now, tell me why you want to find my family.'

Stacey hesitated then asked, 'When did you last speak to any of them?'

'Must be well over a year ago. Bronwen rings occasionally, but certainly not regularly.' Gwen poured tea. 'I ask again, why do you want to find them? Not a problem, is there?'

'We're concerned about their wellbeing,' Heidi said. 'They left their home a little while ago now and haven't been seen since. Do you know where they are?'

'No, sorry, I don't. I find it very strange they've left. Mam always said she'd die in the mountains. On the rare occasion Bronwen rang, we didn't talk about Mam.' Gwen smiled sadly. 'She was a dreadful bully, quick temper; it wasn't uncommon for her to lash out.' She sipped tea. 'Why are you so interested in my family?'

'Stacey and I met your sister when Stacey was working on a story,' Heidi said. 'Bronwen had spoken briefly to a man who was found dead a matter of hours later.'

Gwen shook her head. 'Bron wouldn't have had anything to do with that, not killing someone. Being big doesn't make her a murderer.'

'No, we know it doesn't,' Stacey said quickly. 'Thing is... it's difficult.'

'We have a journal,' Heidi said. 'Your sister recorded long-term, physical abuse directed at you, your sister and your father, for years. Is that how things were?'

'Oh dear.' Gwen dabbed her eyes. 'I never wanted to talk about any of this. It's why I moved away.' She looked at Heidi. 'How did you find me?'

'We matched your DNA records held on an ancestry site with what was found at the house. You registered on the site a few years ago.'

'I did, yes. It was a present.' She sighed. 'Why did anyone collect DNA from the farmhouse?'

'The police were investigating the murder of the dead man,' Stacey said. 'During their enquiries, they discovered your sister was one of the last people to see him alive and obviously had to interview her. A couple of days later, Heidi and I drove out to speak to her.'

'We burst a tyre on the drive along the valley and Bronwen helped us change the wheel,' Heidi said. 'She was very kind.'

'That's nice of you to say,' Gwen said. 'She was always kind to me when I lived there.'

'Why did you leave home?' Stacey asked. 'Bronwen wrote in her journal that your mother drove you out. Mentioned something about some "trouble".'

Gwen sighed and rubbed her eyes. 'There was trouble, yes.'

'You don't have to tell us if you don't want to. We won't share your story with anyone and I promise not to write about it, but it might help us to find your family. We are worried about them. Bronwen wrote in the journal that Iolo was ill and she was finding it difficult to care for him.'

Gwen sighed again and reluctantly began to recount her story.

'It happened a few weeks before my eighteenth birthday. The snowdrops had started to flower and lambing was just beginning.' Gwen smiled fleetingly at the happy memory, then closed her eyes as she slipped back in time. 'The farm was always busy in the spring, molly lambs in the kitchen, weenies tucked up in the warming oven. On the day in question I couldn't do anything right, and ended up dropping Mam's favourite casserole dish. It smashed on the flagstones and she flew at me. I don't know why, but for the first time ever I fought back, caught her off guard and she fell hard.'

Gwen rubbed her eyes again and removed a cotton handkerchief from the sleeve of her jumper.

'Mam glared at me. I saw murder in her eyes and she snatched up the skillet. I shot out of the way. She turned fast and hit Da square in the face. Broke his nose and spilt his lip and cheek, there was blood everywhere.'

Tears began to roll faster down her cheeks. Stacey reached out and took hold of the distressed woman's hand.

Gwen squeezed Stacey's fingers, then continued, 'I... I just couldn't stay. I should have… should have helped to protect Da from her, but I was so frightened. I packed a small bag and ran and I've never been back.'

Heidi topped up the mugs from the teapot and gently pushed one into Gwen's trembling hand. 'Drink,' she said. 'It'll do you good.'

Gwen slurped then she placed the mug on the coffee table, wiped her face and blew her nose.

'I try not to think about it,' she said, 'but I was sure if she set about me, she'd more than likely kill me. Mam was incredibly strong and I was delicate – she called me "The Runt".' She paused and took a deep breath. 'So tell me, how were they all when you saw them?'

Stacey wasn't sure what to tell Gwen. She hadn't expected the awful tale, and she didn't know how to tell Gwen her mother was dead and that Bronwen had killed her. In the elongated and uncomfortable silence, there was a noise in the hall, a sort of quiet thump, like a footstep. Stacey glanced up as the living room door swung open and BB appeared in the doorway.

'It's OK,' she said. 'Gwen knows what I did. I told her as soon as I arrived. Thought I could hide here, but I should have known I couldn't filter into the shadows, not after what I've done.' She walked further inside the room and gently rested an enormous hand on her sister's head. '*Dim crio, cariad. Dim crio.*' Bronwen looked at Stacey. 'So you're here to take me away. Will you hand me over to the police?'

Heidi got to her feet. 'No, Bronwen, we're here to help you.'

Chapter thirty-three

Ben and Jack entered the incident room, helped themselves to coffee and dropped onto a couple of chairs.

'What a bloody waste of time that was,' Ben said. 'I really thought Ryan would be able to tell us something, but he has no memory of the incident at all. Useless!'

'Criminals who use the drug know about this side effect,' Jack said. 'I must admit, I wasn't expecting him to be able to tell us much, but as you say, nothing at all?'

'Some of his reluctance is bound to be down to his hostility towards the police, but you'd think he'd want to help us catch whoever put him in intensive care.'

'Yeah, you'd think,' Jack said.

Ben swivelled his chair to face the board and gazed at photographs of the victims. Pictures of them in life, smiling with friends, happy; the Townsend brothers in a pub garden, pints of beer in their hands. Other pictures showed how they were found in death, pale, naked, displayed prominently in public places.

'Had to be two,' he muttered under his breath.

'What, guv?'

Ben waved a hand at the board and the photographs. 'Posing bodies like that would be impossible on your own.

You would definitely need help.' Ben got to his feet and pointed at the red kite sculpture. 'Doesn't really matter how strong you are, carrying a dead body is bloody difficult, like trying to carry a bag of liquid, flops about all over the place, so you'd have to drag it, but Carrie found no marks on the bodies to suggest that.'

'OK, I'm listening.'

'Let's say you pulled a van up next to The Square. It's late, the street lights are out, locals are in bed and traffic nearly non-existent. Even so, any of that could change in an instant and you don't want to hang about.' Ben nodded. 'Yeah, two people. Carry the body between them, flip it on the kite and away. Speed is what makes this possible and explains why we haven't discovered any witnesses.'

'So now we're looking for a pair? Brothers? Sisters maybe? Partners?'

'Yeah, I reckon that's who we should be looking for.' Ben glanced across the room to Elsa Duffin. 'Did you hear that, Elsa?'

'Yes, sir. I'll check the list of local bad boys who might fit into that group.'

'Thanks. Where are Tegan and Ollie?'

'Builth. Ollie is having another scout about for stray CCTV cameras. Tegan is knocking on doors again, trying to get round the residents we haven't managed to speak to before. She's also going to pop into the Wyeside Arts Centre. The manager – Corrine Ballinger – rang first thing. Kevin Townsend's exhibition is over and he's picking up his work this afternoon. Tegan thought an unthreatening chat and a cuppa might shake something lose.' Elsa shrugged. 'That's what she said anyway.'

'OK.' Ben put his jacket on. 'Jack and I are going off the radar for two or three hours, so man the office and speak to CS Warren if you need any assistance.'

'Where are we going, guv?' Jack asked.

'Back out to BB's place, in the Land Rover. There must be something in the house that will give us an idea where she might have gone. She is a murder suspect, so we must find her.'

* * *

In the tidy kitchen of the house in Monkton, Stacey swilled out the teapot, added new bags and boiling water, and rinsed the mugs in the sink. She put everything on the tray and carried it to the front room, pushing the door open with her hip. Heidi was standing by the window, mobile held to her ear, speaking into the device urgently and quietly. The Llewelyn sisters sat side by side on the sofa and Stacey noticed they were holding hands. Heidi disconnected her call and settled in an easy chair.

'I've just spoken to my father's friend,' she said, 'Edmund Lazarus. He is a brilliant criminal solicitor – got me out of a pretty tight squeeze a while ago – and he'll be delighted to represent you, Bronwen. He's leaving his office now and should be here in a couple of hours. He's a good man. Trust him because he really can help you.'

'You shouldn't have bothered him,' Bronwen said. 'I've told you, we can't pay him and anyway, I am guilty. I did kill my mother.'

'OK, I get that,' Heidi said, 'but let me ask you this; if Myfanwy hadn't abused and beaten all three of you horribly for years, would you have killed her?'

Bronwen shook her head. 'No, of course I wouldn't. She was hurting Da. I just wanted her to stop. I didn't set out to kill her.'

'So, tell me how it happened,' Heidi said gently, 'and I'll tell you whether or not you're guilty.'

'But...'

Heidi held up her hands. 'Just tell me about the day Myfanwy died.'

Gwen squeezed her sister's hand. 'It's OK, *cariad.* You should let them help you, someone has to.'

Bronwen took a deep breath, filled her lungs then began to speak. 'I was out the back, in the workshop, skinning rabbits,' she said. 'Mam had been in a vicious mood all day and I was keeping out of the way.' She stopped speaking and closed her eyes.

'Then what?' Stacey prompted.

'I heard a row start up indoors, lots of yelling, more than usual. I suddenly heard Da yelp, like a dog that had been kicked. He yelped again, louder, so I ran to the kitchen.'

'What did you see?' Heidi asked.

Bronwen rubbed her face. 'As I went in, I saw Mam pick Da up, and fling him across the room. He landed against the hot range and didn't move. I saw... I saw the skin on his arm bubble and he still didn't move.' Bronwen gulped a breath. 'I thought maybe she'd killed him, our lovely Da who'd never hurt anyone and I was so angry. I saw Mam move towards him, thought she was going to hurt him again, so I raised the cleaver and hit her. She fell to the floor. I went to Da, lifted him away from the stove.' She took another breath. 'Poor man. He might as well have been dead. He never walked again after that day, stuck in a chair, unable to move, getting sicker and sicker.' She closed her eyes. 'He refused to see a doctor, couldn't bear the shame.'

'Where is Iolo?' Stacey asked.

'I drove him to Hereford Hospital, left him on the doorstep in his wheelchair and came here. I couldn't care for him anymore. I tried, really tried and failed. I knew he needed proper care and seeing him struggle day after day was breaking my heart.' A sob caught in her throat. 'My best wasn't good enough.'

* * *

Edmund Lazarus arrived on time and after introductions had been made, Heidi drove back to Llanagethin and dropped Stacey in the lane outside Noddfa.

'Would you like to come in for a quick coffee?' Stacey asked.

'No thanks. I need to get home. Finding Bronwen and arranging her some help has cleared the decks a little, but there's loads of work to do on the spiking case.'

'Do you really think Eddie will be able to keep Bronwen out of prison?'

'If he can't, no one can. I think he'll encourage Bronwen to hand herself in, but he'll be there when she does. It'll be a hard-hearted copper who would insist she be held on remand' – Heidi smiled – 'and we know Ben isn't one of those.'

Stacey nodded, opened the passenger door and slipped out. 'Keep in touch, will you?'

'Of course. We'll speak soon.'

Stacey watched her friend drive away and round the sharp bend, then she walked up the front path and let herself into the cottage.

She went to the kitchen, dumped her bag on the table, opened the back door and put the kettle on. Her mobile chirruped as a text message from Ben landed, offering a take-away supper. She smiled and replied with "yes please", then she made a pot of coffee and switched on her laptop. She checked her emails, then created a new document and typed up details of her visit to Monkton. She was so involved with the Llewelyn sisters' tragic story, she didn't notice time passing and nearly jumped out of her skin when Ben walked through the kitchen door with a carrier bag in his hand.

'Hey, *cariad*,' he said. 'Everything OK? You're as white as a sheet.'

'I'm fine,' she said. 'Made me jump, that's all. I was engrossed in my work and didn't hear your car.' She switched off the laptop. She didn't want Ben to know about Gwen and Bronwen, not until Eddie Lazarus had his ducks in a row.

'What are you working on?' Ben asked as he unpacked the carrier bag.

'A feature for Sam. It's not progressing as well as I'd hoped. Extra difficult because although there have been many spiking incidents, the police haven't been able to catch anyone.'

'Any of the available CCTV footage doesn't help us identify the culprits. It's all very poor quality and there's not enough of it.'

'Then post coppers in the clubs. The police are here to protect and serve and I don't know of a single woman who feels in the least protected.'

Ben groaned. 'If I had the staff, I would, but with all the cuts...'

'Yes, I know and I'm sorry, but something has to be done.' Stacey dished out the food. 'Heard anything from the sergeant in Cardiff? Has he managed to lift any prints from the webcam in the smoke detector?'

'Nothing yet but I spoke to Erica and she's going back to work tomorrow. The spiking epidemic is top of her list.' He gulped from his mug. 'It really is time that public venues up their game and invest in some decent CCTV.'

'That's all very well,' Stacey said, 'but that won't stop this happening, it just gives your boys in blue a better chance of catching the perpetrators. Something needs to be put in place to stop it happening in the first place.'

'I agree, but you spoke to the club owner, Jonnie Jones. Look at all the measures he has in place and none of that has stopped this awful business.'

'Heidi thinks there's more to it, especially since we discovered the webcam.'

'Has she shared any theories?' Ben asked.

'Only that she seems convinced the answer will be on the dark web. It's very sinister though, drugging women, taking them to a motel, having someone take photos, then what? What's the point?'

'It seems motiveless, but obviously isn't. That's why it's so difficult to work out who we are looking for. The girl found in the room with Erica couldn't tell us much.' He sighed heavily. 'What is it with some youngsters? She was happy to take the jobs – and the bitcoin she was paid – but didn't seem to want to know more about why she was employed to take the photos.'

'You know I spoke with Emily?'

Ben nodded.

'She told me it seemed odd but then backed up her statement by saying there's a lot of odd stuff on the internet.'

'She's not wrong,' Ben said.

The landline rang and Stacey picked it up.

'Hello, Stacey Logan.'

'Good evening, Ms Logan,' Edmund Lazarus said. 'I'm sorry to disturb, but is DCI Ben James with you?'

'He is yes. Would you like a word?'

'That would be good.' He paused. 'Well done today. I'm guessing you'd rather keep your involvement out of my visit to Monkton?'

'I would for now, and thank you. Hang on, I'll pass you over to Ben.' Stacey held out the phone. 'Eddie Lazarus for you.'

'Who?' Ben asked.

'The solicitor who represented Heidi in her hour of need.'

'Yes, I know. I wonder what he wants.'

'Ask him.' Stacey passed him the phone and began clearing the table.

'Good evening, Mr Lazarus,' Ben said. 'What can I do for you?'

'Good evening, Chief Inspector. Please call me Eddie. I am ringing to ensure you will be at the station tomorrow morning.'

'I'm planning to be, why?'

'I'm representing a client and have advised that the best course of action would be to hand themselves in and I would like that to happen tomorrow. I will obviously be in attendance. Would ten o'clock be convenient?'

'That will be fine. Can you give me the name of your client?'

'Yes, her name is Bronwen Llewelyn. I'll see you tomorrow and bid you a good evening.'

Ben put the phone down and rubbed his eyes.

'What did Eddie want?' Stacey asked.

'To visit the police station tomorrow with BB. Seems she wants to hand herself in.'

Chapter thirty-four

DS Erica Bevan arrived early at Cardiff's central police station, walked into the squad room and discovered DS Willis working behind a computer screen. He looked up and smiled.

'Morning,' he said. 'Good to see you. How are you feeling?'

'Pretty stupid for getting myself spiked, but other than that, fine thanks.'

'Glad to hear it,' Willis said. 'Let me fetch us a cuppa then I'll update you.'

Erica nodded, then she sat at her desk, switched on her own computer and winced when she saw a ridiculously long list of emails awaiting an answer. Willis plonked a mug next to the screen and perched on a chair. Erica sipped from the mug and smiled her thanks.

'Let's hear it then,' she said. 'Tell me what I've missed.'

Willis grinned. 'Only the nicking of a kid in a baseball cap. Spotted in Rascals slipping a white powder into a young woman's drink.'

'Wow. You're kidding right?'

'Nope. He's downstairs in the cells. Security guard locked him in the office at the club and we picked him up from there. I knew you'd be in this morning, so he hasn't been interviewed yet.'

'Do we know who he is?'

'Richard Price, twenty-three, local, got a record for nicking cars.' Willis chuckled. 'Not a happy bunny, with a bit of luck he'll have calmed down overnight.'

Erica nodded. 'Hopefully. OK, you lead the interview and I'll be your number two. Better that way and less likely I'll be accused of not being objective enough. Has he asked for a solicitor?'

'We offered one this morning and he declined.'

Erica got to her feet, drained her coffee and slipped into her jacket.

'Right then,' she said. 'Let's hear what he has to say.'

The detectives walked downstairs to the custody suite and waited in the interview room until Price was brought in and directed to a chair. His eyes widened slightly as his gaze flickered over Erica's face and he looked away quickly. Erica, sure she'd been recognised, tried not to grin as she switched on the recording device and logged the date, time and those present in the room. Sergeant Willis rested his hands flat on a cardboard file, raised his eyes and frowned at the prisoner. The silence lengthened.

Price huffed angrily. 'Get on with it then. You obviously have something to say, so bloody say it.'

'You understand why you're here?' Willis asked.

Price smirked. 'Cos you nicked me. Not sure what for, like, but that guard bloke must have said something bad about me and you believed him.'

'So we're clear,' Willis said, 'you've been arrested on suspicion of administering a controlled substance to others without their knowledge. What I want to know is why you did that.'

Price folded his arms. 'I haven't done anything and you can't prove that I have.'

'How do you know we can't?' Erica asked quietly.

'What?' Price switched his gaze and asked, 'I know you don't I?'

Erica smiled. 'Do you?'

'Why do you think you know my colleague?' Willis asked.

Price shrugged. 'Thought I'd seen her before, that's all.'

Willis opened the file and perused the contents. 'Been a busy boy I see,' he said. 'Ever nick any vans? White Transit Connect ring any bells?'

'What? No. I haven't nicked anything for ages, not since I got done for it. Why are you asking about a van?'

Willis turned a page, slipped out a sheet of paper and slid it across the desk.

'I want you to look at these dates,' he said, 'and tell me where you were on each one of them.'

Price barely glanced at the paper and said, 'No idea. Who knows where they were months ago?'

'They're all Saturdays. What do you usually do on a Saturday night?'

'Dunno. Go out sometimes, stay in others.'

'Think back to last Saturday. You ought to be able to remember where you were last week.'

Price shrugged. 'I dunno. Might have been out I suppose.'

'You were in Rascals weren't you?'

'Uh... no... well, maybe, not all night. Might have been in the Boston Bar too.'

Willis grinned. 'We know you were there. Your mug was captured on CCTV. Actually, we know a lot more than you think, so you'd be better off telling us what you were up to.'

'I wasn't up to anything. Had a drink, a dance, stuff you do at clubs. No law against it.'

'We have footage of you getting into a white Transit Connect outside the Boston Bar at one thirty in the morning. Give us the name of the driver.'

Price said nothing. He glanced at Erica and once again looked away quickly.

'I've changed my mind,' he said. 'I do want a solicitor and I'm not saying anything else until I've got one.'

'Not a problem,' Willis said. He closed the file and got to his feet. 'We'll do our best, but it might be a bit of a wait. You sure now?'

'Yes, I'm sure.'

Willis leaned across the desk and switched off the recording device then a uniformed officer led the prisoner from the room and back to the cells.

Willis smiled at Erica. 'He's as guilty as sin,' he said. 'Really doesn't like having you in the room. I bet you that by the end of the day he'll tell us exactly what has been going on and we get to throw away the key.'

* * *

Stacey huddled on the low wall outside the police station, half-hidden by a thick rhododendron bush, hoping no one inside had spotted her. After Ben had left for work, she'd given him ten minutes to get clear, then followed him to town, parked on a side street and walked to the station.

She checked her watch, saw it was a quarter to ten, and hoped Edmund Lazarus would arrive soon. She'd made up her mind in the middle of the night to go there. Not to take photos or in her role as a reporter, but just to be here so Bronwen Llewelyn would see a friendly face. After all the woman had been through, she deserved that. A chilly wind rustled the leaves of the bush and snuck inside Stacey's jacket. She turned up the collar. A few minutes later a dove-grey Bentley swooshed into the car park. Stacey left her spot, walked closer and sent her best smile to Bronwen who sat in the passenger seat next to Eddie.

Bronwen looked pale and frightened. Her eyes flicked nervously around the car park. She spotted Stacey and half-raised a hand. Eddie pulled on the handbrake, turned off the engine and stepped out as Stacey opened Bronwen's door.

'*Bore da*.' Morning, Stacey said as the large woman left the car. She placed a hand on Bronwen's arm and asked, 'Are you OK?'

'Dw i ddim yn gwneud yn dda.' I'm not doing well.

Stacey squeezed her arm. 'I'm sure you'll be fine. Ben is a good, fair man and Eddie will look after you.'

'Of course I will,' Eddie said. 'All will be well, I'm sure.'

'Why are you here, Stacey?' Bronwen asked.

'Moral support and to let you know I'm thinking of you.' Stacey turned to Eddie. 'How long do you think this will take?'

'Not too long, I hope. We've prepared a statement which Ms Llewelyn will read. All things being equal, we should be able to leave in a couple of hours. Will you wait?'

'I was intending to. Wondered if you'd like lunch at my place before you travel back to Monkton.'

'That would be most welcome, thank you.' Eddie smiled. 'I know where you live and there's nothing you can do here, so go on home and we'll meet you there.'

'If you're sure,' Stacey said. 'Is that OK, Bronwen, or would you like me to stay?'

Bronwen shook her large head. 'You go. We'll follow later. *Diolch yn fawr, cariad*.' Thank you very much, love.

'I'll be in touch if anything changes,' Eddie said.

He leaned back inside the car, removed his jacket and briefcase, then walked towards the main entrance of the station, Bronwen at his side.

* * *

Sergeant Willis and Erica Bevan re-entered the interview room in the basement of Cardiff's central police station. Richard Price was already present and seated next to his solicitor, a woman in her thirties called Val Morgan. They both looked up as the detectives walked in. Erica set the recording device in motion, verbally logged on and took a seat next to Willis. She felt Price's gaze on her. She knew her presence unsettled him and smiled to herself.

'Right then,' Willis said, and glanced at Ms Morgan. 'Have you had sufficient time with your client?'

'I have. Mr Price has a statement he wishes to read.'

'Oh?' Willis leaned back in his chair. 'Let's hear it then.'

Richard Price unfolded a sheet of paper taken from a legal pad and began to read. He gave his name, address and date of birth, then continued.

'I work for an organisation which provides experiences, in particular sham kidnappings. Customers contact the company to book and their details are passed to me. I meet up with the customers and I am instrumental in beginning their experience evening. I escort them to a van. They are then driven to a nearby motel, where I leave them and go home. This is the extent of my involvement. I am paid digitally with bitcoin. I have been involved with around twenty experience evenings in the past and do not believe I have broken the law.'

Price slid the statement across the table towards the detectives and folded his arms.

Erica snorted. 'Is that it?'

'Yes,' Ms Morgan said. 'That's it.'

Willis laughed. 'Instrumental eh?' he asked. 'Sounds more like plain mental to me.' He glared at the prisoner. 'You were seen slipping white powder into a young woman's drink at the bar in Rascals nightclub. You were apprehended by security inside the club and traces of GHB have been recovered from your hands.' He laughed some more. 'Do you really expect us to believe the woman paid for an "experience" which included being spiked? Are you barking mad? What did you say to the receptionists at the motels when you carried a comatose woman past the booking desk?'

Price didn't speak and kept his eyes on the tabletop.

'What is the name of the organisation which sells these "experiences"?' Erica asked. 'Have you any proof it even exists?'

'No comment,' Price mumbled.

'Where did you get the drugs?' Willis asked.

'No comment.'

'Tell us the name of the van driver,' Erica said.

Price remained silent and picked at a scab on the back of one of his hands. Willis leaned across the table and glared at his prisoner.

'Do you have any idea of how much trouble you're in, boy? No? Let me enlighten you.' He nodded at Erica. 'DS Bevan was one of your victims last weekend. She hadn't booked one of these experiences you keep on about. We have CCTV footage which clearly shows you spiking her drink. More of you leaving the Boston Bar, your arm around her waist. You put her in the back of a white van which was later seen at a motel off the M4. DS Bevan was subsequently discovered in a room, unconscious. Also in the room was a young woman taking photographs, and you're trying to tell us this is all part of a legitimate business?'

Price shrugged and kept his eyes low.

'You are looking at a very long sentence.' Willis grinned. 'Any idea what drugging and kidnapping a police officer will get you? Add attempted murder and life with an indefinite tariff is more or less a given.' He chuckled nastily. 'Don't reckon a little fella like you will thrive in jail. Don't rate your chances at all.'

Val Morgan cleared her throat. 'I can't let you badger my client, Sergeant,' she said. 'He has provided a statement and I have advised him not to comment further.'

'Then I don't rate the advice you're giving him,' Erica said. 'As we speak, forensic IT experts are combing through his phone and computer records. They will be able to prove conclusively your client's involvement with these dreadful crimes. If he doesn't talk to us and tell us what we need to know, he'll be found guilty and cop for the lot. With a bit of luck, by the time he's released, he'll be approaching sixty. Job done! Your client's life over before it really starts.' She got to her feet and glared at the solicitor. 'I suggest you take some time to have another chat with your client.' She checked the clock on the wall. 'Interview terminated at 10.49am.' She slapped off the machine and the detectives strode from the room.

Chapter thirty-five

Stacey drove around the bend on the edge of Llanagethin and spotted Heidi's truck parked in the lane outside Noddfa. She tooted the horn, pulled into the drive, got out of the car and discovered Heidi waiting on the front path.

'Hey, you,' Stacey said. 'Been here long?'

'Ten minutes or so. Where have you been?'

'Outside the police station waiting for BB to arrive with Eddie. Wanted to wish her luck.'

'Kind. How was she?'

'Pretty scared but Eddie looked and sounded confident. He's planning to come here for lunch after it's all over. Come in, I'll make coffee.'

Stacey unlocked the door, draped her coat on the newel post, went to the kitchen and put the kettle on. Heidi followed and flopped on the carver.

'I've got news,' she said.

'Good or bad?' Stacey asked.

'Bloody awful.'

Stacey sat at the table. 'Tell me.'

Heidi removed an envelope from the pocket of her jacket, tipped out a small bundle of photographs and lined them up on the table. They all showed images of young women who appeared to be sleeping... including one of Erica.

'These are the pictures from Emily's camera,' Heidi explained. 'Seventeen individuals, all snapped in motel rooms after presumably being spiked.'

'You managed to identify them all? Wow. Did they report the incidents to the police?'

'Five did, nine didn't and... three died.'

Stacey blinked. 'What?'

Heidi separated three of the photographs from the others. 'These unlucky few were discovered in motel rooms by cleaning staff over the last year or so. In every case, paramedics were called. No obvious causes of death. Autopsies found cardiac arrest. Cause of death recorded as sudden arrhythmic death syndrome, or SADS. No traces of GHB, but after the time lag there wouldn't be.'

'Oh shit,' Stacey said. 'That's just terrible. I haven't heard anything about these deaths at all.'

'Why would you? Three different motels, three unconnected victims, three unsuspicious deaths separated by time. Stuff like this slips through the gaps. There is no story.'

Stacey wiped her eyes with her fingers. 'Erica was so lucky.'

'Yes, she was. All the survivors were.'

Heidi made coffee and slid a mug across the table to her friend. Stacey took a large gulp, winced at the heat and spluttered. She wiped her lips.

'So do you know why the women were taken?' she asked. 'And why those particular women?'

'I don't know yet, but hope to soon.' She grinned. 'Baseball Cap Boy was nicked last night at Rascals. Erica told me. Security pulled a blinder and nabbed him in the act. Richard Price is hopefully purging his soul in a Cardiff interview room at this very moment.'

'Well that's good news at least.'

Heidi cracked her knuckles. 'There's more.'

'Really? Good or bad?'

'More curious, but probably ultimately bad.' Heidi opened Stacey's laptop and logged on to her messaging system. 'Angus has been busy and he discovered this.'

Heidi tapped the keyboard and a video clip began to play. Stacey stared at the screen and saw an image of a woman lying on a bed. She had short dark hair, small diamonds in her ears, wore a red cocktail dress and her eyes were closed.

'Oh my God! Is that Erica?'

'Yes and look at the bottom of the screen.' Heidi pointed at a red ticker tape which scrolled by continuously. 'That's displaying all the data from the Fitbit put on her wrist.'

'Where did Angus find this?' Stacey asked.

'He discovered a shadow, like a ghost in the cloud – it's complicated. He knows the file was sent to the dark web, but uncovering the eventual destination will take time – if it's possible at all.'

Stacey rubbed her eyes again and removed her hoodie, the room suddenly too warm.

'How about the order Emily received?' she asked. 'Has that given you any idea what this is all about?'

'It's my opinion that little Emily was used. Like many teenagers, she's desperately naïve. She's broke, she needed the money and was offered a job doing something she enjoys. Her only crime really was not asking enough questions.'

'What does Angus think?'

'That something disgusting is going on and he needs to catch whoever is behind it quickly.'

There was a loud knock on the front door.

'That'll be Eddie,' Stacey said. 'I do hope BB is with him.'

'Stay there,' Heidi said. 'I'll go. We'll talk more about this later.'

Stacey heard the door open and Heidi say, '*Croeso,* Bronwen, Eddie. *Prynhawn da. Sut dych chi?*' Good afternoon. How are you?

* * *

Ben and Jack sat in the window of the local greasy spoon, mugs of tea in front of them, bacon sandwiches ordered.

'I need this, guv,' Jack said. 'That poor woman. What a dreadful tale.'

'Wasn't easy to listen to, I agree,' Ben said.

'What do you think will happen now?'

'What happens in every case. We'll send the papers to the CPS and they'll make the decision whether or not to prosecute, but first we have witnesses to interview, Gwen and her father. One thing is certain, Eddie Lazarus will make sure Bronwen receives the best defence possible.'

Jack nodded, smiled at the waitress who delivered their food, then smothered the still-sizzling bacon with brown sauce and took a huge bite. He chewed thoughtfully then asked, 'How did Eddie Lazarus get involved with this?'

Ben chuckled. 'How do you think? Come on, Jack, you're a detective after all.'

Jack shrugged and took another bite of his sandwich.

'Stacey and Heidi went to visit the sister after Heidi tracked Gwen using records from DNA ancestry sites,' Ben said. 'Clever bit of lateral thinking.' He drank from his mug. 'Neither said a word to me about it.'

'Just as well I reckon. Better this way than arresting BB and dragging her from the house. Do you think she'll be sent down?'

'No idea, but I'm fairly sure we can remove her from the list of suspects on the murder case.'

Jack nodded. 'If it hadn't been for the investigation, we'd never have found her... or Myfanwy's body. Do you know how Iolo is doing?'

'I spoke to a doctor at Hereford Hospital who confirmed he is on a ward and being cared for. I've sent Elsa and Ollie to get a statement. They'll call in and speak to Gwen on the way back.'

Ben's mobile chirped. He peered at the screen and saw a message from Tegan: "You're needed at base." He crammed the last of his lunch in his mouth and stood. 'Duty calls,' he said. 'Tegan wants us at the station.'

Jack drained his mug and followed his boss from the cafe. Five minutes later they walked in through the main entrance of the station and ran upstairs to the squad room. Tegan glanced up from her work as they entered.

'What's up, Constable?' Ben asked, removing his jacket.

'As you know,' Tegan said, 'I was going to try to catch Kevin at the Wyeside yesterday when he came to collect his work.'

'Yes, I did know.'

'Well, he wasn't there. Corrine Ballinger said he hadn't called to cancel and when she rang him she only got a machine. First thing this morning I tried to get hold of him but couldn't so I spoke to the FLO who, as it turns out, Kevin had sent packing.'

'Is there a point to this?' Ben asked.

'Yes, sir, sorry. I spoke to Bill Hill, the caravan site manager. He went to check on Kevin and' – she took a breath – 'found him hanging from the rafters in his studio. He was naked and very dead.'

'Christ,' Ben said and dropped onto a chair. 'Foul play?'

'Too soon to tell, but so far no one's found a note. The body's been taken to Haverfordwest. Local nick has asked if you want to visit the scene.'

'When was Kevin found?' Jack asked.

'Couple of hours ago.'

'OK,' Ben said and hauled himself upright. 'Tegan, ring my opposite number and tell him we're on our way.'

Ben dragged on his jacket and strode from the room, Jack close behind. They got in the car and set off for Tenby.

'What do you reckon, guv?' Jack asked. 'Murder or suicide? Which is more likely do you think?'

'Not a clue. Ask me again when we've had a look at the studio. Put your foot down but make sure we get there in one piece.'

* * *

When SOCO moved in to examine the scene in the studio, Ben and Jack went in search of Bill Hill, the elderly site manager. They found him in a large mobile home, sited close to the entrance of the caravan park. Bill welcomed them inside and made a strong pot of tea.

'We'd like you to tell us what you know about the brothers,' Ben said. 'What you thought of them and what it was like to work for Ian.'

Bill let out a deep breath. 'I'll be honest, I didn't like either of them, Ian or Kevin. Not my type.'

'Why was that, sir?' Jack asked.

Bill snorted. 'London types. People like them will buy up Wales if we don't put a stop to them. Second homes, businesses like this, that have been in Welsh hands for years. They all think they know better than the locals, but if you ask me, having money doesn't make them cleverer than us.'

'Why did you stay on after the caravan park was sold?' Ben asked.

Hill shrugged. 'Where would I go? I've lived on this site for the last thirty years as site manager. Not like I can afford to buy a place at my age. I could never get a mortgage.'

'Sounds to me there's more to it than that,' Jack said.

'Not like I had anything in common with them. Ian was bearable, when he wasn't sticking his nose in, getting in the way. As if I didn't know what I was doing after all these years.' He rubbed his face. 'Bastard even cut my wages when the brothers took over. Told me I only needed pocket money seeing as I lived here rent-free.'

'I wouldn't have been impressed myself,' Jack said. 'Did you challenge him about it?'

'As if he'd listen!'

'What didn't you like about Kevin?' Ben asked.

Hill chuckled. 'You met him. What was your opinion?'

'I'm asking you, sir.'

'Complete wastrel. All that rubbish he painted. Artist? Yeah right. Can't say I was impressed.'

Jack fixed the man in his gaze and said, 'You really didn't like either of them, did you?'

Hill shook his head. 'No, I didn't, but you're barking up the wrong tree. I freely admit I won't miss the pair, but how on earth would I have managed to kill them? I'm an old man, I struggle to walk most days. Besides, I never even met Robin.'

'So you say.'

Hill got to his feet and stuck out his wrists. 'Go on then, arrest me if you think I did it. Slap on the cuffs and get this show on the road.'

Jack didn't react but he didn't drop his gaze.

'Thought not,' Hill said, 'so piss off and leave me alone. I've done nothing wrong.'

The officers left the caravan and walked back to their car.

'Turns out Bill Hill isn't such a nice chap when he's riled,' Jack said.

'No, he isn't and he has a lot to be angry about,' Ben said. 'When we get back to the station, we need to dig into his past. He said he'd lived on the site for thirty years, it'd be good to know what happened in his life to lead him here.'

Chapter thirty-six

Stacey hadn't left her office since the visitors had gone. The information Heidi and Angus had discovered was shocking. Three young women dead. Stacey massaged her temples where a fierce headache had taken up residence, gazed through the window above her desk and spotted a tiny wren hopping about in the bushes.

Smiling, she opened a drawer beneath her desk and rummaged around in the paperclip graveyard until she found a strip of painkillers. She swallowed a couple with a mouthful of cold coffee and looked back at the screen. Before Heidi had left, she had handed over a flash drive containing copies of her research and the information Angus had recovered from the cloud. Stacey had spent a couple of hours learning about the lives of the three teenagers who had died. On the flash drive were links to their Facebook accounts and each contained hundreds of photographs of the girls. Pictures of holidays, friends, pets and selfies of over-made-up faces, new outfits and hairstyles. She swallowed a lump in her throat and went to the kitchen in search of fresh coffee.

While the kettle boiled, she opened the back door. She stood on the step and filled her lungs with mountain air, smelt garden bonfire smoke and smiled sadly. Those poor women wouldn't ever see another autumn. She was about to close the door when Ben appeared at the end of the cottage. She hastily wiped her face.

'Hi, Sherlock. I'd forgotten you were coming. Sorry, there's no supper.'

Ben moved closer and pulled her to him. 'Are you OK, *cariad*? Has something happened?'

She nodded. She didn't want to cry but didn't trust herself to speak. Ben closed the back door and steered her to a chair.

'What's up, Pumpkin? Tell me what has upset you.'

Stacey took a deep, steadying breath. 'Heidi came over and left a flash drive containing her research into the spiking epidemic.' She waved a hand at the laptop on the table. 'Help yourself. I'll rustle up a quick meal.'

Ben frowned, opened the laptop and tapped the mouse to wake it up. He scrolled through the files while Stacey began constructing a tomato sauce for a spaghetti bolognaise. She didn't need to see the images again, she knew she would never forget them.

* * *

After supper, the couple retreated to the cosy living room and stretched their feet out towards the fire in the grate.

'Disturbing stuff on that memory stick,' Ben said. 'Shame Heidi's mate couldn't provide anything tangible – names, addresses, an IP address, something.'

'She said he's working on it. He'll let us know as soon as he finds anything like that.'

Ben nodded. 'I'm assuming Erica's seen this? It's her case after all.'

'Yes, she knows. Did you hear that Cardiff nicked the kid who was doing the spiking?'

'Jack told me. He also said the kid is playing dumb. Cardiff have been granted an extension, so they'll have another go in the morning.'

Stacey snuggled closer. 'Tell me again about Kevin.'

Ben sighed heavily. 'God, what a mess. Initial evidence points towards suicide. Jack found a small canvas with what appears to be a suicide note. Ian's widow confirmed the handwriting belongs to Kevin.'

'What did it say?'

'Usual sort of stuff, goodbye cruel world.'

'No chance the killer got to him?'

'I don't think so. No card found in his mouth, and he wasn't completely naked. Still had his socks and underpants on.'

'Your suspect list is shrinking.'

'I know.' Ben groaned and rubbed his face. 'Impossible to solve a crime without physical evidence or any witnesses. I have no idea where we go from here.' He untangled himself from Stacey's arms, stirred the embers in the grate and added a fresh log.

'Any updates regarding Pete the Pot?' Stacey asked.

'Not really. The magistrate remanded him and he'll go to Crown in due course. Intent to supply controlled substances.'

'I'm so pleased BB got police bail. I can't imagine how someone who'd lived such an isolated life in the mountains would adjust to prison.'

'Hope it doesn't come to that,' Ben said. 'I had a word with Eddie and he's convinced he can prove Bronwen acted to defend her father. He'd helped her to prepare a statement about the abuse Myfanwy dished out to her family – such an awful story. Jack was really rattled by it.'

'BB and Eddie came for lunch before he drove back to Monkton and he seemed confident. How long do you think it will be before the CPS make a decision?'

'No idea. Ollie and Tegan collected statements from Iolo and Gwen and they have been passed on. They matched exactly what Bronwen told us. Eddie hopes the CPS will take the view that a prosecution is not in the public interest. To be honest, I'm not at all convinced a jury would convict. I wouldn't, even though the physical evidence is clear.' He yawned. 'I'm bushed. Fancy a hot chocolate before bed?'

'Good idea.' Stacey uncurled from the sofa. 'I'll make some and bring it upstairs. You can go and warm the sheets.'

* * *

Ben didn't sleep well. He tossed and turned all night, and had to drag himself out from beneath the duvet when the alarm went off at seven. Stacey got up with him and insisted he ate a bowl of porridge before he left for work. After he'd gone, she tidied the kitchen, cleaned out the grate in the living room and put on a load of washing. She carried a mug of strong and black to the office and switched on the computer. While she waited for the machine to boot up, she picked up the phone and dialled her editor's number.

'Sam Jenkins,' he growled.

'Hi, boss,' Stacey said.

'Morning. Are you ringing to tell me your feature is finished?'

'No, not really. Everything has become much more complicated.'

'Oh? Spill the beans then.'

After receiving Sam's assurance that he would keep the information strictly to himself, Stacey recounted details of the fast-moving spiking story, as well as the fact that BB had made a statement to police regarding her mother's death.

'So,' Sam said, 'the cops aren't any closer to solving the murders?'

'No, but their suspect list is shrinking. Kevin Townsend was found dead in his studio yesterday. Looks like suicide.'

'Bloody hell.' Sam took a deep breath. 'How much of this can we print?'

'I'll do some more research and check with the police, but I'll send you a piece about the suicide, and another reporting the arrest of the kid who has been charged with spiking offences. The rest of the stuff can't be reported until we have the full story. No point in only printing half of it, is there?'

'None at all,' Sam grouched. 'Do you think Heidi's friend will be able to find the footage you talked about on the dark web?'

'He's a clever cookie so I'm hoping he can. Whoever is responsible for the deaths of three teenagers, beautiful girls who should have had their lives stretching in front of them, must be properly punished.'

'OK then, send over what you've got and ring me the second we can go public with the rest.'

'Will do. We'll speak again soon.'

Stacey hung up. She reread the two articles, made a few changes, corrected a couple of typos, then emailed them to Sam. She shut off the computer, went to the hall and laced on her boots, then put on a waterproof coat and left the cottage. She needed a walk, she wanted to banish the saturating misery that had seemingly taken root in her heart and hoped a wander along the riverbank would wash the sadness away so she could think more clearly.

* * *

Ben had once again been reviewing the murder case most of the morning so when his phone rang, he answered immediately, glad of the distraction.

'DCI James.'

'Front desk, sir,' a voice said. 'There's a couple here who would like a word with you.'

'Did they say what about?'

'Something to do with the murder in Cilmery it would seem.'

'Really? OK then, put them in the back office. I'll be straight down.'

Ben hung up, shrugged into his jacket and walked downstairs with Jack in tow. Ben pushed open the door of the small room. Sitting at the table was a couple, probably in their sixties, vending machine cups of tea in front of them. The man got to his feet and held out his hand. Ben offered his own and waved the man back to his seat.

'Good morning,' Ben said. 'I'm DCI James and my partner is DS Trent. You are?'

'Mr and Mrs Bailey. I'm Alan and my wife is Anna. We live in Builth, one of the houses near the river.'

'Pleased to meet you,' Ben said, and the officers took seats opposite the couple. 'How can we help? The desk sergeant told me you would like to talk about the murder in Cilmery.'

'That's right,' Alan said. He opened a plastic carrier bag and removed a small black pouch. He unzipped the pouch and slipped out a square device with a screen on one side.

'What's that?' Jack asked.

'The dashcam from Anna's car,' Alan explained. 'She's been having difficulties with it so this morning I took a proper look and discovered a short recording, taken after dark. The image wasn't great, but it looks as though there is someone running across the road.'

Anna took up the story. 'It was the road next to Llewelyn's monument. A few weeks ago, on my way home from my sister's in Llandovery, I drove through Cilmery and the car suddenly squealed at me and put the brakes on. It's a new Toyota. I'm still getting used to it and forgot all about the incident until Alan found the recording.'

'That's why the footage was still stored on the dashcam, because the automatic brake had been applied,' Alan said. 'Anyway, the date rang a bell, so I dug through the pile of old newspapers and saw it had been taken the night that man was killed.'

He passed the device across the table and Jack took it from his hand.

'If you press play,' Alan said, 'you'll see the clip. It is very short, just a few seconds, so don't blink.'

The detectives stared at the screen. Jack pushed play and they spotted a glimpse of a blurry shadow flit in and out of the headlights.

'Play it again,' Ben said.

The clip flickered on the screen for a second time.

Ben looked up at the Baileys. 'We need to keep this for a few days I'm afraid. The desk sergeant will issue you a receipt and I'll return your dashcam as soon as possible.'

'Do you think this does have something to do with the murder?' Anna asked.

'It is possible,' Ben said. 'Think back to that night for me. Did you see anything at all? Vehicles parked in the lay-by? Anyone walking on the road?'

Anna shook her head. 'No, I didn't even see the person on the camera. The alarm on the car made me jump out of my skin and I looked at the instrument panel.' She took a deep breath, reliving the moment. 'I might have swerved a little bit and... oh.'

'What?' Jack asked.

'You know, there was a vehicle in the lay-by, a small van. I saw my lights in the wing mirror as I wobbled.'

'Think carefully, Mrs Bailey. Are you absolutely sure you didn't see anything else? No one by the van? Nothing?'

'No, I'm sorry, that's all I saw.'

Ben got to his feet. 'Thank you for bringing this in. If you wouldn't mind hanging on here a moment. I'll have an officer come down to take formal statements.'

Alan stood and held out his hand again. 'Glad to be of service,' he said.

Outside in the corridor Ben said, 'Go and find a car, Jack. I'll nip upstairs, let Tegan know what's going on and arrange the statement taking, then we'll pay Heidi a visit. If anyone can do anything with that awful grainy footage, she can.'

Chapter thirty-seven

Ben dropped into the passenger seat and as Jack pulled away he tapped out a text message to Stacey: "Sorry. Can't make tonight. Work. Bx". He took hold of the grab rail as Jack sped towards Heidi's basement flat in Brecon. Turning into her road, Jack was pleased to see Heidi's truck parked next to the kerb, and pulled up to the bumper. The detectives left the car, walked down the stone steps and banged on the door. After a few moments' wait, it was opened. Heidi, barefooted, stood on the doormat, wearing an oversized Welsh rugby shirt, a large No.1 on the front.

'Hey, guys,' she said. 'What are you doing here?'

'We need some help,' Ben said. He held out the dashcam in its pouch. 'There's a very short clip on this. I'm hoping and praying you can clean up the image to make it useful.'

Heidi waved the detectives inside, took the device from Ben's hand and padded to her desk. She plugged the device into her computer, downloaded the file and watched as it zipped past her eyes. She replayed it twice more.

'What is this?' she asked.

Ben told her when the footage had been recorded and how it came into his possession.

'Do you think the figure crossing the road is the murderer?' Heidi asked.

'It's the only real lead we've got,' Jack said. 'Any coffee around?'

'Help yourself,' Heidi said as she began to work on the fuzzy video.

The bedroom door opened and Erica walked into the living room, dressed in shirt and jeans, also barefooted.

'Hi, lads,' she said. 'Did I hear Jack say you had a lead?'

Ben smiled. 'Afternoon. Yes, with a bit of luck. Sorry to disturb you both.'

'No sweat. Work always comes first, right?' She crossed the room and peered over Heidi's shoulder. 'Make enough coffee for all of us, Jack.'

'This is rubbish quality,' Heidi muttered.

'We need it fast,' Ben said. 'Any chance your mate Angus could help?'

'It's a one-person job. I can probably do something with it, but maybe not enough for identification purposes.' She glanced up from her screen. 'Don't hover, either of you. I don't function well with an audience.'

Ben and Erica moved away and sat on the long Chesterfield. Jack delivered mugs to the low table, another to Heidi's desk, then joined the others.

'How is the questioning of Baseball Cap Boy going?' Ben asked.

Erica sighed. 'Not great. Got himself a solicitor and read a prepared statement that said practically nothing.'

'Unlike you not to squeeze something out of a prisoner,' Jack said.

'His brief advised him to give a no comment interview and that's what he's done. He's bound to be remanded at court tomorrow, so we'll catch up with him after he's spent a couple of nights in Cardiff jail.'

'I'm surprised to see you here,' Ben said. 'Day off?'

'Early shift,' Erica said. 'Clocked off at two.'

An uncomfortable silence settled in the room, the only sounds the tap and rattle of computer keys and the throaty tick of an antique grandfather clock leaning against the wall next to the front door. Ben resisted the urge to look at his watch and gazed around the flat. He read the spines of books on the shelves, but didn't recognise any of the authors' names. He studied the row of CDs, spotted a few bands and singers he'd heard of, but the myriad of classical titles meant little to him. He was about to suggest he'd come back later when Heidi stood and walked towards the living room area. She held a memory stick in her fingers.

'Have you done it?' Ben asked, scrabbling to his feet.

'As much as I can and as I warned, nowhere near good enough to identify the individual in the road, however...'

'What?' Jack asked.

'I've cleaned up the clip and I'm convinced the figure is male, late teenager, early twenties maybe.'

'How can you tell that?'

'Mainly because of the clothing, the trainers in particular. The headlights hit his shoes and a clearer image was captured.' She topped up her mug. 'Come and take a look on the screen.'

They all crowded behind Heidi as she pointed out the shoes. 'Those are expensive, a must-have for that age group, if you're a lad. Team that up with the hoodie, unlikely that's going to be anyone over thirty. Skinny too, underdeveloped so I say younger.' She tapped the keyboard and the image moved in single frames, then she paused it again and tapped the bottom right of the screen. 'What does that look like to you?'

'The offside, front wing of a vehicle,' Jack said. 'Mrs Bailey was right, there was a van.'

Heidi nodded. 'I'll keep working with this but don't expect miracles. I can only find stuff that is actually there to find.'

'Great, thanks,' Ben said. 'I'll be at the station, ring if you discover anything.'

'Of course.'

'Nice to see you, Erica,' Jack said. 'Good luck with your spiker.'

Heidi showed them out. They got back in the car and returned to the station at a more sedate pace.

'What d'you think, guv?' Jack asked. 'The guy on the video is right for Kevin Townsend.'

'I'd already thought that, but he said he was in his studio all night when Ian was killed.'

'Only really got his word for that though. Mr Hill said he thought Kevin was working in the studio all night, but he didn't confirm categorically he was there.'

'No confessions in the suicide note. Nothing to indicate a guilt trip.' Ben sighed heavily. 'We need to positively identify the guy on the dashcam. Bloody shame more of the vehicle wasn't captured. Number plate would have been dead handy.'

Jack chuckled. 'Yeah, wouldn't it. Trouble is, life nearly always doesn't work that way. Fingers crossed Heidi has some more magic up her sleeves.'

'I'm always grateful she helps us out now and again. Apart from her complete disregard of the rules, she was a very useful copper.'

* * *

Stacey was still struggling mentally due to the facts of the spiking case and wandered around the cottage like a lost child. She'd contemplated trying to get in touch with the dead women's families, but each time she picked up the phone, her fingers refused to tap in their numbers. She wasn't sure that knowing their loved ones had been murdered, rather than dying from a rare and shocking condition, would help any of them. True, the stories would come out eventually, but Stacey was certain hearing such awful news from a police officer was way better than being doorstepped by a journalist. She had covered some dreadful stories in the past but this one had really affected her. Maybe it was because Erica had been a victim and could so easily have been one of the unfortunate few.

Stacey stayed out of the office. She knew if she switched on the computer she would look at the Facebook accounts of the young victims and also knew her heart couldn't bear much more. She caught up on long-put-off chores, mucked out the cupboard under the stairs, dragged in firewood from the log shed, tidied the larder and defrosted the chest freezer, a job she detested. She wished Ben would come over but knew he was busy. When the sun went down she made supper and ate it in front of the telly but couldn't concentrate on the film she'd chosen. Just after nine she gave up, took a hot bath, went to bed early and surprisingly dropped off within ten minutes, mind and body only too happy to shut down.

A couple of hours later, just after midnight, the bedside phone jolted her awake and she snatched up the handset.

'Hello,' she mumbled, voice heavy with sleep.

'It's Heidi. Get up and drive towards Swansea right now!'

'What's going on?'

'Angus has been in touch. He sent a real-time link of a woman lying on a bed in what looks like a motel room. The signal came from the Swansea area. We must find her. Call me when you're close. We're already on the road.'

Heidi disconnected the call and Stacey scrabbled out of bed, dressed quickly, grabbed her kitbag from the office and ran out to the car. She backed out of the drive and shot off along the Llandovery road. The night was cold and clear but a frost had yet to settle so the road was damp, not icy. Even so, she kept a wary eye out for sleepy sheep. Her mobile rang as she turned onto the main road. She answered using the hands-free kit and heard Erica's voice.

'Are you on your way?' she asked.

'Yes, where are you?'

'Heading towards the motorway. There are a few motels around Swansea and we can't pinpoint where the victim is. Meet us at Swansea West, junction 47. ETA?'

'Bit of luck less than an hour.'

'See you there, outside the motel. Get a move on.'

Chapter thirty-eight

Stacey took the A40 as far as Llandeilo, then turned onto the A483, joined the motorway at Pont Abraham and travelled towards Swansea West. Turning into the services, she spotted Heidi's truck parked outside the motel, pulled up alongside and opened her window.

'Found her?' she asked.

'She's not here,' Erica said. 'Heidi is ringing the others. No luck so far.'

'How does the girl look? Are her vital signs on the screen like before?'

'Yes and her blood oxygen levels are dropping. We have to find her soon.'

Heidi finished her call. 'Pont Abraham. Stacey, get in the truck. I drive faster than you.'

Stacey transferred vehicles and Heidi spun the tyres as she powered out of the services, joined the motorway and headed west. Erica began making calls, she rang for an ambulance and contacted the local police station to round up reinforcements.

'How has this happened again?' Stacey asked. 'Baseball Cap Boy is still in custody, isn't he?'

'Yes,' Erica said, 'but his driver is in the wind. Traffic is searching the system for the van he used last time, he might still be on the road. We'll get him, I know we will.'

Stacey peered through the front seats and saw that Heidi was travelling at over 90mph. As the truck blasted past Pontardulais, it picked up a police tail, sirens blaring, lights strobing across the surface of the road.

'Ignore it,' Erica said.

'I intend to,' Heidi said. 'We're only a couple of miles out.'

'Don't let him pass you,' Erica warned and tapped her mobile again. 'I'll see if I can get him to back off. Last thing we need now is a stinger across the carriageway.'

Stacey peered through the back window and swallowed hard as she saw the patrol car only a couple of feet away from the truck's bumper, its siren deafening. A hundred yards from the exit, Heidi signalled her intention to leave the carriageway and hit the start of the slip road, her foot still on the accelerator. Approaching the large roundabout at the top of the incline, she waited until the last moment before squeezing the brakes and slaloming a little, the police car not far behind. Heidi turned into the car park, slowed rapidly, wove through parked cars and pulled up outside the motel.

'Deal with the cops, E,' Heidi said. 'Stacey, come with me.'

Stacey slung her kitbag over her shoulder, scrambled out of the back seat and followed her friend inside the building. Heidi ran past reception, barrelled through a set of double fire doors and began hammering on doors.

'Open up!' she yelled. 'Police!'

Bedroom doors began to swing open, bemused and half-asleep patrons in nightclothes appeared in the corridor. Heidi made a second run, more doors opened until just one, number six, remained closed. With hardly a breath, she let fly with one of her booted feet. Plywood splintered, the door burst open and Heidi dashed inside.

'Got her!' Stacey heard her yell. 'She's bad. Find the bloody paramedics.'

Stacey turned and headed back towards the main entrance, ignoring the many angry complaints flung at her back as she ran. Reaching the glass entrance, she saw an ambulance pull up and a pair of green-clad paramedics leap out. Stacey pushed open the heavy doors.

'This way,' she shouted. 'Room six. Down the hall.' She pointed and they followed her directions.

Stacey went out to the car park. A total of four police cars were now parked next to the truck and Erica stood in the middle of a group of uniformed officers issuing orders. Unwilling to get involved, Stacey turned back inside and approached the shocked-looking receptionist.

'Who booked into room six?' she demanded. 'Tell me.'

'W… w… what?' the young man stammered.

'Simple enough question. Who's in room six?'

He tapped the computer keyboard. 'Says here, Shane Gibbon and his sister. He said she'd had a skinful, so he carried her to the room then went out for coffee to sober her up. He's not back yet. What is this all about?'

'You'll find out soon enough. The police will want to talk to you.'

Stacey quickly took her small point-and-shoot camera and snatched a couple of shots of the man, another clutch of a small gathering of disgruntled, pyjama-clad customers advancing on reception, then returned to the car park. No one noticed as she removed her Nikon from the kitbag and captured the scene, blue lights reflecting off the damp tarmac and emergency vehicles. She sensed movement behind her, turned to see a laden stretcher roll out of the front door and watched as paramedics loaded it into the ambulance. One climbed in the back, the driver slammed the doors, got into the driver's seat and fired up the engine. Siren and lights blared to life as it headed towards the motorway. Not seeing any sign of Heidi, Stacey made her way back to room six.

Heidi was pacing, mobile held to her ear, a smoke detector she had torn from the ceiling in her other hand.

'OK, Angus, I get that ... Yes, I agree,' she said. 'Piggyback is a great idea, just make sure you sit tight and hang on. I want these scumbags like a dog wants ice cream.' She listened. 'Yeah, returning to the flat. No more to do here. I'll check in when I arrive and, Angus, remember what I said. Do not lose touch with this.' She hung up and looked at Stacey.

'What now?' Stacey asked.

'Back to Brecon.'

'What about Erica?'

'She'll find her own way home.'

They strode along the hall, slipped past the heated discussions at the desk and went out to the truck. Stacey settled in the passenger seat, while Heidi had a few words with Erica before climbing in, backing out of the parking space and rejoining the motorway.

'I'll drop you back at your car,' she said.

'What are you going to do when you get home?' Stacey asked.

'Help Angus follow the transmission. An extra pair of eyes never goes amiss in a situation like this.' Heidi accelerated past a slow-moving HGV loaded with steel. 'Not only that, Ben and Jack popped round earlier. Gave me some shitty footage from a dashcam I want to have another look at.'

'Anything I can do?' Stacey asked. 'There must be something.'

'Maybe,' Heidi said. 'Come to the flat. You can keep the coffee coming if nothing else.'

* * *

Stacey did as Heidi suggested, she drove to Brecon, parked behind the truck and let herself in through the unlocked front door. Heidi was at her desk, immersed in cyberspace. She didn't acknowledge Stacey's arrival but grunted when a mug appeared next to the keyboard.

Stacey retreated to the leather sofa, sipped her own drink and gazed around the room, much as Ben had a few hours earlier. The flat was warm and cosy and Stacey was tired. The chase on the motorway had been nerve-wracking, the stress of the situation at the motel exhausting and the soft rattle of the computer keyboard was hypnotic. She nodded and felt her eyes closing, fought sleep – and lost. Hours later, she felt a hand on her shoulder, opened her eyes and saw Heidi looking down at her.

'Fat lot of good you were,' Heidi said. 'Worse than that, you've dribbled on the leather.'

Stacey struggled upright. 'God, I'm so sorry.'

Heidi grinned. 'Just kidding. Take a shower to wake up, then come and have a look at the progress I've made.'

'Is Erica here?'

'No. She's at work. A patrol car caught the van and its driver. The receptionist has also been pinched so Erica has interviews to conduct. Now – shower.'

Stacey shuffled into the bathroom, turned on the shower, stripped and stood beneath the hot jets of water. By the time she returned to the main room she almost felt human. She moved close to the desk and stood behind Heidi.

'Show me what you've got,' she said. 'Do you know where the live feed ended up?'

'Not yet. I spoke to Angus and he's still tracking it while it bounces from server to server right across the planet. He just needs to hang on tight until it lands. I had more luck with the dashcam footage. Take a seat and have a look.'

Stacey perched on a wooden stool and stared at the screen while Heidi called up the short clip and played it through.

'Blimey,' Stacey said. 'Blink and you'd miss it. Where was this taken?'

'A483, Cilmery, next to the monument. I'll slow it down. Take another look.' Heidi ran the video.

'There's someone running across the road,' Stacey said. 'Any idea who?'

'Not really, only that they are probably male and young, however...'

'What?'

'Without getting too technical, dashcams are set up so if there is an accident or a sharp braking event, it records then stores the resulting footage on the device.'

'OK, with you so far.'

'Most of these gizmos also hang on to ten seconds before the incident and ten seconds after. The owner of this one said it was malfunctioning, and it sort of was, but' – Heidi tapped at the keyboard – 'I've discovered the extra seconds. Watch.'

Stacey peered at the screen as the longer recording played.

'Is that a van parked in the lay-by?' she asked.

'Yes, it is,' Heidi said triumphantly. 'Better than that, a number plate.'

'Do you know who the van belongs to?'

Heidi grinned. 'Owned by the builders' merchants in Llanwrtyd Wells.'

'Bloody hell,' Stacey said. 'That's where Idris Jones works. Finder of the body on the bird.'

Chapter thirty-nine

Jack steered through wide metal gates and tried to navigate around the deepest muddy puddles pockmarking the yard at the builders' merchants on the edge of Llanwrtyd. A patrol car containing Ollie and Tegan followed and pulled across the gateway to hamper any possible escape. Jack and Ollie set off towards the timber sheds, Ben and Tegan entered the attached hardware shop.

A short, slightly dumpy, balding man looked up from behind the counter and smiled at his prospective customers.

'Good morning,' he said. 'Shocking day. What can I do for you?'

Ben flashed his warrant card and the man's face lost its smile.

'Is there a problem, officers?' he asked. 'I'm Colin Williams, the boss.'

'Is Idris Jones in today?' Ben asked.

'Yes, he's working in the sheds. Why do you want him?'

'Does the business own a van?' Tegan asked. 'Dark blue Berlingo?' She recited the registration number.

'Yes,' Colin said, 'that's ours, it's parked at the back of the building.'

'Do you allow employees to use the van for private mileage?' Ben asked.

'Yeah, as long as they don't take the piss.' Colin laughed. 'By that I mean no trips to Scotland.'

Ben nodded and Tegan made notes in her pocketbook.

'Do you keep a record of who borrows it?' she asked. 'In case someone picks up a speeding fine or similar?'

'I do, yes.' Colin ferreted about under the counter and dragged out a dark blue binder, its edges split, cardboard fibres peeping out from the plastic cover. He handed it to Ben who peered at the list of entries.

'These entries,' Ben said, pointing to a page. 'Says here that most weekends Idris borrows the van at six o'clock Saturday evening and returns it to the yard on Mondays. Are those entries correct?'

'Bound to be,' Colin said. 'Anyone writing fiction in the log can't use the van again.'

'Looks like Idris borrowed it regularly, more than anyone else.'

Colin nodded. 'He passed his test a few months ago and can't afford his own vehicle. I like being able to help him out, nice lad, good worker. What's he supposed to be mixed up with?'

A movement outside the shop window caught Ben's attention and he saw Idris in handcuffs, being walked through heavy rain and posted into the back of the patrol car.

'You're arresting him?' Colin asked. 'Whatever you think he's done, you're wrong. As I said, good kid. Came up from the Valleys looking for work. Gotta admire that.' Colin squinted through the window. 'What will happen to him?'

'That very much depends on what he tells us,' Ben said. 'Thank you for your assistance, Mr Williams. I'm sorry, but we will need to take the van. I'll send a tow truck and be in touch again soon.'

Ben and Tegan left the shop. Jack and Ollie drove out of the yard with their prisoner, Tegan tucked in behind, and they returned to the station. Idris was booked into the custody suite, his belt, trainers and jewellery removed, replaced by a pair of shower shoes.

'I don't get this,' Idris said at regular intervals shaking his head. 'I really don't get this.'

The custody officer escorted Idris to a cell and after checking the emergency buzzer inside was working, closed the metal door with a clang and turned the key. The officers went upstairs to the squad room to prepare the questioning.

'That was smooth,' Ollie said. 'Nicked him on a charge of supply. Didn't want to tip him off to what's coming. Came with us as quiet as a lamb.'

Ben sat at the head of the table. 'Right then,' he said. 'We'll give Idris a little while before we tackle him. In the meantime, Ollie, go down to the garage and watch SOCO take the van apart. Make sure they don't cut any corners.'

'Yes, sir.' Ollie left the room.

Jack sat next to his boss.

'So, how are we going to play this?' he asked.

'We need to make Idris believe we know more than we do. Unless SOCO finds anything in the van, we still don't have any evidence to link him to the killings.'

'Do you really think he's capable of murder?' Jack asked.

'The footage from the dashcam puts him and the van in the right place at the right time. The trainers we removed from his feet match exactly those recorded on the video, and he was the finder of the first body. Another right place, right time. Unless he can satisfactorily explain what he was doing in Cilmery during the wee small hours, I reckon we've got our man.'

'Do you think he was working alone?'

'I still can't see how that would have been possible,' Ben said. 'We need to lean on him, force him to give up the name of his partner in crime, and discover a motive. I don't think Idris was the mastermind behind this, but what was his reason for getting involved?'

'I'll work with Elsa,' Jack said. 'Maybe he has a sister or someone in the family who has been a victim of assault.'

Ben nodded. 'I'll give you an hour, then we'll go downstairs and have a crack at him.'

* * *

Stacey had arrived home from Brecon still feeling utterly worn out, so she went to bed and slept until lunchtime. When she woke, she made a light lunch of soup and a cheese sandwich. She washed the dishes and, feeling less like a soggy paper bag, went to the office and began work by uploading the photos she had taken at the services. The pictures captured the event perfectly and she began crafting an article to go with them. After an hour or so, the phone rang and shattered her concentration. She answered grumpily.

'Stacey Logan.'

'It's me,' Heidi said. 'Thought you'd appreciate an update.'

'I would, thanks. How did Erica get on with the van driver?'

Heidi made a rude noise. 'Another kid who believes he was working for an online company providing "experiences" for bored teenagers.'

'Did he know Richard Price had been arrested?'

'No, but he received a message from his "employers" to say his partner was sick and to – I quote – "fulfil the contract alone". No bloody use at all.'

'Where did the message come from? Can you trace the sender?'

'I'm doing my best without Price's phone, but I'm supporting Angus. If we can unpick the encryption on the dark web, work out who is behind this scheme and their motivation, the dominoes should tumble.'

'I'm working on an article,' Stacey said, 'regarding the events of last night. Got some great pictures to go with it. I'm hoping the piece will encourage women to take extra care when they go out clubbing, and the club owners to take better care of their patrons.'

'Good idea, but make sure you don't mention the surveillance stuff. I don't want any of the scumbag organisers to come across it and disappear. I want them caught. Buried alive in a fire ants' nest if I had my way. Heard anything from Ben? Do you know if he's nicked Idris?'

'Not heard anything yet, but he's due later for supper and a sleepover.'

'Have a nice evening, but be careful what you tell him.'

'Of course. Has Eddie Lazarus been in touch?'

'He left a message. Said he's waiting on the CPS to make a decision. Iolo is still in hospital and improving, Bronwen is staying with her sister.'

'Fingers crossed then. We'll speak again soon.'

Stacey hung up, then she dialled Sam Jenkins' number and informed him a new article was on its way and that more would follow. She smiled as she ended the call. Even when he received good news, her boss was still grumpy.

She went to the kitchen and began preparing a venison casserole for supper. She opened the back door and saw the rain had stopped. A soggy-looking robin perched on a low branch, a little red ball, feathers fluffed up against the approaching hours of darkness. Stacey took a handful of suet from a storage jar and scattered it on the wet lawn. The bird dropped from the branch to the grass and began searching for morsels before the last of the light vanished. Late autumn was not Stacey's favourite time and she recalled the poem by Thomas Hood, "No flowers, no leaves, no birds! – November!" It summed up how she felt perfectly.

Casserole ready for cooking, she slid it into the Aga, fed another log into the fire box, then went to the living room and put a match to the paper and kindling in the grate. Once the fire had settled, she put the guard in place and returned to the office to finish the article for the newspaper.

Chapter forty

Idris Jones was brought to interview room one by a uniformed officer who settled the prisoner at the table, then retreated to stand against the tiled wall next to the door. Jack leaned over the recording machine, switched it on and verbally logged the date, time and those present in the room before Ben began the session.

'Right then, Idris, before we go any further, you need to know you are entitled to legal representation. If you don't have your own solicitor, we can provide one for you. Do you understand?'

'Yeah, I get it,' Idris said. 'I've already said I don't need one. Ain't done nothing wrong like.'

'If you change your mind at any point, let us know and we'll stop the interview.'

'What would be good is if someone tells me what I'm doing here in the first place. You nicked me for drugs but I'm not a dealer.'

'We've received a tip-off that you've been supplying GHB locally,' Jack said.

'That's rubbish, man. I don't take that shit and don't sell it either.'

'Not what we've heard,' Jack said.

'Then someone is winding you up like. I don't sell drugs.'

Jack shrugged and Ben took over the questioning.

'Tell us again how you discovered Robin Townsend's body on the statue in Llanwrtyd.'

Idris groaned. 'Not this again.'

'Humour me,' Ben said.

'I told you. I saw him in the pub getting pissed with his mates, then later saw him on the kite on The Square. Your girlfriend was with me – ask her.'

'Not just pissed,' Jack said, 'also doped up on GHB which we believe you gave him.'

Idris blinked. 'What? No. I didn't give him nothing. You can't pin that on me. No bloody chance.'

'Peter Butler, aka Pete the Pot, says different.'

'Then he's lying.' Idris folded his arms and leaned back in his seat, trying to look unconcerned.

'We don't think so,' Jack said.

'That's your problem.'

'He's been very helpful.' Jack grinned. 'Doesn't like prison, wants to get out.'

Idris shrugged.

'A witness has come forward to say they saw you in Cilmery the night Robin's brother, Ian Townsend, was also fed copious amounts of the same drug. Found dead, hanging from Llewelyn's monument. What were you doing there?' Ben asked.

'Wasn't me. I weren't there.'

'You told us you were at home in your flat that night,' Jack said. 'Why did you lie to us? I'll be honest, that really doesn't look good. Doesn't do you any favours.'

'I was at home. I'm not lying.'

'Our witness is reliable,' Ben said. 'I have no doubt you were in Cilmery. Just tell us why.'

Idris shook his head and didn't speak.

'Not only that,' Ben continued, 'the work van was seen parked in the lay-by next to the stone.'

'We checked the log at the yard where you work,' Jack said. 'You were using the van that night.' Jack leaned closer to the prisoner. 'I reckon you used the vehicle to take Ian there and then someone else helped you tie him to the stone.'

'You're wrong,' Idris said. 'Just plain wrong and I don't believe you have a witness. This is just a massive wind-up.'

There was a tap on the door. It opened and Ollie peered in, caught Ben's eye and beckoned him out.

Ben got to his feet and said, 'DCI James leaving the room.' He stepped into the corridor. 'What have you got, Ollie?' he asked.

Ollie smiled and held up a small evidence bag. 'SOCO found this,' he said and passed it over. 'A locket, part of a key ring maybe, containing photos of Ian Townsend and his wife. It had slipped beneath the wooden lining in the back of the van.'

'Bloody well done,' Ben said. 'Anything else?'

'They haven't finished yet, but I knew you'd want to see this so I brought it straight over. On my way back to the garage now.'

Ben nodded. 'OK, keep in touch.' He pushed open the door and stepped back inside the room.

'DCI James entering the room,' Jack said.

Ben sat and dangled the plastic bag in front of the prisoner's eyes.

'What's that?' Idris asked.

'A locket belonging to Ian Townsend,' Ben said. 'Found in the work van.'

Idris seemed to stop breathing and Jack chuckled softly.

'Well, well,' Jack said. 'That puts a different light on things. You might as well come clean, Idris. We've got more than enough to charge you with Ian's murder. Physical evidence and a great witness. You're going down, boy.'

Idris closed his eyes, covered his face with his hands and gasped for breath, shoulders heaving.

'You need to talk to us,' Ben said. 'We believe someone else was involved with the murders and attempted murder of Patrick Ryan. Unless you give us a name, we'll charge you with all of it and the court will hand down the maximum sentence. Help us with this and we can put in a word for you. Maybe shorten the jail time a little.'

Idris removed his hands from his face. He was sweating and his eyes were red-rimmed. A solitary tear slipped down one cheek.

'Come on, Idris,' Ben said. 'Do yourself a favour and tell us what we need to know.'

'I need a drink,' Idris said. 'I'm thirsty.'

Ben nodded at the uniformed officer, who slipped out of the room and returned a few moments later with a bottle of Welsh spring water. Idris snatched it, broke the seal and drank deeply. He wiped his wet lips on his sleeve.

'Well?' Jack asked. 'Do you have anything to say? Why did you get involved with these murders? Who recruited you?'

'For fuck's sake,' Idris muttered. 'I didn't kill anyone. Didn't know anyone was going to die.'

Jack pounced. 'So you do know something.'

Idris nodded.

'So tell us,' Ben said. 'I'll help you if I can.'

'They had it coming,' Idris said quietly.

'Tell me why?'

'Cos they were rapists, murderers and abusers, all three of them.'

'To be clear,' Ben said, 'by "three of them", you mean Robin and Ian Townsend and Patrick Ryan?'

Idris nodded.

'How did you know what they had done?' Jack asked. 'Who told you about them?'

Idris shook his head and gulped more water.

'Come on, lad, tell us.'

'Robin was recognised,' Idris said. 'The whole town knew why he'd left London, knew he'd killed his girlfriend and people weren't happy.'

'No one we spoke to admitted knowing about his past,' Ben said.

'They knew. Knew about his brother too, how he'd helped with the killing and how they'd both got away with it.' He took a deep breath. 'Same with that bastard Patrick Ryan, bloody animal, all over the papers he was. People like that shouldn't be allowed to walk around with decent folk. It's not right.' He drank from the bottle. 'Teach them a lesson, that's what he said. Nothing about killing was mentioned.'

'Who said he wanted to teach them a lesson?' Jack asked.

Idris closed his eyes and covered his face.

'Do yourself a favour,' Jack said. 'For crying out loud, give us a name.'

Idris scrubbed at his face and mumbled, 'Derek Brumby in the Stonecroft. The girl who died in London was his best mate's daughter. Told me he nearly had a seizure when Robin walked in the pub and he decided to do something about it.'

Ben immediately called a halt to the interview. Idris was returned to a cell and the detectives ran upstairs to the squad room. Tegan and Elsa looked up as they burst in.

'Ollie still out?' Ben asked.

'Yes, sir. He went back to the garage like you told him to,' Tegan said.

'OK then. Stop what you're doing and come with us, both of you.'

'Where are we going?'

'To nick Derek Brumby. Idris has just told us the man was the instigator of these murders.'

'Bloody hell,' Tegan said. 'I didn't see that coming.'

The women switched off the computers, scrabbled into their jackets and followed Ben and Jack downstairs to the car park. The officers took two cars and sped away from the station towards Llanwrtyd. Twenty minutes later, they pulled up outside the Stonecroft pub. Jack and Elsa made their way to the back of the building, while Tegan accompanied Ben to the front door and stood by his side as he hammered on the old oak.

'Police!' he yelled. 'Open up!'

Tegan peered through one of the windows and spotted Denise Brumby making her way through the bar. Tegan stepped back as the landlady unlocked the door and pulled it open.

'Bleeding hell. Not you lot again,' she said. 'What do you want this time?'

'Where's your husband?' Ben asked.

'Down in the cellar, changing barrels. What do you want him for?'

Ben gently pushed past her, charged down the steep cellar steps and spotted Derek, a crate of bottled beer in his arms. He looked up but didn't speak. Ben took a few steps closer.

'Derek Brumby, I am arresting you on suspicion of murder. You do not have to say anything, but it may harm your defence if you do not mention when questioned something which you later rely on in court. Anything you do say may be given in evidence.'

For a second Ben wondered if Derek would throw the crate at him. He saw the man's arm muscles tense and prepared to defend himself. A shadow at the top of the stairs announced Jack's arrival and Derek, presumably not liking the odds, put down the crate and stood perfectly still as handcuffs were applied. Jack encouraged him up the stairs and into the bar. As soon as Denise spotted her husband, her face lost all its colour.

'What's going on?' she asked. 'Why have you put him in handcuffs?'

'He's under arrest for murder,' Ben said.

'What? No, that can't be right. My Derek kill someone? Not a chance. This is a bleeding wind-up, that's what this is.'

Ben shook his head as Jack guided Derek out of the pub and locked him in the back of one of the cars. Denise barged past Ben and ran outside. She banged on the window of the car.

'Tell me!' she yelled. 'Tell me what you've done.'

Derek ignored her and wouldn't catch her eye. He lowered his head and stared at the floor.

Ben moved closer. 'You need to step away, Mrs Brumby.'

'This is mad,' she sobbed. 'My Derek ain't done nothing. He's a pussycat, not a bleeding murderer.'

'If you're right, we'll let him go, but for now he comes with us.'

The officers got into the cars and pulled away, leaving Denise standing on the pavement in tears.

Chapter forty-one

Stacey dialled Heidi's number and paced impatiently until her friend answered.

'Speak first, you're paying.'

Stacey chuckled. 'Are you and Erica busy tonight? Only I've made a venison casserole and Ben's just rung to say he'll be in late and won't want supper. Fancy popping over?'

'Venison eh? Sounds marvellous. We'll bring some wine. OK if I also bring a plus one?'

'Not a problem. I used my largest casserole dish so there's plenty.'

'Cool. Give us forty minutes. Have you got ice cream?'

Stacey chuckled. 'Always since I met you. Drive safely.'

She disconnected the call, peeled more potatoes and put them in to roast. By the time she had prepared extra vegetables, thrown together an apple crumble and set the table, she heard the rumble of Heidi's truck in the drive. She wiped her hands and opened the front door, anxious to see who the extra guest would be. One of the back doors opened and a slim, lanky lad with an untamed shock of hair, unfolded his large frame and stepped out.

'Hey, Angus!' Stacey called and walked down the path to the gate. 'This is a lovely surprise. How are you?'

'Good thanks, Ms Logan, and you?'

'It's Stacey, you know it is. Come in out of the damp.'

'I think I might be responsible,' Angus said. 'Every time I come to Wales the weather is damp.' He looked up at the cottage. 'Love your place. Been here long? Fancy selling it?'

Stacey laughed. 'Ages and no.'

Heidi stomped up the path, Erica behind her.

'Are we eating *al fresco*?' Heidi asked. 'No? Then shift out of the way, I'm cold.'

'Gosh, you're in a good mood,' Stacey said.

'Sarcasm doesn't suit you and I'm in a foul mood.'

Stacey and Angus moved to one side then followed the women into the warm kitchen. Heidi was already slouched in the carver and Erica was pouring red wine into glasses.

'So tell me what's up,' Stacey said.

'Let's at least start supper,' Heidi said. 'Venison is my all-time favourite and what we have to talk about will make it difficult to swallow.'

'No problem,' Stacey said, knowing Heidi couldn't be pushed.

Stacey ferried dishes of vegetables to the table then added a large, cast-iron pot. Using a tea towel, she removed the heavy lid and a billow of richly scented steam escaped in a mini mushroom cloud.

'God, Stace,' Heidi said, 'that smells amazing.'

She leaned across the table, poured a glug of wine into the contents of the pot and gave them a quick stir. Erica and Stacey dished out and as soon as everyone was served Stacey took the chance to catch up with Angus.

'You still a spy then?' she asked.

Angus laughed. 'If I told you that I'd have to... I'm not a spy. I work at GCHQ.'

'I know that, but you're not a tea boy or a filing clerk.'

'We don't have those anymore.'

'Filing clerks or tea boys?'

'Either.' He glanced across the table. 'I was pleasantly surprised to see these two back together.'

Stacey nodded but couldn't keep the small talk going. 'I'm sorry, Heidi, but I want to know what you and Angus have uncovered.'

Heidi huffed and put down her fork. 'OK, it comes in two parts. I worked on part one.' She took a deep breath. 'This is how the scheme worked. The mastermind behind it – yet to be identified – set up slick-looking websites. On those sites he – or she – advertised lucrative employment opportunities. Too good to be true stuff, unless of course you're a gullible teenager.'

'Then what?' Stacey asked.

'Basically, recruitment. Photographer, kidnapper and driver. Zero-hours contracts, payments for each "job" made in bitcoin. The organiser worked hard at making everything look kosher, and keeping himself anonymous.

'Why did they use different hotels?' Stacey asked.

'Individual crimes were less likely to be linked – we've already proved that. Anyway, a semi-conscious woman carried to room six every Saturday might be noticed, don't you think?'

Stacey nodded. 'So how did webcams get inside the smoke detectors?'

'The driver, Billy Thompson, works as a maintenance man for the motels,' Erica said. 'Once the "order" was received, he made sure the chosen room was set up.'

'When everything is in place,' Heidi said, 'Richard Price dons his baseball cap and spikes a victim – a photo of the chosen woman previously sent to his phone. She is delivered to the room, Fitbit put on her wrist and then the game begins.'

'Game?' Stacey asked. 'What do you mean?'

Heidi waved her fork at Angus. 'He'll tell you the rest.' She fished around in her bowl, speared a large chunk of meat and put it in her mouth. Stacey turned and looked at Angus.

'Go on then,' she said. 'Tell me the rest.'

Angus took a mouthful of wine, swirled it around his mouth, swallowed, then topped up his glass.

'Have you ever been to a casino?' he asked.

'Couple of times, years ago. Can't say I was impressed. I was covering a story, not gambling.'

'So I'm guessing you've never played roulette?'

Stacey shook her head. 'It looked too complicated. Anyway, I'm too mean to waste money on something like that.'

'In a nutshell, punters predict where the ball will come to rest. You can bet in several ways but the main ones are, black or red, or a number. The odds differ depending on the wager. A single number potentially pays much more than black or red.'

'I get it,' Stacey said, 'but what does roulette have to do with the spiked women?'

'It's the same principle, you just change what you're betting on. Red or black equates to lives or dies. The Fitbit records the victim's vitals, so the number option in a roulette game becomes the time of death.'

Stacey stared at Angus, she felt the ground shift and quiver and she gasped for air. 'No, no, no,' she moaned. 'That can't be right. Tell me you're making this up.'

'Sorry,' Angus said, 'I can't.'

'You know who's behind it though, don't you?'

Angus shook his head. 'Not yet, but I'm still working on it – with Heidi's help.'

'Now you know why I wanted to eat first,' Heidi said. 'I've never come across anything this disgusting before.'

'Who would set up something like this?' Stacey asked.

'Someone with money,' Heidi growled. 'Lots of it.'

'Or,' Erica said, 'someone with no money who wants to be rich.'

'Yeah,' Heidi said, 'or that, but the players will be filthy rich.'

'Ben will be here later,' Stacey said. 'We'll tell him.'

'No,' Angus said, 'we shouldn't. He won't be able to stop the scheme without knowing who's involved. Even then, something like this will be way above his pay grade.'

'We can't keep him in the dark.'

'We have to for now. I spoke to Heidi's pa, Freddie, and informed him what we've discovered. As soon as we can identify the gamblers, he has promised swift and harsh action will be taken. He vowed that no one involved will get away with it.'

* * *

The interview with Derek Brumby had been delayed. He had insisted on having a solicitor to represent him and arranging one so late in the day had been a challenge. Ben and Jack finally made a start just after seven. Derek sat at the table, Dick Nyle, the duty solicitor at his side. The recording machine whirred quietly.

'Right then, Derek,' Ben said. 'Before we begin, do you have anything to say?'

The man raised his eyes to meet Ben's. 'Yes,' he said, 'I do.'

'Let's hear it then.'

'It was me. I killed the Townsend brothers and tried to kill that piece of shit Ryan, but I cocked up. Didn't give him enough GHB and I regret that.'

The admission was unexpected. Ben blinked, took several deep breaths and a few moments to gather his thoughts.

'Thank you for that,' he eventually said, 'but you'll need to tell us the why and how.'

Derek nodded. 'The why is easy,' he said. 'They all deserved it. Women suffered at their hands. They were all arrested, taken to court and allowed to walk away, scot-free. That should never have happened.'

'No,' Ben agreed. 'It shouldn't have.'

'Someone had to do something.' Derek rubbed his face. 'I couldn't believe it when Robin turned up in the pub. Made my blood boil. The woman he killed was my best mate's daughter. Beautiful girl, known her all her life, then that... that bastard, blew her life away like snuffing out a candle.'

'So you planned to kill him?' Jack asked.

Derek shrugged. 'Yeah, pretty much, and that creepy brother of his. They were both involved.'

'How did you devise the method?' Ben asked.

'I needed something' – he searched for the word – 'clean. I'm not a violent man. Couldn't stab anyone or beat them to death, so I got hold of the drugs, slipped them in their drinks and well... there you have it.'

'Why strip your victims and display them like you did?' Jack asked.

'To shame them – and you lot for not doing your jobs properly. I wanted to make a point. Too many men prey on women and too many never see the inside of a court, never mind a jail. I wanted the bodies to be a warning to other out-of-control men. Years ago, criminals' heads were displayed after execution. I thought it was appropriate.'

'You know we have Idris Jones in custody?' Ben asked.

Derek nodded. 'Yes, I do. I should never have got him involved and I'm sorry for that.'

'Then why did you?'

'I asked him to get me the drugs and said too much, but he was bang up for it, got involved by accident really. Anyway, we came up with the plan and just got on with it. The Townsends were easy.' He sighed heavily. 'Idris said it had gone so well that we should take Ryan out too and we nearly did.'

'Why did you put those cards in your victims' mouths?' Jack asked.

'Oh, I don't know. Seemed like a good idea at the time, send a message like I said. #MeToo – U2.' He shrugged again.

'Chief Inspector, it's late and we're all tired,' Dick Nyle said. 'Can I suggest we suspend the interview? My client will be better able to provide a full statement in the morning.'

'Yes, I agree,' Ben said. 'A night's rest would do us all good.' He checked the clock on the wall. 'Interview terminated at 19.47.' He switched off the machine and got to his feet. 'We'll continue this first thing tomorrow.'

The detectives left the room, Derek was returned to his cell and Dick Nyle promised to attend at nine the next morning.

Chapter forty-two

Ben pulled up outside Noddfa just before ten and was surprised to see Heidi's truck parked in the drive, and even more surprised when he walked in the kitchen and found it crammed with guests.

'Hello,' he said. 'What are you all doing here?'

Stacey kissed him on the cheek. 'Helping me eat the huge venison casserole I made, only to be stood up. Hope you had a good reason for letting me down,' she said with a smile.

'I was taking a confession statement from the person responsible for the recent murders,' Ben said, 'so yes, a pretty good reason.'

'Wow,' Stacey said. 'Well done. Who was it?'

'Derek Brumby, landlord of the Stonecroft.'

'Derek?' Stacey asked. 'Are you sure? He doesn't strike me as a killer.'

'Nor me,' Ben said, 'but it certainly looks that way. Told us in detail what he'd done.'

'Better open some more wine then,' Angus said, 'being we have something to celebrate. Evening, by the way.' Angus held out his hand and Ben shook it warmly. 'Good to see you again.'

'You too,' Ben said. 'Any of that casserole left?'

Angus fetched an extra chair from the living room and as Ben ate, he told the group what had led to Brumby's confession.

'We called a halt at about eight o'clock,' Ben said. 'We'll take a formal statement first thing in the morning.' He turned to look at Erica. 'How about your case? How's that going?'

'Nearly done,' she said. 'We've nicked the spiker, Richard Price, and the driver, Billy Thompson. Just one more to go.'

'Oh?' Ben asked.

'We wondered how the female victims were chosen. Both scumbags told us they received a photograph on their phones of the woman to target. As yet, we don't know the ID of that individual, but as you can see' – she waved a hand at Heidi and Angus – 'we have some great people working on that. Having the bad guys' mobiles has helped. I have no doubt the sender will soon be identified.'

'I spoke to my opposite number at Cardiff nick,' Ben said. 'He told me you've been able to link many more cases and that it seems three of the victims died. Is that right?'

'Yes,' Erica said. 'It is. Price and Thompson will go to court on murder charges, but I still want the organisers, not just the bottom feeders.'

'What about the girl with the camera you found in one of the rooms?' Ben asked. 'Will she go to court?'

'She will but on a lesser charge. It's obvious she was scammed into her part, she really believed she was just on a job, but naïvety won't protect her completely. More work to do there.'

Ben nodded and glanced at his watch. 'It's late,' he said. 'I'm sorry, folks, nice as this is, I have to get my head down, busy day tomorrow. Good to see you all. We should have a proper get-together when the cases are wrapped up.'

'I agree,' Heidi said. 'Leave it to me and Angus, I'm sure we'll come up with something suitable.'

Ben got to his feet. Drained the last of his wine, kissed Stacey goodnight and went upstairs. He hadn't realised how tired he was and within minutes of slipping beneath the duvet, he was snoring.

* * *

Erica put down the handset of her desk phone and smiled. She got to her feet, slipped into her jacket and went in search of DS Willis. She eventually found him chatting up one of the civilian staff in the canteen.

'Willis,' Erica called. 'We need to make a house call.'

'What, now?' he asked and held up a plate of curry, chips and rice. 'Can't it wait until I've eaten my lunch?'

'Trust me,' Erica said. 'This will be way better than lunch. Round up a couple of uniforms, we might need some back-up. I'll meet you out back by the car.'

'Where are we going?' Willis asked.

'I'll fill you in on the way. See you in five.'

Erica ran downstairs and through the back door into the yard. She got in the car, fired up the engine and impatiently tapped her fingers on the steering wheel. She saw Willis step out of the station and walk towards her. He opened the passenger door, slipped inside and Erica pulled away before he'd put his seatbelt on.

'Blimey,' he said. 'You're in a hurry.'

Erica didn't reply and concentrated on weaving her way through Cardiff's busy streets, a patrol car hard on her heels. She headed into the main shopping area and pulled up in a narrow side street within sight of the Catholic Cathedral. The patrol car parked behind and the officers got out.

Erica left her own car. 'Follow me guys,' she said and began walking along the road.

She stopped outside a sturdy-looking, blue-painted door, with windows on either side protected with thick wire cages. She raised her fist and pounded on the door. She turned to look back towards the main road and apart from the uniformed coppers, saw no one. She pounded again and eventually heard the sound of bolts being shot and the rattle of a chain, then the door swung open. A man in his forties, hair shorn to disguise early balding and dressed in a suit, looked out.

'We're closed,' he snapped. 'What do you want?'

The detectives held up their warrant cards.

'Need a word with the owner,' Erica said.

'Do you have an appointment?'

Willis laughed and pushed the man to one side of the door. 'Don't be daft, boy, we don't need an appointment. Where's his office?'

'Far side of the dance floor. Door marked "Private", left of the bogs.'

The doorman obviously didn't want to get involved with whatever this was and busied himself securing the main door. Erica strode through the empty room, the scent of stale alcohol filled the air, and the carpet surrounding the dance floor was sticky next to the bar. Night clubs during daylight hours always looked sad and dingy. She spotted the door and barged through, startling the man sitting behind the desk.

'This is a private room,' he protested. 'You can't just storm in here.'

Erica flashed her warrant card for a second time and said, 'I think you'll find we can. On your feet. Jonnie Jones, I am arresting you on suspicion of murder. You do not–'

Jonnie surged upright. 'I'm not having this,' he said. 'No bloody way. Murder?' He laughed. 'I own a club. I'm not a hitman. You've made a mistake, a really big mistake.'

Erica ignored his protests and while Willis applied the handcuffs, she finished reciting the caution. The uniformed officers began rounding up laptops, mobiles and other digital devices and the prisoner was escorted from the club.

Chapter forty-three

After spending three hours cramped inside a small interview room taking Derek Brumby's statement, Ben and Jack needed some time away from the station. They walked to the local cafe and ordered all-day breakfasts.

Derek had told them in detail how the two killings, and one near killing, had taken place. Robin Townsend had been easy, he'd said. Pete the Pot sold a quantity of GHB to Idris which he handed to the landlord, who had no trouble spiking the victim's drink. Idris had pulled the work van up to the back of the pub and helped the not quite unconscious man into the vehicle. Once inside – and being in no state to complain – Robin had been stripped, driven to The Square and positioned on the statue. His clothes had been buried in the planters and within minutes, the Berlingo was back behind the pub.

Ian Townsend hadn't been much more difficult. Derek recounted how Idris had contacted the man. He told Ian a few of Robin's mates were planning to meet in the Prince Llewelyn pub in Cilmery to raise a glass to his brother's memory and invited him along.

'We were surprised he turned up,' Derek had said. 'He recognised both of us from the Stonecroft. We had a couple of pints then I spiked one which Ian drank.'

He told how Idris put Ian in the back of the van and drove him to the outskirts of Builth where he was stripped. His clothes were stowed in his own car which Derek left in the Co-op car park. They returned to the monument, hung their victim on the stone and left.

Derek didn't leave out any detail relating to his crimes, and actually seemed relieved to be able to tell the awful story. He told the detectives where he had bought the rope, how many grams of GHB had been given to each man, even how much Pete the Pot had charged him for it.

The confession had been the most detailed and complete that Ben had ever heard. He did not have a single doubt it would hold up in court and all Ben was waiting for was the CPS to notify him of the expected trial date.

The meals were delivered to the window table and Jack smothered his with brown sauce before digging in.

'What a result!' he said between mouthfuls. 'No loose ends at all. I'll bet CS Bunny Warren is pleased with you.'

Ben smiled. 'Seems to be. Offered me some time off. Stacey reckons we ought to take a mini break, but where would we go in November?'

'Somewhere warm. Florida maybe?'

'Oh God no. I'm not a natural flier. Have to be somewhere closer to home than that. I'd be happy with a few days staycation on the mountain. Must admit I could do with it. This case has been hard work.'

'Bloody lovely when it all clicks into place though and we get to send a murderer to jail,' Jack said. 'I feel a little sorry for him. As he told us, he isn't a violent man, just wanted to right a wrong.'

'We better hope not too many others decide to the do the same thing.' Ben sighed. 'That pair of daft plods in Cardiff didn't do us any favours.'

'What happened to them?'

'They accepted "words of advice".'

Jack shook his head. 'How is it going for Bronwen? Any news from Eddie Lazarus?'

'So far so good from what he tells me. The CPS seem to understand a prosecution wouldn't be in the public interest and I agree. Translating the journal really upset Tegan. What that family had to go through. All three have described Myfanwy as an evil woman and the hospital have found signs of past abuse all over Iolo, many old fractures. Poor man.'

'How is he doing now?'

'Better I think,' Ben said, 'but he'll never walk again. His wife snapped his back when she threw him against the iron range, but doctors say they can make life better for him. Plan is he'll go to live with Gwen when he's finally discharged.'

'If Bronwen does manage to walk away from this, do you think she'll go back to the farm?'

Ben shook his head. 'No idea. We'll have to wait and see.'

His mobile rang, he dragged it from his pocket and recognised the station's number on the small screen.

'DCI James.'

'Tegan here, sir. Will you be much longer?'

'Shouldn't be. Why?'

'You have visitors. Heidi Holtz and a man who won't give his name. They say the matter is urgent.'

'OK. Give them a cuppa and we'll make our way back now.'

Ben disconnected the call. 'Seems Heidi wants a word, sounds like she has Angus with her.'

'I wonder what they want,' Jack said.

'Finish your meal and we'll go and find out.'

* * *

Jonnie Jones was booked in by the custody sergeant and taken directly to an interview room. Erica wanted to question the man while he was still rattled by his arrest. She didn't want to give him time to take a breath. She sat on one side of the table and grinned when the prisoner was brought in but didn't speak until Willis had set the recording machine in motion and verbally logged on. A cardboard file rested on the table in front of her, she opened it and flipped through the pages, taking her time. There was no rush. Jonnie was guilty and she could prove it.

'Get on with it,' Jonnie snapped. 'I have things to do and you're wasting my time.'

Erica removed a plastic evidence bag from the file and placed it on the table. Inside was a mobile phone.

She glanced up at Jonnie and asked, 'Do you agree the phone I'm showing you is your property?'

'Well, duh,' Jonnie said. 'I handed it over when you nicked me, so yes, it's mine.'

'Digital forensics have taken a quick look and discovered a quantity of photographs of young women. We believe they were taken by you, inside your club and at the Boston Bar in Cardiff.'

'So? What of it? Photos are photos.' He chuckled. 'No porn on there, so don't bother looking.'

'Why did you take these pictures?'

Jonnie shrugged. 'Why does anyone take pictures?'

Erica frowned. 'I need an answer.'

'I dunno, cos they were pretty I guess. Can't blame a man for liking pretty women.'

'I believe there is more to this than that.'

'Guess that's your prerogative.'

'What if I told you that the young women were all victims of spiking? Fed large doses of GHB slipped into their drinks?'

'That's got nothing to do with me. I run a clean club. Read the local rag. My "Clean Club" made the front page, so I'm not sure what you're suggesting.'

'Merely stating the facts.' Erica took a deep breath. 'How about if I told you that three of them are dead? Overdosed and taken to motel rooms where they were left to die.'

'That's tragic, but I still can't see what it has to do with me.'

Erica nodded then she opened the file again, removed a pair of photographs and slid them across the table.

'Do you know these men?' she asked.

Jonnie cast his eyes over the pictures and looked away.

'No,' he said. 'Who are they?'

Erica tapped the photos in turn. 'This is Richard Price and this is Billy Thompson.'

'If you say so. Never met them.'

'That is very odd. If you've never met, how come you have their phone numbers stored on your mobile?'

Jonnie shrugged again. 'I collect numbers like people collect stamps, doesn't mean I ever ring them, or even remember who they are. I meet heaps of people every day.'

'Do you send these random people pictures of the young women you thought were pretty?'

'What are you trying to prove?'

'That you were involved with the murder of the three women – amongst other things.'

Jonnie smirked. 'Best of luck with that then.' He folded his arms as though he considered the interview over.

'Here's the thing,' Erica said. 'We have solid gold proof that you sent photographs of those women to Price and Thomson. You left a digital footprint behind – more than one actually.' She smiled and leaned across the table. 'You do realise we've got you banged to rights? Game over? You're definitely going down for this, for a long, long time.'

'Course I am,' Jonnie sneered. 'I'm a respectable businessman. Told you, I run a clean club, I donate generously to local charities and my record is spotless. I wouldn't put money on you being able to convince a jury I'm involved with those deaths.'

'And I'm equally certain that we will. Price and Thompson are on remand and neither are enjoying prison. They want out and are being very helpful. I have no doubt that will continue to be the case.'

'You do have a choice though,' Willis said. 'Tell us about your involvement with this, give us the names of those higher up the chain, and we'll put a word in.'

'Yeah, of course you will,' Jonnie muttered.

'Your choice,' Willis said.

Jonnie groaned and rubbed his eyes. 'I've had enough of this,' he said. 'I want my phone call, something to eat, some decent coffee and access to my solicitor. Not another word out of me until my requests have been met. Not a single bloody word.'

'Have it your way,' Erica snapped and got to her feet.

Willis officially ended the interview and turned off the recorder. The detectives swept from the room and headed upstairs as Jonnie was returned to his cell.

'Having his brief here will slow things down,' Willis complained.

'Can't see it will make much difference. The digital evidence is clear. We've got him, Willis, and he won't see the light of day again until he's an old man.' She grinned and thumped her colleague on his shoulder. 'We've bloody got him!'

* * *

Ben and Jack walked upstairs to the squad room and found Heidi and Angus sitting at one end of the room, coffee in their hands.

'Hi, both,' Ben said. 'Didn't expect to see you again so soon. What's up?'

Heidi got to her feet. 'We need a word,' she said, 'somewhere private.'

'That sounds serious.'

'It is.'

'Come to my office then. You OK with Jack being included?'

'Fine.'

The group left the large room, walked downstairs and squashed into Ben's office on the second floor. Angus and Heidi laid claim to the visitors' chairs, Jack perched on the edge of Ben's desk.

'Let's hear it then,' Ben said when they were settled.

Angus told the detectives how he'd piggybacked the signal from the cloud to the dark web, and about the twisted game of roulette he'd discovered there. Ben and Jack listened in disbelief as Angus spoke and didn't interrupt until he finished his report. Angus handed an envelope across the desk. Ben broke the seal and removed a single sheet of paper on which was a list of names. He ran his eyes down the list then looked up at Heidi and Angus.

'Who are these people?' Ben asked.

'The punters,' Heidi growled. 'The sick bastards who played the game.'

'Some of these individuals are household names.'

'Yes,' Heidi said. 'Rich ones without a moral compass.'

'You know I can't handle this case, don't you?' Ben asked. 'This is way out of my reach and to be honest, I'm not sure I want any part of it.'

Jack was reading the list over his boss's shoulder and whistled.

'This is just... well... bloody hell. Can you prove this?' he asked.

Angus nodded and held up a flash drive. 'Everything is on here, FYI only. A secure copy has been stored. Another has been sent to Freddie Holtz.' Angus grinned. 'Maybe he'll go in with a SWAT squad.'

'What, really?' Jack asked.

Angus chuckled. 'Wouldn't put it past him.'

'What does Freddie actually do in Whitehall?'

Angus leaned closer and stage-whispered, 'I think he's a spy.'

Heidi laughed and the others joined in.

'Seems you have everything covered,' Ben said. 'Word of warning though, these names cannot be leaked to the press. Don't want to prejudice any trial – if it gets that far.'

'I promise it'll get that far,' Heidi said. 'Maybe even farther. Those... those... I haven't the words, but they were paying to watch live streamed, snuff movies, and betting on the outcome. What is wrong with humans?' she asked. 'Why do they do such disgusting things to each other and always try to justify their actions?'

'Any royals on that list?' Jack asked.

'No British ones thankfully,' Angus said.

'Why did that woman – Emily Ansell – take photos of the victims? What was that all about?'

'As far as we can tell,' Angus said, 'trophies for the winner. Last living photo of... you get the idea.'

'Do you know who is behind this? The man at the top?'

Heidi nodded. 'Turns out you've chased the man before,' she said. 'A drugs case, manufacture of ecstasy. You knew him as The Colonel. The case papers said he escaped because you couldn't track him on the dark web.'

'Bloody hell,' Jack said. 'That's going back in time. Do you know his real name? Where he is now?'

'We do,' Heidi said and placed a photograph on the desk. It showed a portly man in a flamboyant dressing gown, standing on a sunny balcony with an elaborate metal balustrade. 'Colonel Frank Bradstone, retired. Current residence, Mayfair Guest House in Zamalek – an island in the middle of the Nile, centre of Cairo.'

Ben stared at the picture and asked, 'Any chance we can extradite him?'

Angus grinned. 'No need. He's already on his way.' He glanced at his Breitling watch. 'Landing at Heathrow in approximately three hours. There will be an appropriate welcoming party you can be sure. No need to worry, Ben. Freddie will round them all up, I have no doubt.'

The group fell silent, horrified by what had been happening over recent months, praying those involved would in fact be arrested and severely punished.

'Let's move on,' Heidi said and cracked her knuckles, 'this is done. How about we all get together for a posh lunch at the Caer Beris, Saturday week? Erica and I have already booked a great table in the conservatory, so how about it?'

Ben smiled. 'You're right, we need to move on and lunch sounds like a great idea. We'll see you there.' He got to his feet and shook hands with her and Angus. 'Thank you,' he said. 'Discovering this terrible crime wouldn't have happened without you.'

'Got that right.' Heidi grinned. 'See you Saturday week then.'

> *Extracts from The Mid Wales Times*
> *SPIKING GANG SMASHED – by Stacey Logan*
>
> *In a large investigation involving many officers, Cardiff police have successfully broken up a spiking gang operating in the city's night clubs.*
> *Four individuals have been arrested and charged with varying offences – including murder relating to the alarming increase in this disturbing crime.*
> *It has emerged the heinous activity has cost the lives of three young women in South Wales and consequently, three members of the gang have been charged with murder. One of those arrested was Jonnie Jones, owner of Rascals nightclub. A fourth will appear in*

court on lesser charges. A trial date has been set for the New Year.

TWO POWYS MEN CHARGED WITH MURDER – *by Stacey Logan*

Two local men have appeared in court, charged with the murders of Robin and Ian Townsend, and the attempted murder of Patrick Ryan, earlier in the year.

Idris Jones of Llanwrtyd Wells and Derek Brumby, landlord of the Stonecroft public house in the town, have both been remanded. The case will be heard at Cardiff Crown Court in the next few months. It is understood both intend to plead guilty.

Epilogue

Ben pulled up outside the Caer Beris country manor hotel, on the edge of Builth Wells, nestling in an area of parkland on the banks of the river. Stacey gazed up at the imposing black and white building and its many leaded windows.

'I love this place,' she said. 'Nice idea of Heidi's for us to get together here for lunch. Lovely to have an excuse to dress up, get out of the slobbing-around-the-house clothes for a while.' She smiled, took hold of his hand and held up her ring finger. 'Remember how you gave me this beautiful ring all that time ago?'

Ben leaned across the seats and kissed her soundly. 'How could I ever forget? I've never regretted it.'

'No, nor me.' She returned his kiss.

'Come on then,' Ben said. 'Can't get caught snogging in the car park and I don't want to be late.'

They left the car, walked along a strip of red outdoor carpet and into the spacious reception. The woman behind the desk looked up and smiled welcomingly.

'Good morning,' she said. 'Do you have a booking?'

'We do,' Ben said. 'In the name of Heidi Holtz.'

The receptionist smiled again. 'Ah yes, I have it here. You're in the conservatory, please go on through. The rest of your party have already arrived.'

Ben took Stacey's hand. They walked through the opulent dining room and out into the large conservatory at the back of the old building, overlooking a stretch of green sweeping down to the river. Heidi suddenly appeared at Stacey's side, a huge smile on her face. Unusually she took hold of Stacey's hand, stood on tiptoes and brushed a gentle kiss on her cheek.

'Wow! That's a welcome,' Stacey said. 'You look nice. Is that a new jacket?'

Heidi didn't comment but said, 'Come with me. There's something I want you to do for me.'

'Oh? What's that?' Stacey asked as Heidi pulled her through the long, airy room.

At the far end of the room Erica waited. She wore a long black skirt and a small black hat with a net veil, a large smile on her face and a bright corsage constructed with orchids and the tip of a peacock feather. She raised a hand in welcome.

'Stacey! You came. I'm so pleased,' Erica said.

Heidi rummaged in the tiny pocket of a velvet waistcoat beneath her jacket, removed something small and placed it in Stacey's hand. Stacey opened her fingers and saw a ring, a thick band of gold set with blue diamonds.

'What is this?' she asked.

Heidi laughed and gave her friend another quick hug.

'It's a wedding ring,' she said. 'Best woman keeps the ring safe until it's needed.'

'Oh my God! Are you and Erica getting married?'

Heidi nodded. 'Yes, in about ten minutes, so I'm extremely pleased you arrived on time.' She laughed again. 'And during the wedding breakfast, you can watch your grumpy editor eat the picture of us clubbing. I knew he wouldn't pick you out.'

THE END

If you enjoyed this book, please let others know by leaving a quick review on Amazon. Also, if you spot anything untoward in the paperback, get in touch. We strive for the best quality and appreciate reader feedback.

editor@thebookfolks.com

www.thebookfolks.com

More fiction by Nicola Clifford

NO REFUGE (book 1)

Reporter Stacey Logan has little to worry about other than the town flower festival when a man is shot dead. When she believes the police have got the wrong man, she does some snooping of her own. But will her desire for a scoop lead her to a place where there is no refuge?

THE CONSORTIUM (book 2)

Whilst reporter Stacey Logan is investigating illegal raves in the Welsh countryside, her boyfriend DI Ben James is dealing with a suspicious death. When drugs enter the picture, their two separate inquiries will collide. Can they find a way to collaborate and catch a dangerous killer?

NOT FORGOTTEN (book 3)

When journalist Stacey Logan's policeman boyfriend disappears with little more than a note, she suspects he has been abducted. But his colleagues refuse to pursue her leads. She'll have to go it alone, but must brace herself for the worst.

RIGHT OF SANCTUARY (book 4)

When DC Heidi Holtz's sister Greta joins a cult, she has trouble convincing her superiors of foul play. And there is nothing the detective can do if Greta went by her own free will. Holtz will have to find evidence to discredit the sect, or risk losing her sister for good.

CODDLING MOLLY (book 5)

A teenager is found dead after a fall from a bridge on a winter night in Brecon. Identifying her proves a challenge. DI Ben James and DS Erica Bevan discover links to a drugs gang. But when these crooks bother someone dear to ex-detective Heidi Holtz, she too will jump on their trail.

GONE TO THE DOGS (book 6)

Reporter Stacey Logan is looking into the case of a missing teenager, but she can't help but put her nose into Detective Ben James' murder investigation. Tensions within the community reach fever pitch as events come to a head.

RIVER OF BODIES (book 8)

When a woman and a man's bodies are found in a flooded car showroom during the night, detectives guess that they are the victims of a cuckolded husband. But once again the cops will rely on the increasingly dangerous investigations of reporter Stacey Logan to reach the truth.

GREEN SHOOTS (book 9)

Police are called out to an commune on a country estate. The owners of the land want the environmentalists off their turf. Someone is going to get killed. Let's hope it isn't journalist Stacey Logan, who is heading there for a scoop.

Other titles of interest

After a man confesses in church that he has killed a girl, having wrangled with his conscience the priest tells the police. It would be easy for them to dismiss the confessor as a crank, but DI Knox has a hunch the victim could be a young Canadian tourist who has gone missing. Yet with few other leads, it will take brilliant detective work to catch the killer.

A woman is found murdered. The same night, the office pathologist Jenny Norris goes missing. Worried that her colleague might be implicated, DCI Gawn Girvin in secret investigates the connection between the women. But Jenny has left few clues to go on, and before long Girvin's solo tactics risk muddling the murder investigation and putting her in danger.

Printed in Dunstable, United Kingdom

81407416R00173